FROM THE DEPTHS

JE GURLEY

ISBN: 978-1-925047-54-7

Dedication

I wish to dedicate this book to my wife, Kim, who endures my constant pecking at the keyboard and allows me to create worlds and characters, while forgiving my failure to remember the names of friends and family. She is my constant source of light against the darkness of which I write.

I also wish to thank Severed Press for turning my Southern drawl scribbling into a readable work.

J.E. Gurley

1

Oct. 25, 1962, Caribbean Sea –

Captain Ilya Voshok searched the sky for the pair of American Navy Skyhawk jets with his battered Komz binoculars, but the fog, as gray as his beard and as heavy as his belly, hid them from his view. Their distinctive Pratt and Whitney J52-P8A turbojet engines rumbled briefly to the north, and then to the east. He couldn't help wincing in dread, as they turned and passed over his ship. He thanked providence for the fog. Without seeing them, he knew that their armament consisted of 2x20 mm Mk12 cannons, four AIM-9 Sidewinder air-to-air missiles, and two AGM65 Maverick air-to-surface missiles. The report from the submarine *Velikovsky* had been very thorough. He even knew what time the jets had taken off from the carrier *U.S. Enterprise* thirty kilometers to his east.

His ship, the a thirty-year-old rust bucket freighter *A.V. Pokhomov*, renamed for a 1948 Samolyot rocket plane pilot, had been playing a game of cat and mouse with the blockading U.S. fleet for two days. His cargo, four 30-kiloton nuclear warheads, had to reach Cuba without delay. He was not happy with his orders, but he would obey them to the best of his ability. The freighter *Bucharest* had safely slipped through the blockade, but the *Marcula* had been boarded and its cargo searched before being released. The Russian freighters *Gagarin* and *Komiles* had turned back. He could not. His orders were to scuttle his ship before allowing the Americans to board her. The idea of scuttling his ship was preposterous, especially in light of her cargo.

The jets did not return. His ship was safe for now. He replaced his binoculars in their worn case and hung them on the railing beside him. They had been with him since his first command, a converted fishing trawler ferrying troops across the Volga during the siege of Stalingrad. He had survived that battle, but the odds of surviving this conflict did not look so good. The American President, Kennedy, and the Kremlin leader, Khrushchev, were seeing who had the bigger balls, daring one another to knock the nuclear chip from their shoulders, and neither man was willing to back down. At stake was the fate of the world. President Kennedy's failed coup at the Bay of Pigs in Cuba had made him look like a fool in the eyes of the free world, as did his apparent apathy at the construction of the Berlin Wall. He could not afford to lose face once again in this matter. Fidel Castro was the pawn that the two were using in their private game of chess, and Cuba was the playing board.

For his part, Voshok cared little about Castro, Cuba, or the glorious revolution. He had endured his revolution as a twelve-year-old boy from then Finnish Vyborg forced to fight in a Red Army brigade. He had survived that slaughter, and hoped to survive this test of wills. His only true love was the sea. His ship was home, family, and country, and his only allegiance was to his ship and his crew. He turned to his second-in-command, Stanos Kommakov, a tall, thin man from the White Sea port city of Belomorsk.

"We will attempt a run to Cuba after dark. Please have all the area charts on hand. I do not wish to run aground on some cursed sand bar and wait for the Americans to destroy my ship."

Kommakov, a stolid man of few words, wiped his perspiring brow, nodded, and retreated through the door to the relative coolness of the cabin. Kommakov, by trade a fisherman in the Barents Sea, did not enjoy the muggy tropical air of the Caribbean. He preferred the chilly breezes off the Arctic ice. Voshok took pleasure in the warm breeze, but the humidity clogged his lungs. October in Vyborg, his home, was a far cry from Cuba. The northern winds that howled across the Karelian Isthmus could cut a man in half in mid-winter, but in October, the winds blew mild from the sea. The nights were cold and crisp, a time for vodka and a warm fire, but the days were clear and alive with only a hint of the winter to come. When he had left port, Voshok had watched with regret as the stark white tower of Vyborg Castle slowly vanished over the horizon, as if sinking in the sea. In his heart, he knew he would never see Vyborg again.

His destination, the *Golfo de Batabano,* lay on Cuba's southwestern coast, protected by the *Isla de la Juvented* and a series of small islands. Reaching a safe anchorage would be difficult, especially at night. His cargo had to reach San Cristobal. To fail would mean his removal as captain or worse. Without his ship, he would have no reason to live. He would fulfill his mission or die trying. The biggest problem, aside from the American Fleet, would be the fog. It would provide cover for his ship, but his obsolete radar would make threading the small islands and almost invisible mud flats very difficult. He would need to be eagle-eyed to see his ship safely through.

Kommakov burst from the cabin with a hastily scrawled message in his hand. His face, normally so impassive, was one of abject terror. "This just came through from the *Velikovsky.*"

Voshok took the note, his hand trembling from dread, a sinking feeling in his stomach as if worms were writhing. He knew from his mate's expression that the message bore ill tidings. His first glance bore out his suspicions.

'*U.S.S. Allen M. Sumner* is in pursuit. Estimated interception six hours. Continue a bearing of 84 degrees Southwest until such time *Velikovsky* can provide assistance.'

Voshok was stunned. "Provide assistance? Do they propose sinking an American destroyer?"

"The *Sumner*, designation DD-692, can make 34 knots. Our top speed is 21."

Voshok glared at Kommakov. "Yes, yes, I know, Kommakov. You state the obvious. We cannot outrun her. She also carries six 127 mm guns, batteries of 44 mm and 20 mm antiaircraft guns, and ten torpedo tubes. We cannot fight them off with our pistols."

He had gone over the statistics for every American warship involved in the blockade before shipping out. He knew what he was facing. With only two submarines in the area and a few shore-based aircraft, the Russians were greatly overmatched.

"Full speed ahead bearing 084." He slapped the railing. "I will not lose my ship, and I will not start a war."

He had no choice but run. If the Americans thought he was making for South America, they might leave him alone. After all, they were concerned only with ships attempting to break their blockade. If he had to scuttle, it would be in deep water. The Cayman Trench reached a depth of 7,600 meters. *Let the Americans try to recover my cargo from there.* The ship shuddered as the propellers picked up speed and smiled.

We just might survive this after all.

* * * *

Oct. 26, 1962, Cayman Trench, Caribbean –

Captain Raymond S. Crabtree of the *U.S.S. Allen M. Sumner* stared at the tiny blip on the radarscope fade and reappear with each sweep of the dial. "Are we closing?"

"Aye, aye sir. She's steaming a straight course. We'll make contact in twenty minutes." The radar man frowned as the screen blurred for a few seconds.

"What is it, son?"

"I'm getting some peculiar bounces off the waves. If the seas get any rougher, she might slip by."

As if to emphasize his point, the ship lurched to starboard as a wave struck her amidships. Crabtree braced himself against the bulkhead. He faced a dilemma. He could order a course change and follow the waves to steady the ship, but he might lose the Russian if it suddenly changed course. Or he could continue closing on the Russian and hope his ship held together. They would just have to ride it out.

"What is her captain thinking? We know the *Pokhomov* is carrying nuclear warheads. Does he think we will simply let him slip away into the night?"

He hoped the freighter would make a fight of it. He was eager to draw blood. His father had died in Korea fighting the communists. Now, it was his turn to make them pay.

Lieutenant Mark Bisbee spoke up. "Maybe it's a trap. There's a Russian sub somewhere out there. Maybe we had better move cautiously."

Bisbee's prudence might be called for under normal circumstances, but his reluctance concerned Crabtree. "Now is not the time for caution. The fate of the Free World is at stake. Last plot places the Russian sub forty miles north of us and presents no present threat. The *Sumner* is not afraid of a Russian submarine."

Even in his bloodlust, he had no desire to tangle with a Russian sub. Not for fear it would sink his ship, but because he didn't want to precipitate a nuclear holocaust. Intercepting a Russian freighter was one thing, but tangling with a submarine was different.

"Yes, sir," Bisbee replied, but his nervousness was not lost on Crabtree.

"Have we made radio contact with the Russian freighter?"

"They're not replying."

Crabtree nodded. He wouldn't reply either, if the situations were reversed. He braced against a bulkhead once more as the bow dipped into a wave trough. "When we're within torpedo range, we will attempt one more hail, and then fire a shot over her bow with the 127 mm. If she refuses to yield at that time, I want two torpedoes placed in her side. I want to see that ship on the bottom of the ocean."

"If she's carrying a nuclear cargo ..."

"Mr. Bisbee," Crabtree said, not bothering to hide the exasperation in his voice. "Her nukes will not go off if we sink her. Had you rather see one of those missiles detonate over Washington, D.C., or Annapolis?"

Bisbee licked his lips. "No, sir."

"Very well then, let the depths have them. Instruct the torpedo crew of my orders, and sound battle stations."

A few seconds later, the 'Battle Station' claxon went off, sending the crew scurrying for their stations. Crabtree was proud to see them moving calmly and efficiently. Since arriving in the Caribbean, he had trained his crew ruthlessly day and night. They would know what to do when the time came to act. He left the radar room and struggled up the stairs to the bridge, as the ship suddenly climbed a wave. An ensign handed him a metal battle helmet as soon as he entered the bridge. He removed his hat, laid it on the console, and donned the helmet, carefully slipping the strap under his chin. Stepping outside into the open air, he leaned against the rail, bracing himself against the ship's heavy list. The fog was so thick he could barely see the fantail of the ship. Without radar, they could pass within a stone's throw of the Russian freighter without seeing it.

His choices were limited. He could pursue at full speed, praying that the ship's twenty-year-old hull didn't come apart at the seams, and that the rough seas didn't render his radar useless, or he could reduce speed, and hope the Russian captain didn't realize he was being followed. He chose hard pursuit. The Russian wanted him to think he was on his way to South America, but Bisbee wasn't buying it. Unless somebody had slipped up, and intel had been on the nose so far, the Russian was carrying nukes destined for Cuba. He couldn't allow that to happen.

The full force of the squall struck from the northeast half an hour later. The rain hammered his face as he stared into the deepening darkness, but he ignored it. The Russian was running without lights, but for just a split second, he thought he saw a dark blur atop a wave, silhouetted against the deep purple sky. It disappeared so quickly he thought it might simply have been his desire to see the Russian placing it on the horizon. He chose to think it was real.

"I've got you, you bastard," he whispered into the night. He clenched his right fist around the rail.

The distance between the two ships closed slowly. The *Sumner* was capable of making thirty-four knots on a calm sea, but now she was reduced to less than twenty. The Russian captain must have been a fool to risk his rust bucket of a ship at that speed.

The speaker on the bridge sang out, "Sonar here, sir. I picked up a ping about two clicks out, just astern of the Russian.

The Russian sub. Captain Crabtree gripped the railing tighter. "Stand by depth charges." He smiled as he imagined the look on Bisbee's face when he heard that order. "Do not unload the racks unless the sub makes an aggressive move first. When the Russian freighter is within range, you have my orders."

God help me if I'm wrong.

* * * *

He could not see them, but Captain Voshok could feel the American's presence as a small itch between his shoulder blades. He had experienced the same discomfort during the siege of Stalingrad, as the German *Stukkas* dive bombed his ship and strafed his passengers, raw recruits for the meat grinder that was Stalingrad. He had survived Stalingrad. Could he survive this? A heavy wave crashed into the bow, sending him sprawling across the deck like a bit of flotsam. He fetched up against a bulkhead and fought his way to his feet. He caught sight of the American destroyer less than four-thousand meters to port in a sudden flash of lightning. They could not escape. He had to scuttle his ship, but he could not give the order. Better to let the Americans do the job for him. At least, he would not be around to watch his ship sink.

"The Americans are hailing us again," the radioman announced.

He tensed. Answering them was his last chance at surviving. He could not. "Ignore them," he snapped.

A few seconds later, a flash of light and an explosion a hundred meters off their starboard bow. A geyser of water rose into the air. The Americans were being serious.

"Continue on course," he called out. Did the Americans want to start a war?

"Torpedoes!" rang out from the top look out.

Voshok swung his binoculars to port toward the American warship, expecting to see twin lances of death streaking toward him. He saw nothing.

"What bearing?" he yelled.

"Starboard."

He quickly spotted the wake of a single torpedo six hundred meters away. He smiled as realization dawned on him. Rather than risk his cargo being intercepted, his own countrymen in the *Velikovsky* would assure his death. The ship shuddered and lurched as the torpedo struck the stern, lifting it into the air. The deck rose to smack him in the face. He felt his cheekbones shatter. He spit out a broken tooth with a mouthful of blood. His ears rang from the blow. The aft of the ship disappeared in a bright orange ball of flame. The heat and concussion washed over him, rendering him deaf and scorching his clothing and skin. He struggled to his feet and saw the American torpedoes pass by the bow. The American captain had been a good shot. If not for the *Velikovsky*, the American's torpedoes would have done the job. The American had been robbed of his victory. Voshok forced a smile to his smashed face.

The second explosion shattered the ship's spine. The aft section split apart with a screech of rending metal and fell away. He watched two crewmen, friends, swallowed by a large crack in the deck, engulfed in flames. Lifeboats broke free of their hoists and crashed into the ocean. His countrymen were taking no chances. There would be no time to abandon ship. His crew, which had become his family, would die with him. He regretted that their lives would be sacrificed to the ever-starving beast of politics, but no story of the *Pokhomov's* deadly cargo could ever told by survivors. Her cargo would soon rest at the depths of the Cayman Trench, forgotten by time.

Voshok clung to the railing as the sea washed over him. The captain rode his ship to the bottom.

* * * *

The second explosion ripped the *Pokhomov* in half. Captain Crabtree watched both halves slide into the water. Men and equipment on her decks slid over the side. One burning crewman leaped over the side into the water and vanished. Flames spilled from portholes and rents in the ship's hull. He had never witnessed a large ship sink. It left a dull ache in his stomach. His battle lust died quickly. Instead of elation, he felt as if he were trapped in her hold, water rising around him, filling his lungs with oily water.

He lowered his binoculars and wiped his brow, gasping for air. When he raised his glasses again, the freighter was gone, leaving only a cloud of steam, quickly dispersed by the wind, and scattered debris that would just as quickly be scattered by the waves. He was surprised that both fish had hit. He had fired two torpedoes from a range of two thousand yards. It wasn't a perfect firing solution, but he couldn't afford to let the Russian slip away in the squall. They had ignored his hail and his warning shot. He told himself had no choice, but was he fooling himself?

The dying ship emitted one last groan, a protest at the murder done to her. *Or a promise of revenge.* Of course, the Russians would deny the sinking; deny even that the ship existed. They could not admit to its deadly cargo. His report would quickly be lost amid the reams of paper amassed during the blockade. The world would never know how close to the brink of war it had come.

Captain Crabtree lowered his binoculars and stepped back into the wheelhouse out of the squall, trying to distance himself from his deed. It would soon be over, as would the blockade. The President was rumored to be considering removing American missiles from Turkey, and in return, the Russians would withdraw their missiles from Cuba. No one would know of the deal, but no one would care. The danger was over.

He fumbled a cigarette from a pack of Camels and lit it, trying to hide his shaking hand from the crew. *Now I get the shakes.* He took a puff and glanced at his watch. "Note the time of the sinking, Mr. Bisbee, 2440 hours." He called out to the helmsman, "Take us back to the fleet, Mr. Lee." Standing by the open door, shielding his cigarette from the rain, he thought he heard a long, loud scream rise from amid the debris of the dying ship, but marked it down to his imagination. Still, the sound raised goose bumps on his flesh, and he knew the dead ship would haunt his memory for a long, long time.

2

Oct. 23, 2014, Little Cayman, Caribbean –

Josh Peterman emerged from the emerald green water, ran his fingers through his wavy, blond locks to ease them back into place, and stood, looking up and down the almost deserted beach. Hurricane Clive was still a day out, but the rough surf, the lack of sun, and the scuttling clouds had driven anyone hardy enough to brave the storm into the bars to sip pina coladas. A strong wave surged onto the beach, breaking against the back of his legs with enough force to send him reeling forward. He stumbled and caught himself before falling, but his heels began sinking as the wave retreated, eroding the sand from beneath his feet.

"Enough for today," he muttered and headed for his towel lying on the sand.

Josh, a senior at Texas Christian University, had saved for two years to take this trip to Little Cayman, and he wasn't about to let an impending hurricane spoil it. However, now it would be a total wash out – no sun, no diving, and no women. His anticipated weeklong stay would be shorter than he had hoped. Today, his third on the tiny island would be his last day. He was evacuating with the last batch of tourists on the last plane leaving at six p.m. Only the island's one-hundred-and-seventy or so residents would remain, enduring the hurricane's wrath and fury with the same serenity with which they faced daily life.

Toweling dry as he walked toward to the Sunset Cove Resort, a British Colonial-style, two-story building, he eyed the hammocks suspended between palm trees. He plopped down in one, allowing the nylon netting to enfold him, but after a few minutes, the constant swaying of the tree in the wind brought on a bout of seasickness. The thought of an early dinner on his queasy stomach didn't appeal to him, and he really didn't feel like drinking again so soon after last night's epic binge. *Two-for-one deals should include a warning that the bartender is not responsible for the drinker's inability to know when he has overindulged.*

A grain of sand blew into his eye. As he rubbed it out, he spotted something washing up on shore. The crashing waves rolled it over the sand. It moved. He blinked back a tear and rose from the hammock to investigate.

As he neared the object, some type of animal, the first thing he noted was the teeth, long, curved and vicious, sprouting from both the upper and lower jaws. The gills fluttered as it fought for oxygen. It was still alive. The size of the fish surprised him, nearly five feet in length. It was too dark, almost black, for a barracuda, and didn't have the fins of a shark. It fact, it didn't resemble any other tropical fish with which he was familiar. As he leaned over it for a closer look, the fish wriggled toward him, snapping its jaws at him. An incoming wave moved the fish toward his feet. He leaped back to avoid a bite that would probably have severed his foot.

"Damn!" he exclaimed, looking around to see if anyone saw his startled reaction.

As his mind worked overtime, trying to recall to what species the fish belonged, he noticed several more of the creatures flopping up and down the beach, brought in by the rising tide. It appeared he would have no dearth of specimens to examine. As he considered the possibility of mutations, it all finally snapped into place. His mind reeled, astounded at what he was seeing. The creature was a member of *Anoplogaster comuta*, the common fangtooth, also known as the Ogrefish, but instead of its usual six-inch length, this creature was ten times as large. What it was doing on a beach in the Cayman Islands rather than in the deep dark at sixteen-thousand feet, its usual habitat, feeding on plankton, he couldn't imagine. The storm alone couldn't have brought it up from the depths. Had the tremor that had rattled the island two days earlier disturbed the deep creatures? The news had reported a 5.4 magnitude quake with its epicenter about one-hundred twenty miles south of Little Cayman at a depth of twelve-thousand feet. That placed it in the

Mid-Cayman Spreading Center, an area noted for slides and tremors.

He took a series of photos with his cell phone, laying his watch on the sand as a ruler to indicate the creature's true size. He had to hurry before the tide swept the creature back out to sea. Satisfied with the results, he then attempted to send the photos to his professor at TCU.

"Damn, no bars." He scanned the darkening sky to the southeast. "Must be the storm."

As he entered the resort lobby, the manager, Nigel Hawthorne, met him at the door. Hawthorne, a middle-aged man who was much too pale for living on a tropical island, was going bald, but insisted on combing over his few remaining hairs and plastering them to his scalp. His hand repeatedly flew to his head to replace errant hairs as the wind blew them around. He reeked of patchouli oil.

"Mr., ah, Peterman, I just wanted to remind you about the plane at six p.m. tonight." He stared at Josh with folded hands as he waited for an answer.

"Yes, I remember. I'll be ready."

Hawthorne dipped his head, said, "Very good," and scuttled away.

Josh smiled at Hawthorne's back as he was retreating. Hawthorne was much too nervous for such an easy-going climate, always rushing about, while his employees sauntered from task to task as if it working, personally assaulted their daily routine of *laissez faire*. With his pencil-thin moustache, Hawthorne reminded Josh of a prim and proper mortician. The lobby was deserted. In fact, only three guests remained in the resort. One was a long-time resident, and the other two were a couple from Minnesota leaving on the same plane as Josh.

Josh's room overlooked the beach. He grabbed a cold cola from the room's mini fridge and walked straight through the room to the veranda that all the beachside rooms shared. He plopped down in a white wicker armchair and propped his feet on the railing. The vase of flowers that had fallen from the table beside his chair and shattered during the tremor two days earlier was still there, one of the few signs of visible damage from the tremor. He was surprised the staff hadn't gotten around to cleaning it up, but he supposed they were busy preparing for the hurricane.

He scanned the beach, but it was clear of giant Ogrefish. The tide had washed them back out to sea. He wished that he could have saved a specimen on ice, but it would never have survived the long journey back to TCU. The photos would be proof enough, and perhaps provide a basis for his thesis. Watching the tide eat away the sand, he sensed a twinge of sympathy for the island's residents for when the storm surge arrived. The resort lobby would be flooded, as would most of the island. The island's highest point was barely forty feet above sea level. Even if it survived the ravages of the hurricane's winds, the island would be devastated.

Josh's stomach rumbled, but he had no desire for a large dinner. Instead, he nibbled on fruit from a bowl beside the chair and the remains of a package of potato chips to curb his hunger, wondering how much of his stomachache was due to too much alcohol and how much from fear. He had never been so close to a hurricane before. He had seen photos of the aftermath of one and had no desire to be caught in the middle of one. He also had a fear of flying. He had fought the fear during the entire journey from Texas, tempting fate in his desire to visit the island. Thoughts of flying through the fringes of a hurricane in the dark made him more than a little uneasy.

He pulled out his cell phone and stared at the photos of the Ogrefish. He had dived with sharks and barracudas, and even had a small scar from a moray eel's bite, but meeting giant Ogrefish in the dark depths sent a shiver up his spine. Such creatures couldn't live in a vacuum. They had to eat something, and in turn, something larger ate them. Such was the cycle of nature. Whatever had driven them up from the deep, earth tremor or hurricane, had it also brought other deep denizens to the surface, creatures that would make Ogrefish pale in comparison? He had heard of giant squid, had seen their sucker marks on blue whales. If this was an example of sea life in the depths, what else lurked below?

A gust of wind swept across the veranda, swaying the trees, bringing with it the strong scent of rain. The day was rapidly fading into an early twilight. The surf was rising and powerful waves began to pound the beach. He thought of huddling in the dark confines of the flimsy wooden structure of the resort during a hurricane and shuddered.

He hoped the plane would take off on time.

3

Oct. 23, 2014, eighty miles southeast of Grand Cayman Island
—

Captain Ron Germaine normally wouldn't have accepted a charter for a night dive in such rough seas with a hurricane bearing down, but the two thousand dollars the client offered would help him meet his next payment on his boat, the *Miss Lucy*. An unopened late-payment statement from the bank lay on an end table at home. The fifty-foot schooner was almost forty years old, just twelve years younger than he was, and had become higher maintenance than his alcoholic ex-wife. Under way, with a crew of three, the two-mast schooner required maximum effort from all hands. Now, with the jib, the fore gaff topsail, the mainsail, and the fore sail reefed and secured and the sea anchor out, they relaxed with bottles of well-earned beer.

Germaine kept one an eye on the weather, and the other on the bubbles off his starboard beam. The mass of dark clouds to the east marked the leading edge of Hurricane Clive. Already a Class Three storm, it promised quite a punch. Lightning illuminated the cloud mass like New Year's Eve sparklers, heralding the storm's approach. Already the twenty-knot winds were raising whitecaps that rolled the schooner like a cork in a bucket. It would be a close call to reach port before the weather worsened.

His passengers, three American adventurers from Utah who fancied themselves underwater photographers, were a hundred feet below the ship filming a school of barracuda. He hoped they didn't get eaten, mainly because they still owed him five-hundred dollars for fuel. He had no respect for amateurs, but all three had their diving certificates and professed a hundred hours of dive time each.

From their manner aboard ship and lack of sea legs, he guessed most of those hours were in dive pools back in Utah. He had always imagined Utah a desert state, like Arizona. Perhaps they practiced diving in the Great Salt Lake.

The small remote monitor sitting on the hatch cover relayed what the trio was filming. The camera lights reflected off a writhing silver wall, undulating like satin sails in a breeze. As the camera panned upward, the wall became a fifty-feet-tall whirlpool of circling barracuda. Germaine hoped the greenhorns knew that barracuda bite. He checked his watch and lifted an eyebrow to catch the attention of Chance Bodden, his first mate. Bodden set down his beer and sauntered over, moving with the cat-like grace that made him a natural on the masts.

"What up, Boss?" he asked in his island drawl.

"Those greenhorns have been down almost an hour. They might forget just how much air is in their tanks. Give McCoy a call on the walkie-talkie to remind them."

"Sure thing, Boss."

Seth McCoy was the group's spokesman, an overbearing little man with a penchant for Jamaican rum and arguing with anyone who would listen. Germaine tried to give McCoy a wide berth, but on a fifty-foot schooner, that was difficult. He listened in as his mate called the divers.

"*Miss Lucy* to Mr. McCoy. Come in."

The reply was muffled and interspersed with regulator noise as the diver breathed. The view in the monitor lost focus as McCoy jiggled the camera. "This is McCoy. What do you want, *Miss Lucy?*"

As usual, McCoy managed to sound put upon.

"Watch your dive time, sir. You're almost out of air."

"I'm well aware of our dive time, thank you. We will be up shortly. There are some strange lights below us that I want to photograph."

Bodden shrugged. He was used to McCoy's superciliousness. To Germaine, he said, "We could just leave them here."

Germaine flicked the ashes from his cigarette over the side. He detested McCoy but liked his money. "Tempting as it is, they still owe me money. Give them five minutes and call them again."

Germaine wondered what lights McCoy meant. Most of the phosphorescent sea life was down deep. The storm could be bringing them to the surface. If so, predators would follow. He didn't want his passengers caught in the middle of a feeding frenzy. A few minutes later, he saw lights just beneath the surface off the starboard bow.

"They must be surfacing," he said to Bodden. "Stand by to help them aboard."

He checked the monitor, but it showed only darkness. Curious, he watched the lights off the bow for a few moments before it struck him that there were too many of them for the three divers. The walkie-talkie erupted at the same time.

"My God, it's gigantic!" Panic filled McCoy's voice.

Germaine checked the monitor again, and this time, he saw shadowy shapes and pulsating lights in the darkness. He rushed to the walkie-talkie. "McCoy, get back to the surface now."

"What are those things?" McCoy yelled to one of his companions. "One just swallowed half a dozen barracuda with one gulp. I've got to get a picture of it."

Killer whales? Sharks? It didn't matter. "Negative, McCoy. Surface now."

McCoy ignored Germaine's command. His voice was filled with excitement as he spoke. "It must be twenty feet long. Its head is as big as a garbage can. Bigger. There are rows of lights along its sides." Now there was awe in McCoy's voice, but his breathing rate had increased, eating up his remaining oxygen. Germaine worried that if McCoy didn't surface soon, he would be sucking from an empty tank.

"McCoy?" he demanded.

A second voice blared over the walkie-talkie. It sounded like Cory Radisson, the youngest of the three divers and the only one Germaine could stand. "It's coming at me!"

"Radisson, look out!" McCoy yelled, and then, "My God, he's gone."

The monitor showed bright specks in the water, tiny phytoplankton reflecting the camera lights. The school of barracuda had vanished, but part of a barracuda's tail floated by.

"Get up here fast, McCoy," Germaine screamed, but he knew it was too late. Whatever was down there, it now considered the divers as food. With blood in the water, they didn't have a chance.

"Boss, look." Bodden pointed over the side. Germaine hoped to see the divers' heads surfacing. Instead, he saw a monster.

A creature half as long as the schooner cut through the water just below the surface. Its head was large and bulbous with two massive red eyes. Its black, ribbon-like body ended in a single dorsal fin. Rows of lights running along each side gave it the appearance of a mini-submarine. He recognized the creature from one of the marine books in his small ship's library as a Viperfish, but this one was enormous. What had brought it up from a mile deep? As he watched, several more surfaced. Then the seas came alive with lights. They were adrift in a sea of Viperfish.

McCoy was still alive, or at least the camera was operating. Germaine tried the walkie-talkie. "McCoy! Get the hell up here now." He heard only the sound of very rapid breathing through the speaker. The angle camera swung down, catching a glimpse of McCoy's swim fin. Something large and dark was rushing at him from below – a Viperfish. Lights pulsated behind its head. The swim fin fluttered rapidly as McCoy struggled for the surface, but he was too late. The Viperfish was much faster than he was. With a quick flick of its eel-like body, it lunged at the diver. The camera showed the bulbous head and large red eyes, the enormous mouth yawning wide like a cavern with needle-sharp teeth like stalactites. Then everything went dark. McCoy's brief muffled scream over the walkie-talkie was followed by static. All three divers were gone.

One of the creatures thumped the side of the boat, releasing Germaine from his shock. "We have to leave," he yelled to Bodden. A fish as large as the Viperfish could stave in the hull. Raising the sails would take too long. "Cut the anchor rope and start the engine." Bodden cast a quick nervous glance over the side, looking for the divers. "Forget about them. They're gone." So was his five hundred dollars. That would be the least of his problems. Losing three divers and bringing in a tale of giant Viperfish would earn him a police inquiry and probably cost him his license. Then he remembered the extra camera McCoy had left on the deck. He grabbed it and snapped three quick photos, hoping the black Viperfish would be distinguishable against the dark background.

The sky to the east lit up with a frenzied flurry of lightning. The sea around them pulsed with light as the Viperfish responded, an eerie sight that made Germaine's blood run cold. He had witnessed a lot of strange things on the sea, but the Viperfish were the strangest. The *Miss Lucy* surged forward as Bodden shoved the throttle to full speed. Germaine offered a brief silent prayer for his lost divers and turned to the crew, who were as frightened as he was.

"Secure everything. We're in for a rough ride back."

Gradually, the schooner pulled ahead of the school of Viperfish. Germaine glanced back at the spot where he had lost his three passengers. The area pulsed with lights. Suddenly, a dark shape like the prow of a submarine rose from the water, engulfing dozens of the Viperfish; swallowing them as a whale devours krill. The shape sank beneath the surface, but the lights suddenly vanished. The sound of a hundred whales echoed from the depths, vibrating the *Miss Lucy's* hull. Bodden glanced at Germaine. He hadn't witnessed the dark shape rise, but he knew enough about ocean sounds to know that this sound was different. Germaine shuddered in fear. He knew that in the vicious cycle of life, big fish preyed on smaller fish. What top predator snacked on twenty-foot Viperfish?

He didn't want to find out.

4

Oct. 23, Little Cayman Island, Caribbean –

Josh was going nowhere. No one was. He had arrived at the small airstrip at Edward Bodden Airfield in Blossom Village half an hour early. The winds had already reached gusts of forty miles per hour, and the pilot had expressed his doubts about taking off under such conditions. As badly as Josh wanted off the island, the thought of daring heavy winds disturbed him more than the approaching hurricane. One of Josh's fellow passengers became irate upon hearing the news and loudly voiced his objections. The pilot's concern had become a moot point when a sudden gust lifted the eight-thousand-pound de Havilland twin-engine Otter from the tarmac like a palm frond, and sent it hurdling into a nearby fuel truck. The attendant pumping fuel into the plane barely made it off the field before an enormous explosion lit up the night sky, as plane, truck, and a small nearby storage shed erupted in flames. Fire danced along the plane's sixty-five-foot wings like a line of Vegas chorus girls. Wind whipped the flames into an inferno that quickly consumed everything it touched. All four passengers in the small terminal watched on in silence. As the flames died, so did Josh's hopes.

"Is there another plane?" the irate man asked. "I have to be in New York in two days."

"No more planes, no more boats," the pilot replied, his attention focused on the burning plane.

"You mean I'm stuck here?"

"We're all stuck here," the pilot replied.

"Well, I never …."

The pilot ignored the irate passenger and walked out the door toward his destroyed airplane. His cap blew off and it went scuttling across the field. He stood outside in the blowing rain, his hands on his hips, staring at the wreckage. The lucky fuel attendant came to stand beside him. Neither of them attempted to extinguish the flames. The irate man turned to Josh, his mouth still open from his last unfinished tirade. Josh shrugged, picked up his suitcase, and left, leaving the man, his wife, and the fourth passenger, an islander on his way to Grand Cayman, behind.

The resort car that had delivered them to the airport had already left. Josh staggered with his head bowed into the wind as he struggled his way back to the resort on foot. Palm fronds, plastic bags, and blown sand pelted him in the face. Only his muscular legs kept him upright. A smaller man or woman would have gone pin wheeling in the wind. Heavy waves crashed onto the beach and surged across the road. His shoes and feet quickly became soaked. As if to further enhance his personal discomfort, the rain began as a solid sheet of water that raced down the road toward him. He had nowhere to run, so he kept plodding forward.

He was soaked by the time he walked in the door of the resort. Hawthorne, the manager, stared at Josh for a few seconds, as he dripped a steady stream of water onto the wooden floor; then rushed over to take his bag.

"What happened?" His gaze took in Josh's soaked shirt and pants. He also cast a quick glance at his wet floor.

"The plane's wrecked. No one's leaving."

A brief smiled flashed on Hawthorne's face at the prospect of getting at least another night's income from his guests, but then disappeared with the realization that he would also be responsible for his stranded guests' safety during the hurricane.

"Was anyone hurt?"

Josh shook his head. "No."

"You will be safe here," he assured Josh with a big smile.

The windows rattled, as a strong gust shook the building. Josh tossed Hawthorne a contemptuous look. "You haven't been outside lately."

"We have our own generator. If the power goes out, all I need do is go switch it on."

"Yeah, well they don't work so well underwater." He decided to quit giving the manager a hard time. It wasn't his fault the plane was wrecked. "You'd better send the car back for the others. I don't think they'll enjoy walking." He took his bag back from Hawthorne. "I think I'll change into something dry, if I have any dry clothes left."

As Josh trudged up the stairs to his room, water squishing out of his shoes with every step, Hawthorne rushed to the closet for a mop to clean up the mess Josh had left. Once inside his room, Josh dropped his bag on the floor, stripped naked, and tossed his wet clothes in the sink. He dried off with a towel and dressed in jeans and a t-shirt that he pulled from his bag, thankful for the dry clothing. The French doors to the veranda were swinging wildly in the wind, banging against the wall. He stared into the darkness for a moment before shutting them. When lightning flashed across the sky, illuminating every cloud, every tree, and the raging surf, reminding him of the storm on its way, he closed the drapes as well. He plopped down in a wingback chair, propped his feet on the rattan ottoman, and cursed his luck.

"Damn. I should have left yesterday with the others."

He had thought one more day on the island would help alleviate the bad luck of choosing the worst possible time of the year for his vacation. Now, he was stuck on Little Cayman with no way off. For good or bad, the resort was home for the duration. He took out his cell phone and pulled up the photos of the Ogrefish. Once again, he was struck by the savagery in the creature's eyes, but he decided that he was perhaps anthropomorphizing its normal countenance. The Ogrefish was neither evil nor good. It simply ate smaller creatures to survive, as nature dictated. A large jaw and sharp teeth best suited its chosen prey. Its demonic features were by design, not choice. His frustration annoyed him. He had made one of the greatest discoveries in marine biology in years, and he couldn't even share it with others. He couldn't contact his professor or even phone his parents to let them know that he was okay.

He tossed his phone onto the bed just as a large clap of thunder rattled the windows and shook the building.

"This is going to be a lot of fun," he said in disdain.

Picking up the remote, he tried the television, but the screen showed nothing but snowy static.

"Satellite dish is probably halfway to Mexico," he moaned and replaced the remote.

He sagged into his chair and closed his eyes, but the bright flashes of lightning penetrated his closed lids, and he couldn't escape the strident peals of thunder. It was unlikely that another plane would come until the hurricane had passed, and no one would risk taking him to George Town by boat, even if he had the cash to bribe them. He took heart in the fact that the Caymans had survived numerous hurricanes since their discovery by Christopher Columbus in 1503. He hoped they would survive one more storm.

He tried to force thoughts of the storm from his mind with trivia he had read in brochures downstairs in the lobby. Columbus had named the islands the Tortugas for the many turtles he found there, which early sailors saw as a source of nourishment. Now, the rock iguanas and the endangered Red-footed boobies were more numerous than the turtles. A bright flash of lightning, followed by another window-rattling clap of thunder reminded him of his surroundings. The iguanas and boobies would ride out the storm safely in the mangrove forests, while he was stuck in a forty-year-old, two-story wooden building fifty feet from the beach. The entire island was less than a mile wide and ten miles long, a mere speck in the ocean. It was a sitting target.

The phone beside the bed rang. Had the long-distance lines been repaired? He lurched out of his chair and picked up the receiver. "Hello."

"This is the desk, Mr. Peterman. The restaurant is closed because I thought all the guests were leaving, but I have made sandwiches, coffee, and tea for all of you. Would you like me to bring some up?"

Josh sighed. He had hoped to be dining at the Calypso Grill in George Town. That was now out of the question. "Sure. Thanks. Can you bring up some chips and a Coke? Oh, can you also bring me a bottle of rum?" He needed a drink in spite of last night's escapades. The rum would take the edge off his fear.

"My pleasure, Mr. Peterman. I'm glad to have you back."

Josh wasn't as pleased at Hawthorne was, but he was stuck there, and he was hungry. The lights flickered as he hung up the phone, but quickly settled. A heavy roll of thunder jangled the telephone on the table. His curiosity drew him to the window. He pulled aside the heavy, floral brocade drapes and stared outside. An almost constant barrage of lightning flashes illuminated the beach, or what was left of it. Waves crashed against the palm trees where he had lain in a hammock that afternoon, only ten feet from the front door. Each wave devoured mouthfuls of white sand with hungry wet teeth. The sea beyond was angry, lashing out at the island with all its fury, as if trying to shove the small speck of land into depths of the Cayman Trench from which it had arisen.

He spotted movement on the beach. At first, he thought a buoy or even an old WWII mine had washed ashore. Then, several more appeared, rolling onto the beach with the waves.

"What the hell?"

As he watched, the first sphere uncoiled into a living creature resembling a giant segmented pill bug with a dozen or more legs. It quickly scurried toward the resort. Others followed it. A lump formed in Josh's throat. He recognized the creatures as isopods, *Bathynomus giganteus,* ocean-bottom scavengers that often reached lengths of sixteen inches. However, these specimens were at least five feet long. Normally confined to the depths, he wondered how such creatures could survive out of water, but they seemed to be managing well enough. Within minutes, hundreds of the giant isopods littered the beach moving inland.

He remembered one more thing about *Bathynomus giganteus* – they were carnivorous, meat eaters. They often devoured dead whale carcasses that fell to the bottom. Creatures this size– who knew what damage they could do.

Nigel Hawthorne had seen the creatures as well, except he was foolishly standing bareheaded outside in the rain, frantically waving a broom at them, as if they were stray dogs to shoo away. Josh threw open the door and rushed out onto the veranda.

"Get back inside," he yelled at Hawthorne.

The manager glanced up at Josh, confusion pulling his face into a mask of confusion.

"Inside," Josh repeated, but to no avail.

If Hawthorne heard Josh over the roar of the surf and howling wind, he didn't respond. He returned his gaze to the creatures crawling toward his resort. He shoved the broom into one creature's face. It seized the broom with its maxillipeds, a set of legs designed to draw food to its four sets of jaws. It crushed the wooden broom handle like a toothpick and discarded it. Too late, Hawthorne understood the danger he was in. He began backing toward the porch but failed to see the large stone planter behind him. He tripped over it and fell to the ground. The isopod moved more nimbly than Josh had thought it capable. It crawled over Hawthorne's prone body and began tearing into his flesh with its jaws. A second creature joined the first, seizing one of Hawthorne's arms and ripping it from his shoulder. Hawthorne's agonized screams split the crash of the pounding surf and defied the howling wind to resonate throughout the resort. Josh turned away from the sickening sight, refusing to watch the creatures consume the manager's body.

At the sound of a loud crash downstairs, he rushed back into his room, flung open the door, and stared down in horror at the scene unfolding in the lobby. A score of the creatures had smashed down the front door and entered the building, trailing puddles of water behind them. They milled about the lobby like eager Black Friday shoppers, investigating everything, overturning statues and potted plants, and smashing chairs and tables. One knocked the tray laden with sandwiches destined for the guests onto the floor and gobbled them up in two quick bites. As Josh watched the jaws opening and closing, he was struck by a sense of awe at their complexity, and with terror at their raw power. Such creatures should not exist, but there they were. The giant Ogrefish were no mere anomaly. They were a plague, a plague of deep sea creatures grown to gargantuan size, let loose upon an unsuspecting, unprepared populace.

He ducked back inside his room, snatched up his cell phone from his bed, rushed back out and snapped several photos of the creatures. The irate passenger from the terminal, Wilkins he thought was his name, stepped out of his room.

"What is all this racket?" he demanded.

Josh stared at him a moment before pointing downstairs. Wilkins' eyes opened wide when he saw the creatures.

"They killed Hawthorne," Josh told him.

"Killed?" Wilkins' face contorted into a mixture of disgust and fear. "Call the police," he yelled.

The lights went out, leaving the resort in darkness. Josh waited for the resort's generator to kick in, but nothing happened. Then he remembered Hawthorne saying he would have to switch it on. *So much for that.* The clicking of the creatures' clawed feet scurrying across the wooden floor was even more frightening in the dark. Josh was glad of the flashes of lightning. At least until they revealed Wilkins raising a vase over his head ready to fling it at one of the creatures below.

"I wouldn't do that," he advised Wilkins.

Wilkins stared at him contemptuously, and then threw the vase. It shattered on one of the creature's hard, segmented carapace, but did no damage.

"Those plates are hard as steel," Josh said. "A bullet wouldn't penetrate."

The isopod raised its fore body into the air and focused its attention on Wilkins. Its four antennae waved wildly as it sensed prey, and then, to Josh's astonishment, it began nimbly climbing the stairs. Wilkins retreated to his room and slammed the door.

"The door won't stop them," he yelled at Wilkins, but he knew it was a useless gesture. He noticed several other creatures joining the first in its slow but steady ascent of the stairs.

"Remarkable acuity of senses and agility," Josh remarked.

He paused a moment to observe the creature's progress, then retreated to the dubious safety of his room. He walked onto the veranda and saw hundreds of the creatures swarming onto the beach, and imagined thousands more doing the same all along the island's coastline. No lights were visible anywhere on the island. The storm had knocked out the island's single main generator. In the darkness, muffled by the fury of the wind and surf, no one would hear the creatures coming until it were too late.

Trying to escape down the back stairs would be suicidal. The resort was completely surrounded. His only hope of survival lay in the creatures' only weakness – oxygen, or the lack of it. They were sea creatures. Unable to breathe on dry land, they would live only as long as sufficient oxygen remained in their bloodstreams. Locomotion and eating would quickly consume that stored oxygen. Sea mammals, such as porpoises, dolphins, and whales, could remain underwater thirty minutes to two hours, respectively. The question was how long could a giant isopod remain out of water and survive?

It took the creatures only minutes to reach the second floor, and another minute to splinter Wilkins' door. He heard shouts and loud crashing sounds. Wilkins and his wife's screams thankfully lasted only a few seconds. Josh heard the creatures outside his door and knew it wouldn't take them long to locate him. He quickly slipped on his wet sneakers, stuffed his cell phone in his pocket, and went onto the veranda. Even though he could easily outrun the creatures, their vast numbers and the likelihood of stumbling into them in the dark made escape impossible. With the highest point of the island nearly ten miles away, and only forty feet above high tide, his choices for refuge were few. Between him and the island's highest elevation lay salt water ponds and marshes. If the surf continued to rise, he would be floundering in water filled with either isopods or Ogrefish, a risk he was not willing to take. He searched for an alternative.

One end of the building had a wooden trellis with a dense tangle of climbing roses running from the ground to just below the roof. With the resort soon to become an island and surrounded by deadly creatures, the roof seemed the safest spot. His biggest problem would be the hurricane-force winds. He ripped a decorative fish net from the veranda's ceiling, threw it over his shoulder, and raced for the end of the veranda. He risked a quick peek inside Wilkins' room and wished that he hadn't.

The room was in shambles. Only the bloody legs of Wilkins' wife were visible beyond the bed, but Wilkins' partially stripped carcass lay in the middle of the room beneath a small huddle of the creatures. White bone gleamed obscenely through large open wounds above his hip and chest. One creature was gnawing on Wilkins' head. He was dead, but his eyes were open and staring. Josh fought down a rush of nausea and continued.

The wind, the rain, and the rose thorns made climbing difficult, pricking his hands and legs as he climbed, using muscles he had long ago forgotten. He hadn't climbed since a boy in his uncle's apple orchard in Austin. With blood and rain-soaked hands, he pulled his way upwards toward the roof as gusts of wind threatened to pry him from the trellis. Using a gutter for a foothold, he fought the aches in his arms and legs, and scrambled onto the wooden shingle roof. He lay prostrate for a few moments to catch his breath. Then, securing one end of the net to a drainpipe downspout and the other to the chimney, he wrapped himself in the net as tightly as he could.

The wind buffeted him like a tetherball, bouncing him against the roof. The wind-driven rain made breathing difficult, but he clung to the nylon netting as if his life depended on it, which it did. He could no longer see the isopods, but he could hear the damage they were doing to the resort. After a while, the noises faded. He wondered if the creatures had succumbed to the lack of oxygen, but he didn't dare leave his perch to check. Within an hour, the waves began entering the resort. The entire building shuddered as the heavy waves crashed into it, and then shook as the massive surge of water retreated. These repeated hammer blows of water, combined with the hurricane-force winds, took a toll on the wooden structure. Railings ripped loose and sailed kite-like with the wind. Palm trees bent until they touched the ground, and then, forced beyond even their resilience, snapped in two, their crowns scuttling along the beach like massive beach umbrellas.

The weather report had listed Hurricane Clive as a Category Four hurricane on the Saffir-Simpson Scale with winds reaching one-hundred-fifty miles per hour. At that speed, a loose roof shingle or a splinter from a palm tree would penetrate his flesh like a loosed arrow. Soaked and battered by the wind, Josh held on for dear life. His arms and legs deadened from the cold rain. His ears grew numb with the constant roar of the wind and the incessant crashing of thunder. When a low rumble began to impinge on his senses, he wiped the water from his eyes and gazed out to sea. A wave, marching like a white-helmeted giant, rushed toward shore at an alarming speed. The water in the bay retreated until he could have walked to nearby Owen Island. By the time the wave reached

Owen Island, it towered over the tiny spit of land by twenty feet. The island disappeared beneath the wave, which grew even taller as it entered the shallower water of the bay. The ground trembled until the building danced away from its foundation. The chimney shattered, threatening to drag Josh's net with it. Loose bricks pelted his body. The nylon net dug into his flesh until he thought he would be halved like the child facing Solomon's dilemma. Then, with a sharp snap, the net parted from the chimney. He bounced across the roof, secured only to the drainpipe. He grabbed the gutter with both hands to avoid rolling off. Helpless, he watched the inexorable approach of the island-killer wave.

The wave reached the resort, slamming into the structure with the force of a thousand sledgehammers swung by a thousand John Henrys impacting simultaneously. Thin wooden walls exploded inward, becoming kindling. The veranda collapsed into the raging surf. The beach side of the building dropped several feet, as the sand washed away beneath it. The roof cracked; then split apart a few feet from Josh's legs. The section to which Josh clung fell away. The sudden lurch as the roof slewed sideways caught Josh unaware. His pittance of a meal, chips and fruit, exploded from his mouth. The vile taste of bile mixed with dirty salt water as his mouth filled with ocean and sand. The roof crashed into the surf. The rest of the resort became a disjointed raft of planks and wooden furniture, which was quickly swept beneath the water. His small piece of roof became a raft, swept inland by the crest of the wave.

He had surfed Galveston's beaches a few times and considered himself a decent novice, but nothing had prepared him for the wildest ride of his life. In a dizzying, water-borne journey across the island, he witnessed buildings being smashed, power poles snap, and trees uprooted like plucked daisies. He caught the occasional glimpse of horrified people run down by the powerful wave and tossed aside like litter. The wave carried him westward along the length of the island. Through the wall of rain, he glimpsed an island reduced in width by half and by two-thirds in length. Blossom Village, the airport, and the entire eastern end of the island were gone, submerged beneath the waves.

His tiny raft rolled in the waves, dunking him repeatedly beneath the water, but releasing himself from the net would mean his death. He held his breath as long as he could and came up sputtering each time the raft righted. The wave reduced in height and gradually lost strength as it moved inland. Josh waited for the inevitable crash. His heart raced as he glimpsed a tree rushing toward him. In a brief flash of lightning, the tree moved, revealing a large eye that blinked twice. He braced himself as best he could, but the impact with the creature tore him loose from the net and the roof. He rolled beneath the waves and struck something solid. The impact crushed his chest and forced the air from his lungs. He fought for the surface, but in the dark, beneath the roiling water, he couldn't distinguish up from down. A strange calm came over him as his body settled beneath the waves. He had heard drowning was almost as good a way to die as freezing. In the cold water, he was doing both at the same time. He closed his eyes and embraced the inevitable.

5

Oct. 24, Grand Cayman Island, Caribbean –

Hurricane Clive struck Grand Cayman a glancing blow at two forty-five on the morning of the 24th. Even so, the devastation was enormous. Wind-driven waves surged inland, swamping houses and piling boats into piles of stacked driftwood. George Town suffered eighty deaths with over two hundred reported injuries. More would surely follow as the day progressed. The monetary damage would eventually reach seven-hundred-million dollars, but when balanced against the cost in lives lost and disruption, it paled in comparison.

Ron Germaine's schooner, the *Miss Lucy*, had ridden out the storm anchored in deep water on the leeward side of the island. It had suffered damage both from the hard voyage and during the storm. A cracked jib spar, a lost sail, some loose planking along the bow, and damaged rails would be costly to repair, but he had been very lucky. He chuckled as he considered his luck. His ship had survived and his crew were safe, but his passengers, all three of them, were gone, devoured by sea monsters. He hadn't reported their deaths to the authorities yet. He hadn't drunk enough scotch for that, but he knew he would eventually have to. He briefly considered reporting them as simply missing during the storm, but lying usually brought more problems than the truth, even one as unbelievable as sea monsters.

Bodden, his mate, sat on the hatch cover staring into the water. He had said very little since returning to port. Though this wasn't unusual for the taciturn Bodden, Germaine sensed some deeper reason for his silence.

"What do you think of all this, Chance?" he asked.

Bodden lifted his head and glared at Germaine from beneath the brim of his battered cap. His dark eyes bore the same haunted look Germaine had once observed in a man picked up after twenty days at sea alone on a raft.

"That storm was evil."

"Evil?" Germaine stared at his mate, but the look of fear on Bodden's face indicated he was dead serious.

Bodden nodded. "She was no simple blow. She brought devils up from the Deep. Bad luck will follow us."

"Bad luck?" Germaine waved his hands around. "What do you call this? Three passengers dead, my ship damaged, and the whole damn island almost wiped out."

"No, I mean bad luck for us. We escaped death last night, but it will not stop. It will come for us. We will all die."

"Shut the fuck up," Germaine yelled, fed up with his mate's melancholy. "You want to jinx us?" Predictions of doom didn't sit well with him. It was like calling down the wrath of God.

Germaine glanced at the video disc he had taken from McCoy's monitor. The quality was poor, but with it, he might manage to keep the authorities from arresting him and impounding his boat. It probably didn't matter. Once the story of the deaths circulated, he would be out of business anyway. No one would ever charter a death ship.

"Gather up McCoy's and the other passengers' belongings. If I report it now with all the commotion, the authorities might not investigate too thoroughly." He didn't really believe that, but he needed to snap Bodden out of his funk.

Bodden rose from his seat and went below. Germaine stared at the island. Most of the trees were now broken stubs sticking up from a land scoured by waves. Once pristine Seven Mile Beach was littered with debris, and the houses nearest the shore were gone, swept from their foundations and carried inland by the water. He hadn't seen his home yet. It was on the east side of George Town on a low rise. Hopefully, it had survived the worst of the devastation.

He glanced down at the disc in his hand, sighed, and dropped it over the side. It didn't sink, but it would float ashore and become just one more piece of flotsam no one would notice. No one would believe his story, even with a barely viewable video. It would be better to take his chances.

After Bodden had gathered the dead men's things, they lowered the launch. He left the other two crewmen aboard to tidy up. Germaine had Bodden land the small craft in George Town Harbour near the town. The masts of sunken sailing yachts protruded from the water like a drowned forest. Buoys torn from nets, bits of flotsam and jetsam from sunken or beached boats, broken boards, and bags of trash littered the surface. The Port Facility building was gone. Only a scar of rubble remained. The Bayshore Mall and the Pier Market, where tourists had once sought bargains, were piles of shattered brick and twisted steel. Germaine shook his head in disgust, as he watched one young man grab an armload of blue jeans from one of the few standing shelves and run off. Even in a calamity, looters profited.

"I need to check on me mum," Bodden said.

Germaine, too wrenched by the scene of destruction, nodded. He watched Bodden make his way through the piles of debris until he disappeared, and then began walking up Harbour Street. Parts of the road were missing, crumbled into the sea. Of Elmslie United Church, all that remained was a steeple lying on its side. Germaine thought it a profane desecration of the holy. He resisted the impulse to ring the church bell to toll the dead. Fort George, a small colonial-era fort constructed of native coral and limestone in 1790, was an historical ruin, partially demolished by a developer a few years earlier, but the fort had weathered the storm better than most modern buildings. It still stood sentinel on the shore guarding the remnants of George Town as it had for two-and-a quarter centuries.

The streets of George Town were clogged with rescue vehicles and hastily erected first aid stations. Survivors sat on the curb waiting their turn to see the deluged medical personnel. On the way to his home, Germaine passed men, women, and children with broken bones, open wounds, and battered bodies. All had the hollow-eyed lost look most survivors of a catastrophe exhibited. There was amazingly very little talking. Aside from some low moans from the injured, a few children crying, and the soft scuffle of feet shuffling on the sidewalks, the city was eerily silent.

He also passed sad rows of bodies covered with sheets. Grieving families huddled around the bodies of lost loved ones. Even their sobbing was soft, as if in deference to others' grief. Some lifted sheet after sheet to find their missing among the dead. It was a heart-rending sight, made even more horrible by the fact that he recognized some of the families of the dead and many of the injured. A few glanced up at him, but said nothing. What could they say? How could he reply? He was alive. Their loved ones weren't. Red Cross workers drew blood from donors for the injured in alleys beneath tarpaulins slung between shattered buildings.

He spotted Orlando Mason, the island's Royal Cayman Island Police Chief Inspector, wearing his uniform jacket over his pajamas. He was barefoot. The Chief Inspector stood in front of the courthouse directing the rescue crews to several of the numerous collapsed buildings. Every now and then, a shout rang out as a survivor was pulled from the wreckage, but such joyous shouts were few and far between.

From his boat, at first glance, the town had been spared the worst of the storm, but looks were deceiving. Buildings that appeared untouched from a distance revealed empty interiors upon closer inspection, their contents, even entire upper floors, ripped from them by the powerful surge and deposited hundreds of yards away like garbage on a heap. He held out little hope for his house.

He stumbled past families dragging waterlogged furniture from flooded homes and past automobiles overturned by the storm, slowly growing numb to the enormity of the desolation. The Annex Field was now a small pond. He had watched many soccer matches there on warm Sunday afternoons. It would be some time before such an event happened again. The Butterfield Roundabout on Sound Road was clogged with stalled vehicles. Two policemen directed a bulldozer as it shoved automobiles aside to clear a path for emergency vehicles. He winced as the dozer rolled a new Mercedes onto its side and ground it along the pavement.

Sound Road seemed to be the boundary for the storm surge. Beyond it, most of the damage came from high winds rather than water. He was surprised to see his home still standing. The rise upon which he had built it was just high enough to avoid the worst of the storm surge. Some roof tiles were missing, and two shutters had been ripped off by the winds. His satellite dish antenna was folded like a taco. The plywood he had secured over the front window before leaving was gone. A broken limb from the sixty-year-old Poinciana tree that he had nurtured for twenty-five years had smashed the front window. A carpet of its red-orange blossoms and leaves littered the walk.

Inside, only the front room had suffered damage from wind-driven rain through the broken window. Water dripped into the sink from a leak in the roof. He had worked up a sweat on the long walk. He took a Kalik beer from the refrigerator and twisted off the top. The electricity was off and the beer was warm, but it quenched his thirst. He sat in his favorite leather chair in the front room, staring out the broken window. Eventually, he would have to spread a tarp over the roof and put up more plywood over the window, but for now, he just relaxed. Slowly, his lids slid over his eyes. The beer slipped from his hand and fell to the floor. The tensions of the last twenty-four hours had drained him, emotionally and physically. Sleep wouldn't solve his problems, but his body needed it. After a few minutes, he snored softly.

* * * *

He awoke just before sunset. Refreshed from his long nap, he set about making his house weather tight. He secured a fresh plywood board from the garage over the front window with screws. Next, he dragged out his ladder, scaled the roof, and draped a plastic tarp over the hole above the kitchen, securing its edges with boards and nails. He mopped the water from the front room's wooden floor and hauled the soaked throw rug to the rubbish bin. His couch and one of the chairs were soaked, but he hoped they might dry out before they mildewed. Afterwards, he opened a can of stew and warmed it over the gas burner. The stew, a beer, and a piece of bread became his supper.

His repairs done and his belly full, Germaine summoned up the courage to report the missing divers. He retraced his steps through the rubble to the courthouse, but the police were all busy in the town and around the island, helping search for missing people. He could wait. He was in no hurry to end his career. The long lines of injured had disappeared, either sent home or transferred to a hangar at Owen Roberts International Airport converted into a makeshift infirmary. Island power was still out. Portable generators supplied power for light stands to aid the workers in the darkness. Outside help hadn't yet arrived, held up by the hurricane. He joined a work crew digging into the rubble of a collapsed two-story apartment building. After two hours of backbreaking labor, they discovered two bodies and a lone survivor nestled amid the debris in a corner of a stairwell. Around nine o'clock, he took a cigarette break and walked down to the harbor. He sat on an overturned crate, enjoying a smoke, and watched the waves roll in.

George Town was his home. He and it had weathered many storms and a few hurricanes over the years. Clive had been a bad one, but the island would recover. Islanders were a hardy bunch, self-reliant and industrious. It might be days before substantial aid arrived from other countries, but no one sat on their haunches waiting. The priority was to get the island back in shape for tourists. Tourists meant dollars, yen, and euros, the lifeblood of the local economy. His own livelihood was dependent on tourists. Once word circulated about the deaths on his boat, he might have to look for another job. At fifty-one, he was young to retire and too old to start over. He might make a living fishing, but it was a hard, hand-to-mouth livelihood and one he hoped to avoid.

A scratching noise drew his attention to the water. At first, he thought the small dark objects climbing the sea wall were red crabs, but they had already made their yearly migration to the sea. As he watched, hundred of the strange creatures came ashore. Remembering the giant Viperfish, he approached them cautiously. It was dark, but they reminded him of some type of insect, and bore a passing resemblance to horseshoe crabs. They varied in size from a few inches to almost a foot in length. When several of the creatures zeroed in on him, he became alarmed and began backing away. He flicked his cigarette at them. They swarmed it. He removed the letter from the bank he had picked up in his house and shoved in his pocket. He rolled it up, lit it on fire with his cigarette lighter, and tossed it at the creatures. They rushed it, but quickly retreated from the heat. By the flame's light, he swore the creatures were giant sea lice.

Sea lice, common in Caribbean waters, infesting fish and even hapless swimmers, were tiny creatures, plankton, eating flesh and drinking blood through siphon mouths. By this time, thousands of the sea lice had crowded onto the beach and road. Germaine decided discretion was the better part of valor. He ran to the center of town where the rescue crews were still working, yelling a warning as he went. People stopped and stared at him as if he were drunk, but otherwise ignored him. He continued running, but smoking, a sedate lifestyle, and lack of exercise had weakened his constitution. His lungs ached and his legs became leaden, but he knew that if he stopped, the sea lice would catch up. He didn't know how they could survive out of water, but they were doing a good job at it.

He heard the first screams behind him a few minutes later. He stopped long enough to glance back toward the town. Illuminated by the work lights, he witnessed a scene of absolute horror. The lice leaped on people from piles of debris or scurried up their legs, completely covering their bodies. Some beat at the lice with their hands and fists; others simply ran screaming in panic. One man, inundated by the creatures, stumbled into one of the light racks, knocking it to the ground, extinguishing it. In the darkness, the screams continued. Germaine crossed himself and just kept running. He didn't stop until he reached his house. He slammed the door behind him and locked it, though he knew it would do little good against the creatures. He needed a weapon.

He went to the garage where he kept his five-year-old Mini Cooper. It needed a valve job and hadn't run in weeks. He didn't have the money to repair it. He couldn't escape in it. Handsaws, battery powered drills, hammers – none would be effective as weapons. Finally, his eyes settled on the small acetylene torch he had used to make repairs on his rudder. He grabbed it, checked the tank – half full – and went back outside. Picking an area barren of grass, he made several trips and piled scraps of dry wood from his garage in a circle around him, doused it with petrol, and waited.

He didn't have to wait long. A few people ran past him trying to escape, but from the sounds of horror coming from the eastern end of the island, the creatures were also coming ashore from North Sound. The island was less than a mile wide at George Town. There was nowhere to run. A woman rushed toward him, her back and legs swarming with sea lice the size of Palmetto bugs. Her face was a mask of terror. Suddenly, she stopped running. A strange gurgling sound came from her throat, and she collapsed with white foam dripping from her mouth. The creatures' stings were poisonous, something else he had to avoid.

He ignited the wood and it burst into a circle of flames. The first creatures crawled into the flames and were immediately consumed, bursting from the heat, spraying blood and intestines around them. The blood, he assumed, came from their victims. The others stopped a few feet away. Their antenna waved as they sensed the heat. Within minutes, he was surrounded. Every now and then, another sea louse or two would attempt the circle of fire, but quickly died. All too quickly, his fire began to die. He splashed his remaining petrol on the flames, trying to urge them higher, but with no more wood for fuel, the last flames flickered and died.

As if on command, the sea lice surged forward over the dying embers. He lit the torch, set it for a wide flame, and fanned it around him. The sea lice popped like popcorn as the hot flame touched them and they exploded into flames.

"Come on, you little buggers," he yelled, "Come eat some fire."

He spun in a circle to keep them from creeping up behind him. The creatures crawled over the bodies of their dead. Soon, a foot-high wall of burning sea lice surrounded him, making it more difficult for the remaining creatures to get at him. The flame on his torch grew weaker. He tried cranking it up, and then checked the gauge and saw that it was almost empty. He failed to notice one creature launch itself at him. It landed on his leg. A sharp pain lanced through his calf. His head almost exploded in agony. He brushed the creature off with his hand, but the damage had been done. Blood trickled down his leg. The strong odor of blood seemed to drive the creatures into a fury. They redoubled their efforts to get at him. He waved the torch frantically, roasting them as quickly as he could. His leg was growing numb, but he knew that if he stumbled or fell, it would all be over.

When the torch sputtered its last flame, he beat at them with the tank, swinging it with the hose like a medieval mace. He was still flailing at them when they stopped moving. Their bodies were shaking, their antennas quivering. After a few seconds, they curled up and quit moving. He dropped the torch, his arms aching from the effort of swinging it, his chest heaving as he tried to catch his breath. Carefully, with his still numb leg, he stepped over them, kicking at them with the toe of his shoe. They were dead, unable to survive long out of water. He had won the war.

His leg throbbed and his vision was blurred. He hoped a single bite wasn't fatal. Too dizzy to stand, he sat down beside the sea of giant dead lice and lit a cigarette. As an afterthought, he held his lighter to one of the dead creatures until, with a satisfying pop, it exploded. He inhaled the cigarette smoke, but it had the stench of petrol and death on it, so he tossed it aside.

6

Oct. 24, Adrift off Little Cayman Island, Caribbean –

Josh opened his eyes, not quite certain if he was in heaven or hell. He tried to move, but his body sent messages of pain shooting through his nervous system. He had to be alive. Death couldn't hurt so much. He felt as if he had been bitch slapped with a shovel. His chest was on fire. He lay back down and concentrated on opening his eyes. The light stabbed his eyes, forcing him to shut them immediately. Slowly, he tried again. Thankfully, the sun was hidden behind clouds, reducing its glare. By his estimate, it was mid-morning. The slight bobbing of whatever he was lying on meant he was adrift. He turned his head to one side, reeling from the effort and the rush of nausea, and scanned his surroundings. He saw wooden roof tiles, water, and nothing else. A ten-feet-square section of the roof had become a raft, saving his life. He was battered, hungry, and thirsty, but he was alive. He wondered how many other residents of the island had survived.

He remembered the wave, the isopods and the Ogrefish. With a start, he quickly scanned the water, but saw nothing. He also remembered … something else. The imaged flashed in his mind, an image illuminated by a flash of lightning, a head and an eye … He shook his head to clear it and regretted the action, as he threw up salt water and the remains of his last meal. *My imagination*, he thought. He assessed his situation. He was adrift in the middle of the Caribbean after a major hurricane. He had no supplies, and it was unlikely that anyone would come searching for him. If the damage he saw during the storm were any indication, there would be casualties enough to deal with on land.

Carefully, he sat up. His ribs ached and his right arm was numb from being twisted in the net, but he didn't complain. It had saved his life. Other than a few scrapes, some shallow cuts on his hands and face, and a plethora of bruises, he was all right. A distant speck north of him could be Little Cayman or even Cayman Brac, but it didn't matter. He had no way of reaching them other than by swimming, and the current was moving him away from land. After what he had witnessed, he was reluctant to get in the water.

In spite of the cloud cover, the heat was insufferable. He had no shade and no way of quenching his growing thirst. Food would be a problem, but not before, he died from thirst. For a moment, he wished he hadn't survived, but the horrific vision of the creatures devouring Nigel Hawthorne made him take back that wish. He remembered his cell phone. He took it from his pocket, but was dismayed to find it didn't work. He carefully removed the cover and spread it out to dry, hoping the battery was still good. He searched his pockets to see what his survival depended on. The pickings were slim. He had his wallet, some change, a small pocketknife, and a few half-melted mints he had picked up after a meal – not much of a survival kit. He popped one of the mints in his mouth to get a little saliva flowing.

Once, he saw a fin break the surface a few hundred yards away. Whether it was a shark or a dolphin, he couldn't tell, but it came no closer. Sharks were the least of his worries. Giant isopods and Ogrefish didn't exist in a vacuum. Whatever had produced them had probably created other enormous species. He attributed their emergence from the depths to the hurricane, but as to what force, man or nature, they owed their existence, he had no clue.

Individual species long thought extinct or myths kept turning up – a *coelacanth* in the waters off South Africa, giant squid in the Sea of Japan, enormous Oarfish in California, giant stingrays, and photos of a possible *Mauisaurus* in Loch Ness. His professor had caused a stir during one lecture by proposing that Godzilla could exist somewhere in the deep, a product of underwater nuclear testing in the fifties and sixties. Having seen an armada of giant carnivorous isopods and six-foot Ogrefish, Josh wasn't as quick to dismiss Godzilla now.

Sleeping used less energy than remaining awake. He tried napping, allowing the steady rhythm of the waves to lull him to sleep, but each time he awoke from dark, troubled dreams that would not leave him even while awake. The waters he once thought so serene, so full of life, now were the home of nightmarish creatures. They could be lurking just beneath him, ready to devour him as they had Hawthorne.

No, Isopods don't swim. They walk. They walked onto the beach. Nothing to fear from them out here.

He chuckled. "Now, all I have to worry about are giant Ogrefish," he said aloud, then laughed again.

Get a grip, Josh, he chided himself. *Don't fall apart this early.*

Since he couldn't sleep, he passed the time listing whatever sea creature popped into his head by Kingdom, Phylum, Class, Order, Family, Genus, and Species. He deliberately ignored the giants he had seen, though someone would have to classify them eventually. It bothered him that he couldn't remember to which species the six-gill shark belonged, *griseus* or *warreni.* He knew the genus was *Hexanchus.* Finally, he remembered that the bluntnose six-gill shark was *Hexanchus griseus,* and that the six-gill saw shark belonged in its own genus, *Pliotrema warreni.* His satisfaction at solving that mystery dissolved as two fins appeared just yards away – sharks. He mentally kicked himself for calling his own demons. By their metallic bronze-gray coloring, the rear curved first dorsal fin, and long rear tip second dorsal fin, he recognized them as silky sharks, *Carcharhinus falciformis.* He judged their size to be around seven feet long. He had encountered them once before while diving along the Caymans' North Wall. They were more nuisance than aggressive. Relief swept over him when he saw that the pair was herding a small school of bar jacks, *Caranx ruber.* Josh had speared and eaten the tasty game fish numerous times. Bar jacks usually remained around the reefs, feeding on crustaceans. The storm had driven them out into deep water. Now, the two-feet-long fish would provide a snack for the silky sharks.

Better thee than me.

After a while, the sharks left. To his surprise, he discovered that he missed their presence. At least they were known to him, and not some hellish creature dredged up from the deep. The day wore on. The invisible sun baked him, dried out his skin and parched his throat. He splashed water on his skin, but knew better than to quench his raging thirst with salt water. To do so would mean a quick, agonizing death.

As bad as the day had been, night was worse. After the sunset, a light breeze reduced the temperature, leaving him shivering. With no moon, he sat bobbing with the current in utter darkness. He could barely discern the other end of his small, makeshift raft. He forced the idea of some deadly creature lurking just out of arm's reach from his mind. Again, he tried sleeping, but each time, the nightmares were too strong, the memories too vivid. The smell of the creatures, the sight of the blood, and the roar of the giant wave rushing at him overloaded his sleeping senses. He sat huddled, trying to conserve his body heat. The calories he expended heating his body would reduce the time he could survive adrift. His shoes were gone, sucked off by the giant wave. His shirt was in rags. He tucked his feet beneath him in a lotus position to keep them warm.

He reassembled his cell phone, and to his delight, it worked. He had no signal with which to contact anyone, but by occasionally using its flashlight feature, he drove back the all- encompassing darkness. He considered playing some of his game apps to pass the time, but couldn't deplete his battery. He pulled up the photo of the Ogrefish. His professor's lecture on Godzilla jostled a few memories. How could such a creature as giant Ogrefish or isopods evolve? If only one species suddenly grew in size, the cause could be natural, but two species? That involved something more than natural selection. What could stimulate growth in an animal – radiation, growth hormones, some toxic substance? Mankind had been using the oceans as a dumping ground for decades. Anything poured into the rivers or on land eventually made its way to the ocean. The oceans had become a cauldron of chemicals, and with the Japan reactor disaster, radiation. However, that was on the West Coast. What could account for uncontrolled growth in the Caribbean? He knew he wouldn't find the answer sitting on a piece of roof.

He spent the night in frigid misery. How the tropics could be so damned cold eluded him. He longed for a fire, but even if he had a lighter or dry match, he couldn't risk burning his only means of transportation. Every sound, every splash became a monster intent on his death. He tried to pray, but found he couldn't. He had grown up a Christian, a Southern Baptist, but the lure of women, drugs, and booze proved stronger than the word of God. He never considered himself an atheist. Perhaps agnostic was closer to the mark. If there were a God, Josh had never felt his touch. Science had become his religion, marine biology, his philosophy. All other pursuits were merely distractions. By his senior year, even women and drugs had taken a distant fourth. Alcohol had become his drug of choice, and even that, he consumed in moderation, except for this vacation.

Before morning, a tiny sliver of moon broke through the cloud cover. He relished the small amount of illumination it provided. The sea shimmered like a satin sheet. The waves shattered the moon's reflection into thousands of miniature moons dancing on the ocean. He stared at one cluster of lights for several minutes before realizing that it was moving – a ship. He grabbed his cell phone with the instinct honed by an era of instant communication, but he had no signal, nor a number to call if he had. Instead, he turned on the flashlight and waved it over his head. He knew this might be his last chance at rescue, and hoarding battery power served no purpose. To his dismay, the lights soon vanished over the horizon.

He ate his last mint, letting it dissolve slowly on his tongue. It deceived his stomach but not his intestines. They growled and writhed like a nest of vipers. He regretted eating nothing but chips and fruit at the resort the day before. He would kill for a Snickers bar or an apple. A bout of coughing set his chest on fire from the pain in his bruised ribs. The passing of the ship almost broke his spirit, but he refused to give into despair. To quench his thirst, he used his penknife to jab the tip of his finger. It hurt like hell, but he put the finger in his mouth and sucked the blood. The few calories it provided wouldn't do much, but the liquid eased the ache in his throat.

He waited. When dawn came, he greeted the sun with mixed blessings. While he craved its light, its heat was his enemy. The sky was still overcast, but frequent breaks in the clouds turned his small raft into a wooden hotplate. He imagined himself slowly cooking, but that brought on a bout of hunger. He searched the water for fish. He repaired the net as best he could and lay on the edge of the raft with his pocketknife handy. The odds of a fish getting close enough for him to snare it in the net and stab it with the knife were miniscule, but he had nothing to do but wait, watch and hope. No fins broke the surface, and no seagulls ventured near the raft. His hunger mounted.

As the day progressed and the temperature increased, he passed in and out of consciousness. He knew he was suffering from heatstroke, but he could do nothing about it. He rolled over on his stomach to keep the sun from blinding him. He had heard of men lost in the desert or in the snow going blind from excessive sun exposure to their retinas. During his periods of unconsciousness, his nightmares attacked him. He struggled against invisible demons. Once, he awoke half off the raft, his right arm and shoulder in the water.

Night came again, as exorable as death, as dark as the inside of a coffin. He knew he couldn't endure another night in the open, let alone another day. He considered suicide, but he didn't have the strength to let the deep take him, or the courage to open his veins with the penknife. Against his better judgment and the voices inside his head, he endured.

As he lay staring into the darkness, his eyes half closed from dehydration, a light appeared in the distance. Was it another ship or the same one? Or was it just an illusion? He lacked the strength to lift the cell phone above his head, so he held it in his hand on the deck and wiggled it. He ignored the pain. After what seemed like an interminable time, the lights came closer. He began yelling, but his voice cracked. The taste of salt water touched his parched lips. He was crying.

* * * *

Oct. 25, Cruise ship *Neptune*, Caribbean –

The ship sliced through the waves like a yacht, riding smoothly with hardly a shudder. The ship's captain, Luther Amos, smiled to himself as the slight vibration of the engines passed from the deck and traveled up his legs, endowing him with a sense of power. The throb of the engines, the salt tang of the breeze on his deeply tanned face, the clean, crisp lines of his vessel – for Captain Amos, there was no place nearer heaven than the bridge of the *Neptune*. The *Neptune*, catering to a smaller, more discerning class of traveler who preferred luxury and comfort to the carnival atmosphere of some of its larger sister lines, had anchored in one of Jamaica's safe harbors during the worst of the hurricane. Now, her captain was making up for lost time, pushing the ship's engines to maximum to reach Bermuda on time. He was determined that no delay should mar his otherwise exemplary fifteen-year record as captain of the Bahamian-registered cruise ship.

The ninety-six passenger hadn't minded the extra day layover in Jamaica because of the weather. A gala ball had directed their attention from the storm to the freely flowing river of booze from the well-stocked bar and the extravagant buffet presented by the ship's award winning chef. The ship's itinerary was always somewhat lax, allowing the passengers to vote for lingering in or avoiding any port during the seven-day cruise. At over twenty-seven hundred dollars per passenger, he overlooked this slight discretion as a matter of passenger satisfaction. His passengers expected their whims to be catered to, and his staff and crew of sixty-one offered them their complete time and devotion. A spa and fitness room with sauna, a small casino, a theater providing both live entertainment and movies, two pools, and a complete marina with kayaks, small powered craft, scuba and snorkeling equipment, and jet skis made certain no passenger lacked leisure pursuits. If these offerings weren't sufficient or too vigorous, the ship also boasted a large library of books and videos, or a passenger could simply relax in their cabin.

Captain Amos checked his watch, a black Movado Ceramic Chronograph given to him by the company on his tenth anniversary. The thousand dollar watch was his prized possession, a reminder that hard work paid off. 11:00 a.m. – time to make his rounds of the decks to mingle with the passengers. They expected the captain to give them a bit of his valuable time, so he obliged. It wasn't his favorite part of the day, but over the years, it had become routine, like checking the time.

He began on the sun deck by strolling through the lounge, nodding to the Hollisters and the McGraths playing a game of bridge, exchanging a few words with the Lemonds and the Schusters listening to Isabelle Sikes belting out tunes at the piano bar, and nodding politely to Mr. Crabtree, who, as usual sat alone sipping a gin and tonic. This time, he didn't make his escape quickly enough.

"Captain," Crabtree called.

Amos turned and smiled. "Mr. Crabtree," he greeted as he touched the brim of his hat.

"Will we be over the Deep on the 26th?"

Raymond Crabtree's fascination with the Cayman Trench bordered on an obsession. He had often seen the ex-Navy captain pouring over old Navy charts festooned with copious hand-written notations.

"We'll be on time, Mr. Crabtree. We will be passing over the Trench just after midnight tonight."

Crabtree nodded. Captain Amos couldn't recall ever seeing the man smile. He took no part in any passenger events or shore excursions, instead staying locked up in his cabin except for meals and his twice daily gin and tonic in the lounge. His reasons for the voyage were his own, but Captain Amos considered even one dissatisfied passenger a blot on his record.

"There is a dance tonight, Mr. Crabtree. Will you be joining us?"

To the captain's surprise, Crabtree smiled. However, it was not a smile denoting pleasure, but a malicious one, as if the man was savoring a private joke.

"No, Captain, I have another reunion to attend."

When Crabtree picked up his drink and stirred it with his finger, Captain Amos took it as a sign of dismissal. He continued his rounds, but his meeting with Crabtree left him with a feeling of apprehension. Whatever Crabtree's reunion was, it didn't bode well for the reputation of the company. He had no grounds for confining him to his cabin, but he would take the precaution of having a steward keep close tabs on Crabtree.

As he reached the Main Deck, the aroma of lunch being prepared met him at the galley door. The chef and his fifteen assistants scurried around the kitchen, dicing vegetables, stirring pots, grilling steaks, and baking bread. He tried to watch their progress without getting in their way, but at a scornful glance from the chef, he left. The dining room was decorated in his favorite colors, coral and beige. The round tables were covered in white cloths and the high back rattan chairs in a floral pattern of red and white. Vases of fresh flowers graced each table. It was a relaxing room, he thought, one designed to aid the digestion and to encourage lingering. Already, several tables were full. His captain's table at the front of the room was empty as usual. He took breakfast and lunch alone, mingling with passengers only at the evening meal.

Strolling through the corridor, he greeted several passengers, shook a few hands, and posed for several photographs with enamored wives. Outside on deck, though the day was still cloudy, several passengers lounged around the pool or played shuffleboard. His cryptic conversation with Raymond Crabtree had dampened his mood. He postponed touring the engine room and returned to the bridge. Hurricane Clive had passed and the sea was calm. The day was cloudy but full of promise. Why then, did he feel so apprehensive? He had crossed the Trench over a thousand times without mishap. Why was this voyage different?

He rubbed his watch without thinking, as he often did when nervous. His crew glanced at him but he ignored them, keeping his eyes peeled on the horizon, searching for what... he didn't know.

* * * *

Raymond Crabtree leaned on the aft rail of the Sun Deck of the *Neptune*, staring at the water churned up by the propellers. Inside the Trident lounge, a party was going full tilt. He had no desire to party or to mingle with his fellow passengers. His trip wasn't a vacation. It was a voyage of discovery, a sojourn of memories. His stomach rumbled, either from the last gin and tonic he had gulped down, or from the cancer that was gnawing away at his insides. It didn't matter. At seventy-one, he was ready to die. His wife Molly had died four years earlier, and his two children hardly kept in touch anymore. He didn't miss them. Both were precocious brats squandering their lives in the accumulation of wealth, leaving them empty and devoid of human kindness. He regretted that they came from his loins. They would die as alone and as bitter as he was.

Death held no mysteries for him. In his twenty years in the Navy, he had witnessed death in so many forms that they melded together as one massive killing spree. Vietnam had not been a real war, but men had died nevertheless.

The captain had promised that the ship would be over the Trench shortly after midnight. The timing was impeccable, an omen. He remembered watching the Russian freighter break apart and sink on October 26, 1962, just after midnight. 2440 hours to be exact. Its sinking had haunted him all these years. The sound the ship had made as it went down had been a scream, a scream echoing down forty-two years, weaving itself into every fiber of his being, until he had awoken too many nights in a cold sweat with the sound still ringing in his ears. It was a Siren call, beckoning him to join it. He didn't know why a single event in his long life would demand his full attention, haunt his nights. It was as if some cosmic string tied him to the Russian freighter, yanking him downward in a slow spiral into the briny depths.

It seemed appropriate somehow, that he should end his life where the nightmares had begun. Lying in bed while cancer sapped his remaining strength and consumed his body held no appeal to him. He had considered a bullet, but that seemed too mundane, too easy. At forty minutes past midnight, he would quietly climb over the rail and launch himself into the cold, wet void. He would sink to the bottom, joining the captain of the Russian freighter he had killed. It had not been a stand up fight. The freighter had been unarmed. It had been an execution. The Russian's blood had stained his hands for almost half a century. Only the cold, clean ocean could wash it off.

An inebriated couple, the man staggering slightly, passed him without noticing him. He had avoided contact with his fellow man on the cruise. He had no patience for idle conversation or polite smiles. If Molly's lingering death and his own disease had not eaten away his life savings, he would have chartered a small craft for a solitary visit to the place his life ended and his hell had begun.

Instead, he had chosen the *Neptune*. Even the name was an omen, the God of the Deep.

He lit a cigarette and inhaled a lungful of smoke. He had quit on his doctor's advice for ten years, but over forty years of a two-packs-a-day habit had taken its inevitable toll. His desire for a cigarette had remained with him every single day he had gone without. Now, cigarettes and alcohol sustained him. It didn't matter anymore. He was near the end of his quest. He checked his watch – 2030 hours. In just over four hours, it would be all over, except for the dying part. That would come as welcome relief from a life filled only with pain and regret.

As he exhaled, he spotted a light in the distance. At first, he thought a small fishing boat was chancing the seas after the hurricane, but the manner in which the light moved and then began to blink on and off, reminded him of a signal. He debated bringing it to the captain's attention. What did someone in distress matter when his life would end in four hours? Nevertheless, his years as a naval officer, and then a New York City cop were too ingrained to ignore it. He knew that he would lose sight of the light if he went to the bridge or the lounge. Instead, he began yelling, "Man overboard!" at the top of his lungs.

7

Oct. 25, *Neptune*, Cayman Trench –

Josh's heart pounded as the ship changed course. They had seen his signal. He collapsed onto the roof weeping for joy. He waited the twenty minutes for the ship, a three-hundred-foot cruise ship, to reach him. He would have done a happy dance if he thought his raft wouldn't capsize and his legs would hold him erect. From his seated position, just inches above the water, the ship was a city of lights gliding on the water. Curious passengers lined the railing, staring down at him. Some cheered; others raised glasses of wine or mixed drinks and saluted his salvation.

A large door opened just above the waterline in the aft section of the hull, and two men launched a Zodiac raft down an extended ramp. When the Zodiac nudged up against his roof-raft, he tried to stand, but found his legs too numb to support him. He rolled into the raft and allowed one of the men to sit him upright.

"You're a lucky bastard," the man said. "If a passenger hadn't spotted you, we'd have passed you by."

"Thank you, thank you," Josh gushed. He wanted to kiss the man's hand, salute him … something to show his appreciation.

As they returned to the ship, a third crewman tossed a nylon rope to the man in the raft. He secured it to a metal ring in the bow and sat back while a winch hauled the raft up a ramp of rollers into the ship. Eager hands helped Josh out of the raft, handed him a blanket and a cup of hot coffee. The coffee burned his parched lips, but sent a rush of warmth through his chilled limbs. He downed the coffee in three large gulps and returned the cup to the crewman.

"The doctor will want to examine you," the first man said. "What are you doing all the way out here?"

Josh didn't want to sound delirious. He decided to withhold describing the creatures that attacked the island. He especially didn't want to mention what he thought he had seen. "The hurricane. A tsunami washed over Little Cayman. It looked like it flooded the entire island."

"Little Cayman?" the man gasped. "God Almighty. That's terrible news. I heard it was rough in Grand Cayman, but we had no idea how bad it hit the other islands."

"Did you ride out the storm?"

"No. We anchored in Jamaica until she blew over. We're headed for home port in Hamilton, Bermuda."

Josh nodded. "I need to find a flight home."

"Where's home?"

"Texas."

"You're a long way from home. The storm is making northwest toward the Yucatan. It will miss Texas. You can catch a flight out of Bermuda. Come on. We'd best get you to the infirmary, and then clean you up."

Josh allowed the crewman to help him down the corridor to the bow of the ship. He tried not to stare at the gawking passengers and crewmen they passed along the way. His rescue was a bit of excitement for them, something to discuss over drinks. He presented a pitiful sight. His shirt was half torn off his body. His shoes had disappeared during the storm. All he needed was a beard and long stringy hair to pass for Robinson Crusoe. Somewhere along the way, someone shoved a glass of wine into his hand. Dehydrated and suffering from sunstroke, the alcohol was probably the last thing he needed, but he drank it anyway. It was his way of celebrating his salvation.

The ship's doctor was an emaciated older man with thin black hair and dark brown eyes. The glasses he wore perched on the end of his nose were thick and heavy. His sunken cheeks highlighted his high cheekbones. He eyed Josh over the rims of his glasses as the crewman ushered him in.

"Well, well, a real patient. I'm so used to sea sickness, stomach disorders from over indulging, and sprains from shuffleboard tournaments that I'm eager to examine a real medical emergency. Sit down, young man. I'm Doctor Chase."

Josh climbed up on the table and examined the infirmary. The doctor was not a tidy man. Magazines, medical journals, and newspapers littered the desk and an empty glass sat on top of the file cabinet, where Josh suspected he might find a bottle of liquor filed under 'L' for lush. He removed the remains of his tattered shirt, wincing as he did so at the pain in his shoulder and his sunburned skin.

The doctor's latex-gloved hands were cold as he listened to Josh's chest and heart. He peered into Josh's eyes and nodded.

"Except for sunburn, some bruises, and a few aches and pains, you're the epitome of health, young man."

He wiped Josh's exposed skin with a solution that stung as it was first applied, but gradually reduced the pain. He slapped iodine and a Band-Aid on a couple of the worst cuts and scrapes, removed his latex gloves, and tossed them in the garbage.

"A little rest and some hot food and you'll soon be as good as new."

Sleep was the last thing Josh wanted. The nightmares were worse than lack of sleep. "I could use a good meal," he said.

"The cabins are all full, and I doubt you would want to bunk with the crew." He smiled at the crewman who had helped Josh to the infirmary. "You can stay here. I have an empty bed in the next room. We'll send a meal to you. Any preferences?"

Josh didn't feel like being picky. His stomach growled in appreciation of the offer. "A Coke and anything would be nice."

The doctor smiled. "Anything it is." He turned to the crewman. "Have the chef send down something light. We don't want to tax our guest's stomach."

Doctor Chase showed him the empty patient room. In spite of his aches and pains and his fear of sleep, the bed was inviting, but he was too grungy to soil the clean sheets.

"Can I take a shower first?"

"Certainly. I'll see if we can find you some clean clothes. I'm sure one of the crew or perhaps a passenger would donate a few things."

After the doctor left, Josh stripped off his ragged, filthy clothes, and stepped into the shower. The needle jets pricked his sunburned skin, but he ignored the pain, luxuriating in the hot water as it scoured clean his body. After a few minutes, his legs began to give out. He reluctantly turned off the water and toweled off. Underwear, socks, shorts, and a pullover shirt bearing the *Neptune* logo sat folded on a chair. A pair of used Adidas sat on top of them. He had just finished dressing when the steward returned with a tray of food. He appeared to be no older than Josh. He set the tray on a table and pointed to the items as he called them out.

"Ice, two Cokes, bread, butter, potato-basil soup, herb-roasted chicken, baked potato, and steamed vegetables. For dessert, we have ice cream."

Looking at the food made Josh's mouth water. He marveled at the amount. The tray held enough food for two men. Even starving, he would never be able to eat it all.

"Would you care to join me?" he asked.

"Oh, no, sir. Thank you, but I must return to my duties, unless you need something else."

"I think this will do."

The first thing he did was open a Coke and pour it over the ice. More than water or even the glass of wine, the Coke quenched his thirst. He began his meal with the soup and was astonished at the taste. It was the best potato soup he had ever eaten. The fresh basil complimented the Yukon potato, and the heavy cream and butter made the soup rich. Just a hint of leeks edged it beyond a simple soup to a delightful course starter.

He seldom cooked and normally ate his meals in the college cafeteria or his neighborhood bar. The food had seemed adequate, but after tasting the soup, it paled. He wanted to eat it all, but decided to sample his entrée. The chicken, like the soup, exceeded his expectations. He had thought the food at the resort had been good, but this meal put it to shame. He could tell that the chef loved his work and made certain that his cooks didn't scrimp on portion or flavor. He envied the passengers. His stomach began to complain halfway through his meal. He set it aside for later and skipped desert.

A knock at the door surprised him.

"Come in."

An older man opened the door and stood staring at him. His gaze was intense and slightly intimidating, but his gaunt face and pallor spoke of a man of ill health. He wasn't dressed like any of the crew and was therefore a passenger. Josh assumed he was a patient.

"Doctor Chase isn't in."

The man continued to stare, making Josh uncomfortable. Finally, he said, "I'm Ray Crabtree. I'm the one who spotted your light."

Josh smiled at him. "Then I have you to thank for saving my life."

"Just in the right place at the right time. You okay?"

"The doctor says I'm fine, just sore, exhausted, and sunburned."

Crabtree nodded. "I was gonna jump."

Now it was Josh's turn to stare. He wasn't certain he had heard correctly. "Jump?"

"Over the side. It's why I came on this voyage."

"That's pretty rash. Any particular reason?"

Crabtree's lips creased into a slight smile. "Long story. You wouldn't be interested. Let's just say that I'm dying, and something drew me here to this spot."

Josh didn't understand. "This ship?"

Crabtree shook his head. "The Cayman Trench. I watched a Russian freighter sink here forty-two years ago today. It's haunted me my whole life."

Josh understood how something could haunt you. "Do you still want to die?"

"I don't know. Seeing your light did something. It's like I was supposed to find you. Now, I'm sort of confused." He shrugged. "I don't know."

Josh pointed to his tray of food. "Want something to eat?"

Crabtree smiled and pulled a small silver flask from his pocket. "I've been drinking most of my meals lately. Want some gin?"

Josh decided to be sociable. After all, the man had saved his life. He didn't really like gin, but he held out his glass of Coke. "Maybe a splash to sweeten it up."

Crabtree poured a liberal amount in Josh's glass and took a long swig from the flask. Josh took a sip from his Coke, hoping that whatever ailed the man wasn't catching.

"I'm going to die soon. Cancer. This keeps the pain down. I figured here would be a good place to end the pain for good. I had talked myself into it. I was a sailor. They say drowning is a good way to go."

After his near drowning during the tidal wave, Josh wasn't sure he would agree, but then he wasn't facing a long, lingering death by cancer. Suicide always seemed easier than it was. The last step off a roof, the millisecond before pulling the trigger, the last pill – that was when reality hit. He was glad he had disturbed Crabtree's schedule. The man had saved his life. He couldn't save Crabtree's, but he could delay the inevitable. Crabtree could always jump overboard later if that was what he wanted.

"I almost drowned. I'm glad I didn't."

Crabtree nodded. He was silent for a moment, and then took another sip. "I've still got time to do it. It's another two hours until 2440. We'll see. I just thought I should see who I saved. Glad you made it."

"So am I. Thank you again."

Crabtree turned to leave. Over his shoulder, he said, "The sea gives and the sea takes. You were lucky. It wasn't your time."

He decided to try one more time. "Maybe it isn't yours either."

Crabtree smiled. "We'll see."

He left before Josh could say anything more.

"Strange man."

He didn't want to judge Crabtree. An old man dying of cancer deserved an easy out if he wanted it, but the idea of drowning on purpose sent shivers through Josh. Aside from the tidal wave, he had nearly drowned once when his regulator quit working on a dive while he was fifty feet down examining sea anemones. He had reached the surface safely, but the thought of swallowing ocean water and suffocating had stayed with him. After that dive, he now always double-checked his equipment.

Satiated and afraid to sleep for fear of nightmares, he decided to go for a stroll on deck to see if the fresh air would help keep him awake. The infirmary was on the main deck in the bow of the ship.

The corridors were mostly deserted but a party was going on in the lounge. He avoided it and chose a side door onto the outside deck. The water was calm, reflecting the moon's rays like a dark mirror. From the deck of the ship, the ocean appeared serene and peaceful, but Josh wondered what creatures lurked beneath the surface.

Sixteen-thousand feet below his feet, deep in the Cayman Trench, the Beebe Vent Field spewed black copper-rich fluids into the water at over seven-hundred degrees. Only the extreme pressure at that depth prevented the water from instantly exploding into steam. Entire ecosystems of bacteria, algae, crustaceans, tube worms, and other deep sea creatures fed on the nutrient-rich water pouring from the fumaroles, living in a pitch black void that sunlight had never touched. This deep realm was the source of the giant isopods. In turn, larger creatures, such as the Ogrefish, preyed on them. Nine-thousand feet below that, in the bottom of the Trench, his fertile imagination had no trouble conjuring horrid monsters that made the isopods pale in comparison. The firm decking of the ship beneath his feet ship was more comforting than had the fragile wooden raft that had saved his life.

He attributed his gloom to survivor's guilt. Hawthorne, the Watkins, possibly everyone he knew or met on Little Cayman, might be dead from the isopod attack or the tidal wave. He debated informing the captain of what he had witnessed, but even with the photos in his cell phone, he doubted he would be believed. He wasn't sure he believed it himself. It now all seemed like a dream; one of the horrible nightmares he had been experiencing.

In the distance, the water sparkled, a scintillating reflection of the October moon. He was admiring its beauty, and then noticed that the moon was behind a cloud. What was causing the strange, pulsating light? The sea was alive with fireflies. As he watched, he detected a pattern. It wasn't single points, but lines of flashing lights, like strings of Christmas lights. The tightness in his chest eased as the lights moved farther away out of sight.

"Oh, there you are, Mister Peterman," Doctor Chase said.

Josh wanted to ask the doctor if he had seen the lights, but restrained himself. Hallucinations might get him confined to a hospital bed. "I needed some air."

"I trust your meal was adequate."

Josh rubbed his belly and smiled. "Excellent food. I needed to stretch my legs a bit after being confined on my raft for so long."

"You were quite lucky on that account. If the roof hadn't caved in beneath you, you might have found yourself floundering."

Or eaten. "Luck there and luck in your finding me."

Chase smiled. "Good luck all around." He gazed at the horizon. "We just got a report that Grand Cayman got hit hard." Josh shivered. The doctor saw him and frowned. "Are you all right?"

"Yeah, I'm okay. Did many die?"

"Over a hundred. The storm surge inundated George Town."

"Storm surge?" Josh asked, afraid to bring up the subject of isopods. "Is that all?"

Chase stared at him queerly. "The storm surge and high winds. Why?"

"Nothing. Just wondering."

"They were asking for assistance earlier, but they're off the air now."

Josh's face paled and his heart skipped a beat. "Off the air?"

"It's not uncommon. Shortage of petrol for the generator and all that. We're detouring to lend assistance. We have several doctors as passengers on board. I guess I'll soon be busy." He paused, and then said with a stern voice, "I think you need a bit of a lie down. You look terrible."

Josh nodded. He was tired. "Maybe so."

"I'll help you back to bed."

His knees were weak. He allowed the doctor to escort him back to the infirmary. He swallowed the sedative the doctor offered, stripped, and crawled into bed, troubled by the news of George Town. Had the isopods struck there too? Should he warn the captain?

While he was trying to decide, the sedative began working. Exhausted by his ordeal, he gave up the fight and fell asleep, hoping his dreams didn't become nightmares.

* * * *

Crabtree's mind was in turmoil. A whirlwind of thoughts and memories swirled around, refusing to let him focus. For three months, he had planned for the final moments of his life, convincing himself that fate had decreed he met his end where his nightmares had begun. Spotting the survivor had placed doubts in his mind. He was going to die. The Big C would see to that. Giving himself to the sea had seemed the perfect solution – no body, no funeral, not even a grieving family, or at least one that would grieve for long. Now, he had doubts. Was saving the Peterman kid a last chance at redemption or a sign that he was being stupid? Peterman had fought to stay alive. He could see it in the kid's blue eyes. They were almost as haunted as his. Yet, he didn't give up.

The party in the lounge below him was still blasting full volume. People were spilling out onto the main deck and infringing on his space on the sun deck. He relinquished his spot on the fantail rail and went forward to the bow where fewer people gathered. The salt spray tingled on his face, reminding him of that October night in 1962 in pursuit of the Russian freighter. He never learned the captain's name. No record of the ship existed in the Russian archives. His own log was purged, and he and his crew sworn to secrecy. He had told no one, not even his wife. Maybe if he had, the ghosts wouldn't rise up from the depths to haunt him.

To the west, the ocean glittered as if on fire. Flashing lights blinked rapidly, like a traffic light, except in blues, yellows, and reds. Whatever was causing the strange lights, they looked like ghosts in the water, the spirits of the dead rising from their watery graves. He stared at the phenomenon with a growing sense of dread. Was it the Russian freighter beckoning him to join it? The incorporeal lights began flashing in unison, hypnotizing him. When the lights abruptly disappeared, releasing him, rather than being relieved, a deep foreboding descended on him. The air smelled of gloom and death.

The ship shuddered beneath him, rattling the empty glasses on a table beside a deck chair. The sea was calm. The *Neptune* was slicing through the waves cleanly and effortlessly. He had heard that they were headed for the Cayman Islands to offer assistance. He was unconcerned since he hadn't planned on living past midnight. Perhaps the shudder was just the ship as it changed course. He fixed a star above the horizon. After a few minutes, it hadn't moved.

No course change.

The shudder happened again, this time shaking the entire ship. The glasses crashed to the deck and shattered. Deck chairs bounced across the deck. He grabbed the rail with both hands to prevent being thrown forward. This time, a loud screeching sound, like ripping metal, accompanied the shudder. The ship began to slow.

Sheared propeller? Warped shaft? Whatever the cause, it had damaged the ship. He glanced toward the bridge and noticed men running from it toward the engine room. It seemed their rescue voyage to the Caymans would be delayed. The lights remained on. The music and noise from the lounge continued unabated. The passengers weren't even aware of the problem. *Just as well. They'd probably panic.* He fought his curiosity. As a former captain, he wanted to help, but he knew as a seventy-one-year-old man, he would be useless. He leaned his back against the rail, lit a cigarette, and watched.

Ten minutes later, the ship came to a complete stop. If it was a minor problem, the mechanics could deal with it. The ship had a well-equipped workshop. If not, they were adrift. It seemed fitting that this spot should attempt to hold him captive. It had imprisoned his mind for over forty years. Perhaps it had trapped his soul as well. He smiled. Maybe he wouldn't have to take his own life. That the ship might sink with him aboard seemed somehow appropriate.

The bow lifted so suddenly that he flew through the air, landing hard on the deck ten feet away, knocking the breath from him. His right shoulder and hip sang out in agony from the impact. The bow slammed back into the sea, sending a wave of water cascading over the deck. He rolled over and fought to breathe until the water receded. A shadow passed over him, something large, like a crane's boom, but the *Neptune* carried no crane.

The silence after the impact faded, filling with the screams of frightened and injured passengers. The ship's klaxon began to wail. *Battle stations*, he thought, and then giggled. "Maybe the Russian freighter's ghost rammed us."

The shadow came again. He focused on its dark form. At first, he thought of sea monsters – kraken, giant cuddle fish, and monstrous squid – but this creature resembled a segmented worm. Appendages sprouted from the ventral and dorsal sides of each segment. The upper appendages were frilly, waving in the air. The lower appendages ended in small claws. The creature had attached itself to the railing by several sets of rear legs, rearing over the deck with its forward section. It was well over fifteen feet long and iridescent like opal. The head, when it turned toward him, had four spots that might have been eyes. A circle of fleshy protuberances surrounded a short snout that bristled with sharp teeth, or rather serrated extensions of the mouth material. A foul-smelling secretion dripped from the creature's body onto the deck.

More of the creatures appeared over the sides of the ship, crawling onto the deck. Crabtree climbed to his feet and hobbled to the door to the main deck. He had spotted a fire axe on the wall earlier. He grabbed the axe and swung with all his strength at the creature's head. The blow was feeble, but the blade embedded in the flesh beside the mouth. The creature reared, yanking the axe from his hands. It shook its head side-to-side in an effort to dislodge the axe. Mucous splashed onto Crabtree's arm. The liquid burned his skin. As he wiped it off, he noticed tiny creatures swimming in the mucous. His arm erupted in fire as the creatures burrowed into his flesh.

The giant sea worm fell back over the side into the ocean, but an army of its brethren took its place. Dozens crawled up the side of the ship and along the deck. Their multiple, clawed legs dug into the metal hull as if it were cardboard. The *Neptune* was under siege. Other passengers began to notice the creatures. He turned toward a scream in time to witness one of the creatures smash a man to the deck and begin devouring him, ripping chunks of flesh from his torso in a mad frenzy of gluttony.

The worms were dangerous, but not large enough to lift the bow of the ship. Something else, something much larger, had done that. His arm was growing numb, but his skin was writhing as the tiny parasites bore through his flesh. He laughed. "Looks like cancer won't be the one eating me after all." He forced himself to the rail. Directly below him, one of the worms was crawling up the ship. He watched its tail disappear onto the main deck. *That ought to liven up the party,* he thought. He couldn't lift his arm to read his watch, but he knew it wasn't quite midnight, the witching hour. If a ghost could direct living creatures, he knew the Russian captain was reaching out to him.

"I'm here, Captain!" he yelled as he fell over the rail. In his plummet, he dislodged one of the creatures. They landed in the sea together. The water was colder than he had imagined as he sank below the surface. He made no effort to swim to the surface. He caught a brief glimpse of something almost as large as the ship, something dark and sinister slicing through the water. The sea worm beside him disappeared into a maw the size of a subway tunnel. An eye, deep ebony in color with a vertical red pupil stared at him for a moment, the eye of the devil. The pressure of the creature's passage pushed him aside.

Far below him, flashing lights beckoned him downward. He closed his eyes and allowed his body to sink. It was a long way to the bottom. He was certain the clock would strike midnight somewhere along the way.

8

Oct. 26, *Neptune*, Cayman Trench –

The nightmare became reality. Josh awoke on the floor drenched in sweat, his heart jackhammering against his sore ribcage. The silent scream from his nightmare became real and echoed through the door and down the corridor, but it wasn't his. He rubbed his bruised hip.

"What the hell happened?"

He knew he hadn't rolled out of bed in his sleep. His bed had catapulted him onto the floor five feet away. Someone screamed again. He scrambled to his feet and dressed so quickly that he put his shirt on backwards. He slipped on the Adidas without lacing them and spilled out the door into the infirmary. Medical supplies and equipment lay scattered over the floor. He stepped over a broken flask of foul-smelling liquid, yanked open the door to the corridor, and entered pandemonium.

Several people lay on the floor of the corridor stunned. More raced down the corridor screaming. A second massive shudder as the bow lifted sent them reeling. Josh braced himself in the doorway and avoided another spill. The ship settled back into the water with a screech of metal. *Had they hit something?* The ship's klaxon began wailing, a high-pitched whistle that caused even more panic.

"We're sinking!" someone shouted, racing from his cabin with a life jacket half on.

Josh went inside the room and looked out the porthole, but could see nothing, no ship, no island, in the darkness. He could see that the ship wasn't moving. Fear of being cast adrift once more propelled him outside to the lifeboat station. He raced up the stairs to the main deck, reaching the door just in time to see a giant worm snap off a man's head. The headless corpse fell to the deck spurting blood from severed arteries.

After his previous encounters with two giant sea creatures, Josh took the advent of a third such monster in stride. His analytical mind dismissed the horrible death of a fellow passenger and noted the features of the creature. It closely resembled one of the polychaete worms inhabiting deep thermal vents. By the segmented body, tubercle gills, and tentacles surrounding the mouth, it was a member of *Alvinella pompejana*, or Pompeii worm, better known as Bristle worm for the bristle-like gills sprouting from its dorsal side. They were extreme thermophiles, able to survive temperatures around volcanic vents that would cook other creatures. Most grew to lengths of only five inches, though a few reached several feet, but the creature facing him was fifteen-feet long.

After consuming the man's head, the Bristle worm began eating the body. The sharp, raspy teeth literally raked the flesh from the body. The grisly scene snapped Josh from his marine biologist mode into one of survival. From the screams and sounds of panic outside, more of the Bristle worms stalked the main deck. He reversed directions and found the stairwell to the sun deck. The drunken revelers, some injured by the bucking of the bow, but unaware of the real danger, were spilling out of the lounge into the corridors and outside deck to determine what was happening. They walked right into the mass of attacking Bristle worms. It was a massacre. Bristle worms pounced from the roof or the railings, snatching hapless passengers in their jaws. The press of bodies from behind forced many directly into the bloody melee. One of the lounge's large glass doors shattered under the weight of several of the creatures. They crawled onto the dance floor, where Doctor Chase and several crewmen were busy attending injured passengers.

Without thinking of the danger, Josh snatched a fire axe from the wall and pushed his way through the crowd. Many of them, seeing an axe-wielding man panicked, thinking he was the cause of the turmoil. A crewman held one creature at bay with a table until the worm splintered the table and crashed its body on top of the unfortunate man. Another worm loomed over Doctor Chase. Josh attacked the creature in its only vulnerable spot, the colorful gills sprouting from its back. He hacked at them, severing several before the Bristle worm turned its attention to him. He swung with all his might, planting the axe in the center of the creature's head. It squealed in pain and fell at his feet.

He had no time to consider his victory. More of the creatures now forced their way inside the lounge. He grabbed Doctor Chase and pulled him away just as one of the Bristle worms lunged at him.

"My patient," the doctor protested as he fought Josh's hold on his arm.

"Your patient is gone," Josh replied.

The Bristle worm settled on the doctor's patient for its meal. There were far too many of them to attack with one axe. He needed a more powerful weapon, a gun.

"Come on," he said, tugging on the doctor's arm.

"Where are we going?"

"The bridge. If there are any weapons aboard ship, they'll be in the weapons locker on the bridge."

"This is a cruise ship, not a Navy vessel. We don't have a weapons locker."

Josh stopped mid-stride. "No guns?"

"Security might have a pistol or two for emergencies."

Josh glared at the doctor. "You don't think this is an emergency?"

"Do you think a pistol will stop that?" Chase waved his arm behind him to indicate the creatures."

Chase was right. A pistol would be less effective than an axe. Josh's eyes fell on a bulletin board in the corridor. A glossy poster with a photo of a woman in a short skirt shooting clay pigeons from the deck of the ship sent his mind into high gear.

"What about shotguns?" He pointed to the poster.

"They would be in the supply room in the lower level." He stared at Josh in disbelief. "But they're loaded with birdshot.

You're not seriously considering facing one of those creatures with birdshot?"

"It's better than an axe."

Chase nodded. "I'll come with you."

Josh considered his options. Doctor Chase knew the ship and he didn't, but he was an old man and they might have to move quickly. He decided now was no time for diplomacy. "Are you up to it?"

Chase shot Josh a weak smile. "I can't do these people much good as a doctor. Maybe I can help save a few."

The stairs to the lower levels were crammed with people trying to escape in both directions. Josh fought to be heard over the turmoil.

"Go to your cabins!" he shouted. "Lock yourselves in."

No one paid attention to him. He looked at the doctor, and Chase shook his head sadly. The passengers were in a panic and reasoning with them was useless. The lower level contained fewer cabins and was less crowded. Josh started down the corridor, but Chase stopped him.

"One more level," he said.

"Isn't the launching bay down here?"

Chase opened a hatch marked 'crew only'. "The supply room is near the engine room."

The first thing Josh noticed was the absence of sound. The ship's massive engines were silent. The second thing he noticed was the two feet of water in the corridor. The ship was sinking.

"That blow to the bow must have opened a seam."

"Could those things do that much damage?"

Josh wondered the same thing. "No, maybe we collided with something else, perhaps a partially submerged wreck damaged by the storm."

"Not likely," Chase countered.

Josh decided it was time to come clean. "There's something else out there, something big enough to damage a cruise ship."

Chase's face turned white. "God help us if we have to evacuate the ship. I don't understand what's happening. What are those things? Where did they come from?"

"Up from the deep, the bottom of the Cayman Trench. Those creatures are giant mutated Bristle worms. They're normally a few inches long."

"That's impossible."

Josh pulled out his cell phone and showed Chase the photos of the Ogrefish and the blurry images of the isopods. As Chase stared at the photos, his lips compressed to a fine bloodless line and his gaunt cheeks tightened. His eyes began blinking rapidly, as if trying to dispel the images from his mind.

"The Ogrefish were nearly six-feet long instead of six inches. The isopods are normally a few inches, maybe a foot in length. I saw them eat people. They almost had me for dinner. Little Cayman was overrun with them. I doubt anyone was left alive for the tidal wave to kill."

Chase leaned against the wall, trembling. His voice broke as he asked, "Is it the end of the world?"

Josh shook his head. "Something is making deep sea creatures grow to gigantic size and something else is driving them from the deep."

As Josh's words sunk in, the doctor recoiled in horror. He turned away from the horrible, impossible images on the cell phone. Josh gave him a few seconds to pull himself together. They didn't have time for him to fall apart.

"Let's go find some shotguns."

Chase nodded and meekly followed Josh. He splashed through the cold water until he reached a door marked 'Supply Room'. Thankfully, it was unlocked. Chase pointed to a locker beside a rack of scuba gear. The door was locked, but using a steel bar as a lever, he managed to pry open the door. Inside were ten pump-action shotguns – six Remington 870's and four Mossberg 500's. Josh didn't know much about shotguns, but he had hunted as a teenager with his father who owned a Remington. He knew how to pump it to load it, and which end the shot came out. With creatures as large as the Bristle worms, he didn't need to be an expert. Besides, unlike whitetail deer, the Bristle worms weren't hiding. They were attacking.

He grabbed two shotguns and a box of shells. Doctor Chase reluctantly picked up one of the Mossbergs and examined it. "I've never fired a gun before."

Josh took the Mossberg from the doctor and loaded it. He handed it back to Chase and demonstrated how to hold it. "Press it tightly against your shoulder. Point it at one of the worms and pull the trigger. It's a twelve-gauge, so it has a kick. When you fire, pull the cylinder back to pump another shell into the chamber. You've got six shells. The Remington holds seven. Oh, and Doctor, make sure I'm not in the way when you shoot."

Chase nodded. He held the shotgun at arm's length as if it were a germ. Josh hoped he got over his fear of firearms quickly. He slung one of the Remingtons over his shoulder by the strap, grabbed the other with both hands, and went back into the corridor. The water had already risen another foot. The water was frigid.

"Feel how cold the water is. It should be warm. Something is bringing the deep cold water to the surface. That's why these creatures are appearing."

"How do you know so much about it?"

"I'm studying to be a marine biologist. If I live through this, I'll be able to write one hell of a paper."

"If we live through this," Chase repeated.

As they emerged into the main deck corridor from the crew entrance, they faced one of the Bristle worms in the middle of the corridor hovering over a partially consumed corpse. Blood covered the wall and dripped from the creature's mouth. Josh raised the shotgun and fired. The birdshot did little damage from a distance of twenty yards. Josh started walking toward it, firing as he went. From ten yards, chunks of flesh began flying off the creature. At five yards, a shot directly into its open mouth blew its brain out the back of its head. The creature roared and reared until its head brushed the ceiling, knocking out the lights, and then collapsed.

Josh stared at the dead creature. Chase walked up and prodded it with the barrel of his shotgun. The end of the barrel came away slimy.

"Dead," he pronounced. He reached out to touch the slime.

"Don't!" Josh yelled.

Chase looked at him curiously.

"It might be infested with parasites."

Chase jerked his hand back and wiped the barrel on a chair.

Like the isopods that had come ashore at Little Cayman, the Bristle worms were creatures of the sea, extracting oxygen through gills. Given the enormous size of their bodies, the effort of scrambling about on the ship should quickly exhaust their blood oxygen supply. Gills do a poor job of extracting oxygen from air, but the creatures seemed determined to make meals of the passengers.

Reaching the main deck, Josh saw crewmen attempting to lower lifeboats over the side. Passengers, unaware of the nature of the danger, crowded the deck around the lifeboat stations, impeding the crewmen. One lifeboat, half-filled with passengers, tilted abruptly as one of the winches jammed, spilling the passengers into the sea. The worms immediately attacked them. Now, everyone was aware of the danger. As they tried to flee the area, they collided with a phalanx of Bristle worms waiting in the pool area on the fantail.

Josh flung open the door, and he and Doctor Chase began firing into the mass of creatures. A man wearing a purser's uniform rushed up to them. Josh handed him the third shotgun. The three weapons did little actual damage, but the noise drew the creatures' attention away from the passengers. Several of the creatures returned to the water. *To breathe*, Josh thought. As the remaining worms advanced, their shots began to have an effect. The head was the creatures' weak spot, the only area not covered in hard chitin. Though none of the three was expert shots, they began to make headway. Within minutes, five of the creatures lay dead or dying on the deck.

In his zeal for killing, the purser strayed too close to the creatures. When his shotgun was empty, he hesitated before retreating to reload. This was all the time the creature nearest him needed. It reached down and snatched the purser into the air, almost severing his body in half. The man's agonized screams distressed Chase. He fired his last shell into the purser's body, killing him instantly. Josh said nothing as he attacked the creature.

Finally, the fantail was cleared of the creatures, but they still infested the ship. The bow of the ship was noticeably lower than the stern and the entire ship was listing to starboard by ten degrees. The *Neptune* was sinking fast. Two of the six lifeboats had successfully launched, but Josh didn't give them good odds of surviving. Two of the remaining lifeboats were shattered, useless. The third was abandoned, wedged tightly against the side of the ship by its list.

The ship shuddered and went dark as the rising water flooded the generator room. The Bristle worms abandoned the ship *en masse*, struggling to the rails and falling overboard, almost as in fear. At first, Josh attributed the vibration to torque from strained metal. However, as the bow lifted several feet and the ship rolled even more to starboard, he knew he was about to meet the top predator of the food chain. The sudden lurch of the ship threw him to the deck. He slid across the deck and came to rest against the side of the hot tub. As Doctor Chase slid past, he grabbed the doctor by the arm and held on. He thought the doctor's weight was going to wrench his shoulder from its socket, but the ship settled back to its normal list. The two men stared at each other in dread.

A head, twice as large as one of the lifeboats, loomed over the railing atop a long, sinuous neck. Reptilian eyes the size of manhole covers stared down at them, reflecting red in the moonlight. He recognized the creature as the one he had briefly glimpsed on Little Cayman, the one that had upended his raft. With dizzying speed, the long neck shot forward, and a mouth filled with long, sharp teeth, curved inwards for grasping prey, snatched one of the remaining Bristle worms from the deck above. With two quick bites to dismember the creature, it disappeared down the monster's gullet. Josh held his breath, afraid to speak or move, as the head and neck slowly sank back into the water.

The two men remained where they were for long moments, quaking in fear as the stern began lifting into the air, while the bow sunk deeper into the black waters. Their ship was going down and would carry them with it if they didn't move, but the thought of being once again adrift at sea with giant Bristle worms and the gargantuan reptile frightened Josh more than drowning did. As the remaining lifeboat swung away from its davit and away from the side of the ship, Josh threw off the fear immobilizing him.

"Come on, Doctor," he yelled.

The two men raced for the lifeboat and climbed inside. Josh fought to release the forward davit as the lifeboat hit the rising water. If he couldn't free it, the sinking ship would drag the lifeboat to the depths with them aboard. He squeezed the lever as he tried to knock off the slip ring, but the pressure of the boat was too great. The bow of the lifeboat began to go under. He pressed with all his strength and freed the ring just in time. He had no time to free the rear line. He placed the barrel of the Remington against the securing mechanism rope and fired. The pin exploded and the cable released. The rear of the lifeboat dropped several feet into the sea and finally settled to an even keel. Josh cranked the small gasoline engine and began pulling away from the doomed ship.

"Wait. There might be others in the water," Doctor Chase warned. "We have to save them."

Josh's first instincts told him to leave as quickly as he could, but the doctor's words struck home. He nodded and continued toward the bow. A small knot of people bobbed in the water a few yards away from the ship. He stopped the engine, and he and the doctor helped them into the boat. As he turned to search the other side of the ship, the *Neptune* groaned its death song and rolled onto its starboard side. Four massive parallel rents in the hull of the bow revealed the interior of cabins. The gouges appeared too natural to have been inflicted by a collision. The water roiled with bubbles, as the ship lifted its stern into the air in a graceful dive for the depths five miles below. He grabbed the tiller and pointed the small craft into the darkness away from the sinking ship. The gargantuan reptile's head lifted one more time as the head darted to snatch a Bristle worm, or a survivor from the water. Josh hoped it was a worm.

Twice in one night, he was adrift at sea. He glanced at the stars to get his bearing and pointed the small craft toward Jamaica, which was two hundred miles away.

9

Oct. 26, George Town, Grand Cayman, Caribbean –

At dawn's first light, Germaine surveyed the island of death. His steps crunched the carcasses of thousands of sea lice as he marched toward town. The stench was sickening, overpowering. He brought his shirt up to cover his nose. He followed the path of destruction by the bones of the human dead, stripped clean of their flesh, lying white and shiny in the morning sun. The creatures had not left enough for the ravens or red crab to feast on. He was certain there would be survivors on the upper floors of the hotels and in out of the way spots on the island, but they remained where they were, hiding in fear. He alone was brave enough or foolish enough to venture out.

His fear of losing his license over the dead divers was gone. There was neither authority left to report them to, nor anyone remaining alive to concern themselves with three dead out of thousands. Over forty-five thousand people lived on Grand Cayman, with thousands of visitors on the island at any one time. Even with the threat of Hurricane Clive looming, Germaine estimated fifty thousand people were on the island yesterday. Now, perhaps only hundreds remained alive.

There was nothing left for him on Grand Cayman, no reason for him to remain. His ex-wife, if she had survived, could have the house and the note. He located a dinghy on the beach and rowed back out to the *Miss Lucy*. He was surprised to see Bodden sitting on the rail.

"Any more of the crew here," Germaine asked, as he pulled up alongside his boat.

Bodden shook his head and pointed to smears of blood on the deck. "No bodies, no food left. Things scattered and ripped up, but the hull is solid."

"You saw what happened last night?"

"I saw. Took my scooter and went to the Bluff. Figured higher was better."

The Bluff was the island's highest point at one-hundred forty feet. Bodden's decision had saved his life.

"What do we do now?" Bodden asked.

Germaine thought it typical of Bodden to defer to his judgment. The amicable and easy-going Bodden hardly disputed any decision Germaine made. Normally, he accepted the responsibility without thinking. Now, he dreaded the heavy burden of leadership. They couldn't wait for help, and trying to ride herd over a bunch of panicked tourists didn't appeal to him. His last attempt at being in charge of people had ended poorly.

"Load up what we can find and light out for Jamaica."

Bodden nodded, grabbed a mop, and began cleaning the blood from the deck.

With a crew of two, sailing the schooner to Jamaica was out of the question. Instead, they would rely on the engine. While it wasn't the best maintained engine in the Caribbean for lack of funds, Germaine trusted it more than in two men's ability to furl the sails quickly in an emergency. The broken rails and messy cabins could wait. Much to Germaine's delight, the engine cranked with no problem. He brought the *Miss Lucy* into the harbor, and to the concrete pier. A small leak in the starboard chine where side and bottom of the boat met trickled water into the bilge, but Bodden sealed the leak with caulking material and pumped the water from the bilge.

On shore, they sifted through the debris of several stores, ferrying canned good, bottled water, and ammunition for Germaine's .45 to the boat. He filled the *Miss Lucy's* fuel tanks with gasoline and rolled three, fifty-five gallon drums onto the deck, lashing them securely with rope. By the time they were ready to cast off at around eight a.m., several people had gathered on the dock watching them. Bodden glanced in his direction, but Germaine shook his head. They didn't have room for refugees, and he was through with paying passengers. He turned his back on the shore and the survivors so he wouldn't have to see their faces, perhaps some he might recognize, as he ordered Bodden to cast off. He ignored the forlorn shouts from the survivors as the *Miss Lucy* pulled away from the dock.

Jamaica lay four-hundred and eighty five miles to the southwest. Even pushing the engine to its top speed of eighteen knots, it would take *Miss Lucy* almost twenty-four hours to reach Jamaica. He and Bodden would have to take turns at the wheel. He trusted Bodden's navigation, but doubted he would sleep during the voyage. The hurricane was over, but Germaine knew worse things than a storm lay between them and their destination.

At fifty-six years of age, Germaine considered what he could do with his life. The deaths of McCoy and the others would never come to light amid the deaths of so many others, but the memory of it would haunt him forever. Charters for an aging schooner like *Miss Lucy* were too infrequent for a steady income; too many shiny, sleek power yachts to compete with. He had relied on hauling light freight and fishing to supplement his income. Maybe it was time to devote himself to freight and fishing entirely, or give up the *Miss Lucy* altogether and become a landlubber.

Germaine had never felt at home on land, even in his own house in George Town. Land was too unyielding, too steady, and too sedate. The sea undulated gently, was as still as ice, or heaved like a demon bronco, but it was never sedate. It held mysteries in its depths and raised questions in his mind. Now, with what he had seen, even more so. He had spent his entire life at the edge of a depth almost as deep as the Marina Trench but had never considered it except as a tourist attraction. It was an entirely unexplored world. There were things down there no man had seen, and now they were coming up. If every deep in the Seven Seas disgorged its monsters, man would have to abandon the sea, become a creature of the land and the sky. The thought of abandoning the sea frightened him more than the creatures he had seen.

The sky was slightly overcast but otherwise clear. They sailed steadily in a calm sea until dark. Night was when Germaine worried. Then the ocean became a dark mirror reflecting the moon and stars. What lay beyond the mirror was invisible, lurking like shadows and nightmares. They ran with no lights, fearing to attract any creatures around them. The chances of two ships running with no lights colliding with each other was small, and Germaine knew the waters of the Caribbean better than most men. He didn't fear the dark or what he might encounter. He feared what lay beneath the keel.

Bodden cooked a meal of rice and stew, but Germaine's appetite was gone, taken from him by the sea lice rampage against his fellow islanders. Bodden sat on the forward hatch eating his meal while staring out to sea. Never one to speak if he didn't have anything worthwhile to say, Bodden had become even more taciturn since the attack on the island. He had not said anything about how he had survived the attack or if his family was safe. Germaine didn't know if Bodden had returned to the *Miss Lucy* out of devotion or if, like him, Bodden had no other place to go,

When Bodden took the wheel, Germaine busied himself by straightening the mess the sea lice had caused in the cabins. A few of the creatures remained, dead and decaying. Germaine scooped them into a bucket with a wooden boat hook and tossed them over the side. Every item of food on board, even canned goods, had suffered damage. Clothing, bedding, extra sails – anything chewable – had been targeted by the creatures. As he threw everything overboard, he realized that he was leaving a trail of jetsam behind the *Miss Lucy*. He hoped nothing followed it.

Finally, exhaustion won out over his fear of sleeping. He had postponed sleep as long as his body would allow. He threw a blanket over the bare wooden boards of his bunk and slept.

* * * *

Oct. 26, *Neptune* Lifeboat #3, Cayman Trench, Caribbean –

The lifeboat contained seven survivors – five men and three women. Most, including Josh, were in various stages of shock. Only Doctor Chase seemed impervious to recent events. He busied himself administering to his patients from the small stock of supplies in the boat's first-aid kit – aspirin for pain, bandages for wounds, and antibiotics for two people infected by parasites from the Bristle worm mucous. One of the passengers held a flashlight for him as he worked.

Josh examined the lifeboats supplies – a GPS unit, a radio, a signal-flare gun with five flares, ten gallons of water, and food that, stretched, would last the seven survivors two days. They had only the gasoline in the small, five gallon tank. After they exhausted that meager supply, they would have to row. He had retained his Remington, but had only three shells remaining. He had lost the box of ammo during the evacuation.

Almost from the beginning, one passenger, a former marine named Krajack, gave him a hard time. When Doctor Chase had insisted that they remain in the area until morning to search for survivors, both Josh and Krajack had argued against it, but Josh had finally relented. Krajack was not so easily dismissed.

"Who placed you in charge," he demanded.

"I'm just driving," Josh replied. "Doctor Chase is in charge."

"How so?"

"He's a ship's officer."

"I demand we make for the Caymans now."

Josh was exasperated by Krajack's attitude. "Look, you can take charge if you want. I don't care, but we're not going to the Caymans. I came from there. Little Cayman is gone, and we were on our way to Grand Cayman to help them after the storm. They've got enough troubles."

"I say we put it to a vote."

"No votes. Show them the photos," Doctor Chase said.

Josh passed around his cell phone, explaining, "These things came ashore on Little Cayman. You saw what attacked the ship. There's something else out there, too, something bigger."

"Bigger?" one woman asked. "How big?"

"Big enough to sink a ship," Chase replied.

"I still say we go to Grand Cayman," the marine continued, but with less conviction than earlier.

"Well, we're not," Chase said. He glanced at Josh. "We're going to Jamaica. Hurricane Clive didn't do much damage there," he turned to Krajack, "as you well know. When we get close enough, we can use the radio to call for help."

This seemed to satisfy Krajack, or at least he said nothing more. Chase moved closer to Josh and whispered, "I'm worried about the two infected people."

"Is it contagious?"

"I don't know. It's not the infection I'm worried about. That's secondary. The parasites are voracious. I've never seen anything like it. There's nothing in the kit for parasites."

Josh checked the fuel. "We should have enough fuel to get us most of the way to Jamaica. Maybe we can contact a ship before then, and get them some help."

Chase nodded. "I hope so. Otherwise ..."

Josh didn't want to waste their small stock of precious flares, but he fired two at fifteen minute intervals while they were still in the vicinity of the wreckage, hoping to get a response from one of the other lifeboats. No one answered. He tried the radio with the same results.

Of the five passengers, only two were a couple. Each of the others had lost someone aboard the *Neptune*. One woman had watched her husband being eaten by a Bristle worm. The others held out meager hope that their loved ones made it into one of the other lifeboats. From the radio silence, Josh didn't think any of the earlier lifeboats had made it away safely.

Josh had lost no one, either on Little Cayman or aboard the *Neptune*, but he understood their grief. His high school sweetheart, the girl he had planned to marry, had died in a car crash during his first year in college. His grades had suffered so badly that he had considered dropping out, but school was all he had left. Sometimes clinging to hope was the only rope a drowning person is thrown.

The night seemed unending, but dawn revealed a clear sky and a calm sea. The oppressiveness of darkness dissolved with the sun's first rays. They were still adrift, but they had survived into a new day. Wreckage littered the sea, already spreading by the tides. Soon, nothing would remain to mark the *Neptune's* grave. Satisfied there were no more survivors, Josh pointed the boat away from the *Neptune* toward Jamaica.

The two infected people were getting worse. Their color was ashen and their breathing labored. Josh could see the fear in the other passenger's eyes. Doctor Chase's frustration at his inability to ease their suffering was written in his haggard face. Jason suspected Chase's fondness for alcohol had driven him to seek a job as ship's physician, but neither his bedside manner nor his compassion for the sick had diminished. He ministered to their needs continuously, forgoing sleep.

By mid-morning, the woman, whose name he never learned, succumbed to her illness and gasped her last breath.

"We have to remove her body from the boat," Chase said, shocking everyone, even Josh.

"Over the side," the Krajack protested. "Ridiculous." He eyed Josh. "There will need to be an inquiry."

"Shut the hell up!" Chase snapped. Reining in his anger, he said more calmly, "We need to get rid of her body because I don't know what will happen to the parasites infecting her after she dies. They might seek a live host."

Josh nodded. Burial at sea was a custom as old as sea travel. Unfortunately, they had nothing with which to wrap or to weight the body. In the end, they simply lowered her gently into the water and restarted the engine, leaving her behind. He was glad the other patient was comatose and didn't witness the lackluster burial.

Less than three hours later, the second patient died. They repeated the procedure. However, this time, Jason noticed the dead man's skin writhing as the parasites sought their freedom.

"Hurry," he urged.

Krajack became frightened, dropped the dead man's head, and scurried to the opposite end of the boat. In his haste, he dislodged the fuel line. Gasoline spilled into the boat and the engine sputtered and died, as the fuel line fell over the side. As Jeff struggled to roll the corpse over the side alone, several half-inch long creatures emerged from the man's flesh and fell into the boat. He let the man drop into the water and began stomping the creatures with his foot. None escaped his wrath. He cast Krajack a deprecating glance and removed his shirt to wipe up the spilled gasoline. When he reconnected the fuel line, he noticed that almost half their fuel was gone, spilled into the water. It took several attempts to restart the engine. He resumed his place by the tiller and pulled away from the floating corpse. They had been in the water less than eight hours and had already lost two of their number and half their remaining fuel.

The motor sputtered and died two hours later. The sudden silence after so many hours was eerie. Several of the passengers who had been dozing woke with a start. According to the GPS, they were still over a hundred miles from Jamaica.

"Looks like we row from here," Josh said.

"Can't we rig a sail?" one of the women asked.

"With what? We don't have anything to use for a sail unless we strip naked, and there's no wind."

The woman sat back defeated. Josh chided himself for being so aggressive in his argument. They were frightened. So was he. The lifeboat had only one set of oars. They would have to take turns at rowing. Besides himself, the youngest person in the boat was in their fifties, so Josh volunteered for the first shift. After the slow but steady progress with the motor, the boat appeared to be glued to the water. If not for the faint wake behind them proving that they were moving, Josh would have ceased his effort.

The sun beat down on his naked back, rekindling his sunburn. His other aches and pains quickly awakened. His shoulder throbbed incessantly. He bit his lip and rowed. He silently sang a tune by the Goo Goo Dolls to keep his rhythm, *Long Way Down*. He supposed his mind had unconsciously lifted the song from his memory as a reminder of what lay below them, urging him to row faster. After two hours, exhausted, he relinquished his position to Krajack, who proved to be fitter than he appeared. To Josh's surprise, Krajack handled the oars expertly, the blades biting the water with each stroke for maximum thrust. Josh was beginning to believe they would reach their destination.

He relieved Krajack as the setting sun kissed the razor-edge horizon, turning it a soft gold. Doctor Chase passed the passengers a cup of water and a protein bar, their second meal of the day. Josh quickly downed his, knowing his body needed to replace the energy he had expended rowing. They would spend another night on the water, and at their present rate of speed would be lucky to reach Jamaica by noon. Josh settled into the steady rhythm of rowing, the oars slicing the water with hardly a ripple. His mind wandered. He fought the images of the Bristle worms attacking the ship and concentrated instead on the beach at Little Cayman before the night of the isopods.

A thud on the bottom of the lifeboat drew his mind back to the lifeboat. It was quickly followed by several more. He stopped rowing. The water beside the boat began to swirl as something just beneath the surface circled it. Finally, their visitor surfaced, a twenty-feet-long Viperfish. Its long, sinuous, eel-like body brushed the boat, almost upsetting it. The creature's bulbous head filled with dagger-like teeth yawned menacingly. To Josh's horror, a dozen more of the creatures surfaced around the lifeboat.

"What do we do?" Krajack asked.

Josh almost laughed that the ex-marine was asking his advice. "Sit still. No one talk," he warned the others. "Maybe they're simply curious." To satisfy his own curiosity, he took several photos of the Viperfish with his cell phone. They flashed their colors in response to his cell phone's flash. Chase warned him silently to stop. He heeded the doctor's advice.

For several heart-stopping minutes, nothing happened. The Viperfish continued to circle the boat like rampaging Indians circling a wagon train. Then, one of the creatures tired of investigating and attacked. It rammed the side of the boat with enough force to lift it hit several feet into the air.

"Hang on!" Josh yelled.

The boat rocked precariously but resettled right side up, but the creatures became more agitated. They repeatedly jostled the lifeboat, opening up several small leaks. When Josh saw Krajack stand and lift an oar into the air with an expression of fear and rage on his face, he knew the ex-marine was making a big mistake.

"Don't," he yelled, but it was too late.

Krajack smashed the oar into the head of one of the creatures. A second Viperfish grabbed the oar in its mouth. Krajack and the Viperfish wrestled for possession of the oar for several seconds. The Viperfish won, almost yanking Krajack into the water. Off balance, he fell to the gunwale, striking it hard with his chest. Before he could recover, the Viperfish released the oar and seized Krajack's head, snapping it off cleanly above the shoulders. Krajack's lifeless body fell back into the boat, flailing madly in its death throes, spraying everyone with blood. Thinking quickly, Josh grabbed Krajack by the feet and shoved the dead man's body over the side. Before anyone could stop him, he picked up the shotgun and shot Krajack in the chest. Doctor Chase stared at him in horror as he dropped the shotgun, picked up the remaining oar, and used it to propel the lifeboat from the midst of the feeding frenzy.

The water behind them churned with the feeding Viperfish, but none of the creatures were following as he had hoped. It was slow rowing with only one oar, but he gradually increased the distance between the Viperfish and the lifeboat. Chase continued to stare at him.

"I had to do it," Josh explained. "Those things had tasted human blood. Krajack was dead. He didn't feel anything."

"Why shoot him?"

"We needed more blood."

The woman who had suggested a sail was incredulous. "You used him to chum the water."

Josh nodded.

"It was disgusting," she said.

Josh stared at her. "You're welcome to go back and bury him."

She averted her gaze and said nothing more. Trying to reach Jamaica with one oar was hopeless. The current moved them away from Jamaica faster than they could row. They were adrift in a vast sea with little chance of rescue. The limited range of the radio meant that a rescue vessel or plane would have to be within a few miles to hear them, and the signal flares were difficult to see even at night. His cell phone was still charged, but had no reception. Josh convinced the doctor to open a package of crackers and a can of stew, hoping a real meal would lighten the mood, but most, including him, possessed little appetite in spite of their gnawing hunger. They settled back, each wrapped in his or her private thoughts. Josh passed the time bailing out the lifeboat with the empty stew can, but the water poured in almost as quickly as he could bail. They were in dire danger of losing their boat.

The sea finally swallowed the sun, leaving them in darkness. A northeasterly wind picked up, bringing with it a cold breeze. The waves rose, rocking the lifeboat. With the passing of the sun, their resolve weakened.

"We'll never reach Jamaica," Rawlins complained as he replaced Josh at bailing. "We'll die here."

"We have food and water," Josh countered.

Rawlins, a thin, wiry man in his late sixties, waved his hands about frantically. "We have those … things out there. They'll find us again."

"Keep bailing," Josh said. Rawlins stared at him angrily. "We'll take two hour shifts while the others sleep." Rawlins resumed bailing.

The moon rose just after ten p.m., relieving some of the darkness but none of the tension. Now they were five – Josh, Doctor Chase, Rawlins, and the two women, Clarice Bivens, a housewife from Des Moines, and Mary Elizabeth Hart, a retired teacher from West Palm Beach. Bivens had not yet accepted that she was likely a widow; clinging to a slim hope that her husband had survived the sinking. Rawlins admitted that he had travelled with a female companion, not his wife, but seemed little disturbed at her death.

Josh noticed a glow beneath the water some distance away, but said nothing, fearing to alarm his fellow passengers. He was relieved when the lights disappeared to the northwest. He allowed the rocking of the boat to lull him to sleep. If not for a low droning sound …

He sat up with a start, cocked his head to one side, and listened. Satisfied that he had heard something, he took the Very pistol and fired a flare into the air. The red flare arced over the sea before disappearing.

"What is it?" Chase asked. The other passengers were looking at him as well. They had heard nothing.

Josh ignored their questions as he loaded a second flare into the pistol, fired and waited. He hesitated using the last flare. The droning grew louder. A few minutes later, a spotlight swept over the lifeboat.

"A boat!" Rawlins called out.

When the spotlight swept away, Josh saw a sailboat a few hundred yards away. Two men stood on the deck, one controlling the spotlight. He began to wave his arms along with the rest of his fellow castaways. They were saved.

10

Oct. 27, *Miss Lucy*, Cayman Trench, Caribbean –

Just after sunset, Bodden spotted an overturned lifeboat off the starboard side. Germaine brought the ship alongside and killed the engine. He switched on the spotlight and played it over the lifeboat. The boat belonged to the *Neptune*, a hundred-passenger cruise ship he had heard of out of Bermuda. A large piece of the stern was missing, shattered by some great blow.

"No bodies," Bodden said.

"No, it's been in the water awhile."

He restarted the engine and continued south. An hour later, they encountered more debris – deck chairs, life vests, pieces of wood, shuffleboard sticks, bottles, and even a suitcase, but no bodies. It was enough evidence to rule out debris accidently dropped over the side.

"The storm could have sunk her," Bodden suggested.

They both knew the captain of the *Neptune* would have sat out the hurricane in a safe harbor, Jamaica or Haiti. Something other than the weather had sunk the passenger liner. He didn't want to dwell on what.

"There's nothing we can do," Germaine replied. He killed the spotlight, cranked the engine, and resumed his original heading. To be safe, he turned on the electronic fish finder he had traded a case of illegal Jamaican rum for. He didn't want anything sneaking up on him from below.

A week earlier, Germaine would have said that night was his favorite time aboard ship – the moon and the stars reflected in a calm sea, a cool breeze on his face, the darkness erasing the worries of the day. However, tonight he wanted to slink across the

Caribbean like a mouse, drawing no attention from whatever lurked beneath the deceptive calm of the water, every real and imagined reflection of light bringing chills to his spine. He gripped the wheel so hard his hands ached.

After midnight, Bodden relieved him at the wheel. He sat in the bow staring into the darkness. He almost missed the first flare, catching it only from the corner of his eye as it fell into the sea. At first, he dismissed it as a falling star, but as the second flare arced skyward, he motioned for Bodden to steer toward it. He spotted the lifeboat a few minutes later and focused the spotlight on it. The lifeboat held five people. He didn't mind leaving the survivors on Grand Cayman, but he couldn't leave people adrift at sea.

"Pick them up," he called to Bodden.

Bodden expertly pulled the *Miss Lucy* alongside the lifeboat. Germaine helped them aboard. By the looks of the battered and leaking lifeboat, they were lucky it was still afloat.

"Welcome aboard the *Miss Lucy*," he greeted them. "I'm Captain Germaine. He's Bodden."

The thin, older man in a uniform spoke. "I'm Doctor Chase of the *Neptune*. Have you located any other survivors?"

"Survivors? No, no one."

"Are there many ships searching for us," a woman asked.

"No one knows about you. I'm on my way to Jamaica. What happened to the *Neptune*?"

Josh set their few supplies on the deck and spoke up. "This may sound mad, but it was attacked by sea monsters."

Germaine laughed. "Mad? Maybe, but if so, we're all mad. I'm from George Town. It was overrun by swarms of giant sea lice."

Josh was stunned. The attacks weren't a local phenomenon. "I was on Little Cayman. There, it was isopods and then a tidal wave during the hurricane. I was adrift, and the *Neptune* picked me up. Viperfish attacked our lifeboat and killed one of the passengers."

"Viperfish." Germaine growled. "I've seen 'em. So, this is your second rescue. You have the luck with you, boy." He looked down at the lifeboat. "Cast the boat adrift and we'll be on our way."

A soft, steady pinging came from the wheelhouse. Germaine jerked his head toward the sound. "What is it, Bodden, fish?"

"Too big for fish and moving too fast."

Germaine turned to his new passengers. "It may be more Viperfish. Get below and grab some food. We're leaving."

"I think it's bigger than Viperfish," Josh said.

Germaine stared at him. "What do you know?"

"We saw a sea serpent. It rammed the *Neptune* and sank it."

Anything that could sink a passenger liner deserved respect from a distance. "How big was it?"

"Two-hundred- feet long, maybe more. It has a long, reptilian neck and head. I'm a marine biologist, and I've never seen anything like it."

"The sea's spitting up a lot of things I've never seen." Germaine looked at Bodden. "Maybe we can outrun it?"

Bodden shook his head. "It's making twenty-five knots."

Josh glanced at the gasoline drums. "I have a plan, captain."

"I'm open to suggestions."

"Give me enough fuel to run the lifeboat engine. We can load a fuel drum on it, punch holes in it, and set it on fire. If the sea monster goes for it, maybe we can cook it."

Germaine considered their options. They had none. "Okay."

The four of them, Josh, Doctor Chase, Germaine, and Rawlins, rolled the drum over the side and into the lifeboat, almost overturning the lifeboat. Josh leaped in, removed the bung with a hammer, and let fuel spill into the boat. He siphoned a couple of gallons of fuel into the empty fuel tank and cranked the outboard engine. The boat strained against the rope.

"It's here!" Bodden called out, as Josh made the leap back to the *Miss Lucy.* The lifeboat moved as a wave hit it. Josh lost his footing, fell overboard and went under. He could feel the displaced water as something large swam beneath him. He struggled to the surface and grabbed Germaine's outstretched arm. The captain hauled him back aboard.

While Germaine stood by with a knife, Josh struck a match and tossed it onto the lifeboat. It sputtered and went out.

"There's too much water in the boat," he said.

"Use the flare gun," Germaine suggested. "Do you still have flares?"

Josh removed the Very pistol from the lifeboat supplies. "One," he said.

"Then don't miss," Germaine advised as he cut the rope.

The lifeboat slowly pulled away from the schooner in a tight curve. The head of an enormous creature rose from the water just ahead of the lifeboat and continued to rise until half its body was on the surface. The beast was colossal, looking like a submarine. The head hung suspended forty feet above the water. The creature resembled a photo of the Loch Ness monster, except it had a shorter head and longer fins. The boat and the creature were fifty yards away. Germaine stared at Josh as he aimed the Very pistol, praying he didn't miss. He fired the pistol and watched breathlessly as it sailed over the boat and hit the sea monster in the head. The creature bellowed in rage. Just as he thought all was lost, the flare bounced off the monster's head and tumbled into the lifeboat. The boat burst into flames, and then struck the creature just as the fuel drum exploded. The explosion lit up the night. Burning fuel spread over the water and around the creature, engulfing it in a pool of fire. Bellowing, it endured the flames for another minute before submerging.

Germaine slapped Josh on the back. "I think you did it."

"I don't think we killed it. We had better get out of here before it decides to try again."

"I'll push the engines 'til they bust."

"No! I suggest you use the sails. I think the creature is attracted to sound. That's why it went after the lifeboat. It was probably following you."

Germaine gulped. Maybe it had been fortuitous that he had encountered the lifeboat. "I've only got one crewman."

"I can help. I'm no sailor, but I can follow orders."

"Show him what to do," Germaine said to Bodden.

While Germaine dropped the centerboard, Bodden and Josh raised the jib sail, mainsail, and foresail. In spite of Josh's inexperience, the job went smoothly. The fore gaff topsail was ripped and useless, but the three sails were sufficient to catch the breeze. Within fifteen minutes, they were under way. They quickly left the burning and sinking lifeboat behind. Germaine hoped they had left the creature behind as well.

* * * *

Josh was now afloat on his forth sea vessel, if he counted his roof-raft ride from Little Cayman as his first. He was thankful that Germaine had spotted them and hoped that he had repaid the captain's generosity with his fire ship idea. Sir Francis Drake had used fire ships against the Spanish Armada at the Battle of Gravelines in 1588. While Josh's hastily improvised interpretation involved a sea monster, something in which Drake might well have believed, the concept had been sound. He harbored no misgivings that luck had played a major part in the outcome.

Raising the schooner's sails had been hard work. His palms still burned from the rope burns. If his belief that the creature targeted sound or vibrations, they might be safe. It was a big if. Satisfied he had done all he could do, he joined his fellow survivors. They were a haggard bunch. Mrs. Bivens and Mrs. Hart still wore salt-stained formal gowns. Finally succumbing to their grief at the deaths of their husbands, they had little to say to anyone. Rawlins wore slacks and a dirty white shirt. He had discarded his tie in the lifeboat. He appeared to be coping on the outside, but Josh noticed a few nervous tics and shakes of his head that indicated that he was still having trouble with the situation.

Doctor Chase still wore his bloodstained uniform. The journey had taken a hard toll on him. He appeared gaunter than before, and his steps were slower as he moved about the cabin. Bodden loaned Josh a shirt that was two sizes too big, but he badly needed a bath. Bodden cooked them all a meal of bacon and eggs. It was the best meal Josh had ever eaten, or it seemed so. His memories of other meals were too hazy to recollect. It occurred to him in a moment of mental clarity that recent memories were not only more vivid, but actively sought to diminish the potency of older memories. Each time he tried to remember something good in his past, grisly images of monsters and of people dying flooded his mind.

Josh finished his meal and carried a cup of coffee to the captain. Germaine sat on a stool, steering the boat with one hand, while searching the frequencies on the radio dial with the other.

"Any luck?" Josh asked.

"Nothing clear." Germaine switched off the radio.

"Too bad. I need to contact my professor."

"What about your cell phone?"

"No reception."

"Does he have internet?"

"Of course. Why?"

Germaine smiled. "This may be an old tub, but I do have a satellite dish with an internet connection. I don't use it much, but it works. We're on battery, so make it short. We might need the juice later."

Germaine pulled his battered old laptop from a cabinet, hooked it up, and logged on. Josh downloaded his photos and sent them to his professor at TCU. The reply was swift, taking only fifteen minutes.

"Josh. Glad you're all right. I was worried. Amazing photos. The large creature resembles a *ceresiosaurus calcagni,* an extinct reptile from the Triassic. Fascinating. I contacted the Navy, only to discover that they are aware of numerous strange reports from the Caribbean. The Navy has requested our cooperation and discretion, so in keeping with my views on the dissemination of dangerous information, I urge you to refrain from sending photos to anyone else. I am flying to Jamaica on the first available flight. Meet me in Kingston. I'll attempt to charter a boat.

Gerald Hicks, M.S., PhD

Head of Depart of Marine Biology

Texas Christian University

Josh was briefly puzzled by his professor's admonition to refrain from sending the photos to anyone else. Then, he realized the professor feared the e-mail would be intercepted and meant just the opposite. Recalling a former colleague now at Woods Hole Oceanographic Institute in Massachusetts, he forwarded a copy of Hicks' e-mail and the photos. The professor's comment about chartering a boat could mean only one thing – he intended to capture the creature. It was a foolhardy quest. As much as Josh would welcome the opportunity to study the creature, he would try to dissuade the professor from this folly.

He shut down the computer and went back to Germaine. "The U.S. Navy is getting involved."

Germaine's expression at the news was grim. "Good, blow the bloody things to hell with depth charges."

"My professor is meeting me in Kingston. We'll need a boat. I assume you're available for charter?"

"If the price is right. I don't sell my life cheaply." He took a sip of his coffee and set the cup on the windowsill. "You going after it?"

"It would seem so."

Germaine shook his head. "It's a death wish."

"I'll try to limit Professor Hicks' curiosity to photographs."

Germaine looked away in muted pain as Josh mentioned photographs. "I've never met a biologist or a photographer yet who didn't push the limits." He took another sip of coffee to disguise the catch in his throat.

Josh needed to know more about Germaine if he was to work with him. "What happened on Grand Cayman?"

Germaine's eyes glazed for a few seconds. At first, Josh thought he would refuse to answer. "A group of photographers charted my boat. They were licensed, but not very experienced. We were on a night dive off the North Wall, when a school of those Viperfish attacked. All three divers died. I ... I couldn't do anything but watch. The next night in George Town the sea lice attacked, thousands of them, as big as lobsters. It was a damned massacre. Me and Bodden pulled up stakes and left."

Josh now understood the captain's bitterness. He had lost a charter group, his friends, and his home.

"Something caused these creatures to grow to tremendous size. Then something else, an earthquake or the hurricane, brought them up from the depths. The big boy we just met, the ceresiosaurus, is the top predator. He followed them. Sauropteoygian reptiles have been extinct for over two-hundred-million years. How it survived," he shrugged his shoulders, "I don't know? It seems nightmares have come alive."

Germaine sighed, "Maybe it's the end of the world."

Josh walked to the door of the cabin and stared out into the darkness. "No, it's just nature breaking free of normal constraints."

"Well, nature's doing a great job at kicking our ass."

"Nature has a way of correcting itself. Maybe if we study these creatures ..."

"Kill them; then study them. You'll learn nothing by dying."

"For a man so intent on their deaths, why did you agree to let us charter your boat?"

"It's how I make my living, that and fishing. You'll need my expertise," he added.

"I'm sure we will," Josh agreed.

"Just how do you catch a sea monster?" Germaine asked.

Josh scratched his head. He had not given the idea a lot of thought. Capturing a two-hundred-foot reptile was remarkably different from capturing a dolphin or turtle.

"There are a couple of drugs that should be effective – MS-222 or Propofol."

"Do they eat it? Do you put it in the water?"

"No, it's injected."

Germaine scowled. "So you tranquilize the creature, and then try to keep out of its way until it goes to sleep. You have to be some special kind of fool to try that."

Josh laughed. His thoughts were along the same lines, but he knew Professor Hicks wouldn't miss the opportunity to study a new species, and he couldn't let the professor try it alone.

"I guess you're looking at one."

Germaine shook his head and continued steering them toward Jamaica and an uncertain future.

11

Oct. 27, *Pandora*, Caribbean Sea –

The freighter sliced through the blue-green Caribbean water headed south. She showed no flag, and no name marked her black hull. No lights showed from her gray upper structure. Her captain and crew called her the *Pandora,* though no official papers bore that name. Two months earlier, the *Pandora* had sailed under the name *Kiya Maru* with a Kyoto registration. Six months before that, it had been the *Sea Maiden* out of Lisbon. Its mission was top secret, known only to a handful of men in Washington. This was nothing new for Simon Knotts. He had captained the black site freighter around the world on missions of equal importance for ten years, expecting no reward or public recognition for his efforts. He believed in what he was doing and trusted his crew implicitly. They were the best trained crew on the seven seas, hand-picked for their expertise and experience.

Knotts' own experience had been not in the Navy, but as a Marine. He had participated as a fresh-faced recruit in the Invasion of Granada in 1983 and as a captain during three tours of Iraq during the Gulf War in 1991. Working his way up from captain to major had taken three more years. An IED in Afghanistan had damaged his leg, forcing him limp with a cane, and ending his military career. He retired as a lieutenant colonel in 2004. The Central Intelligence Agency had approached him a year later. Since then, he had worked for the Company, which its employees quietly knew as the CIA.

Fourteen-thousand feet beneath the *Pandora's* keel, four Russian nuclear warheads from the Cold War era lay in their watery grave in the debris of the Russian freighter, *A.V. Pokhomov,* a casualty of the Cuban Missile Crisis. Knotts had been born two months before the Crisis, but he knew all about it or thought he had until given the specifics of his mission. Like most Americans, he had not known of the *Pokhomov's* sinking.

His primary mission was to retrieve the warheads. The *Pandora* had indulged in similar clandestine salvage operations many times, acting as a CIA black site, a mobile operations center. He had no concerns about that part of his dual mission. His secondary orders were somewhat more esoteric. He was to obtain, alive and intact if possible, the sea monster responsible for sinking the cruise ship *Neptune*.

Knotts didn't believe in sea monsters, but his superiors did and considered the rumors about the creature reliable enough to send the Navy missile frigate *U.S. Andrews* to investigate. The *Andrews* was forty miles to their south in pursuit of the creature. He had seen blurry photos taken by a young marine biologist and news footage of the carnage in the Caymans, but he still had doubts. Until he saw the creature with his own eyes, it was a myth. Myth or not, it didn't really matter to him. He would run the mission as if such a creature existed.

His priority was the nukes. Four, 30-kiloton warheads in the wrong hands would be disastrous. On the other hand, a nuclear warhead bearing an unmistakable Russian nuclear signature, exploded in Tehran would divide Middle East loyalties to the breaking point, allowing the U.S. to move in with financial aid and military protection. Such political schemes were beyond his pay grade. His job was to get results.

He had a secret weapon, a deep submersible vehicle, or DSV, DSV-5 to be exact, named the *Nemo* after the captain of the *Nautilus*, not the cartoon fish. With it, he could reach the area where the Russian freighter rested fourteen-thousand feet beneath the surface. Built to withstand the crushing pressure at that depth, the submersible could locate and retrieve the warheads.

The records of the incident had been buried in military archives for decades, known only to a handful of men who were sworn to secrecy. Most were now dead, but a historian given permission to cull the archives for a book found the captain's log of the *U.S.S. Allen M. Sumner,* the destroyer that had sunk the freighter. He, too, was sworn to secrecy, but like most academicians, confided his findings to a few friends. Word had finally reached the widespread and eager ears of the Company, and the *Pandora* had been given her mission. It was while training was under way that his second set of orders had arrived.

Knotts' cabin was vastly superior to most captains' quarters on freighters. His spacious suite had a private bath, a sitting room, and a king-sized bed. An adjoining office with a conference table served as a meeting room. Around this table now sat five men, Craig Devers and Lyle Matthews, the two men who would operate the *Nemo*, weapon's specialist Mike Bates, chief engineer Roy Starnes, and ship's doctor Millard Fenton, who would monitor the submersible's crew during their dive. At one end of the room, a sixty-inch flat-screen monitor displayed a depth map of the Cayman Trench, the *Pandora's* destination.

"Gentlemen," Knotts began, "You already know our mission ..." He ignored a few quiet chuckles until they died down. He stood, hobbled to the screen using his black lacquered cane, and pointed to a spot on the map. "This is the best-guess position of where the *Pokhomov* sank. This is a standard salvage operation, but at depths, we have not yet challenged. That is what it is – a challenge. You two," he nodded to Devers and Matthews, "know your job. I expect you to complete operations in one dive."

"What about this bug hunt?" Bates asked. More laughter followed.

"You know as much as I do, gentlemen. You saw the photos and read the report. The *Neptune's* captain was considered a reliable source. A flyover the morning after the sinking found debris in the water but no survivors. The few survivors from Grand Cayman all report the same things, giant bugs since identified as sea lice attacked and killed thousands. There were no survivors from Little Cayman except the marine biologist who took the photos of the creature."

"Y'all want me to throw a lasso around this thing?" Matthews, a cowboy from Arizona asked, exaggerating his drawl for effect.

Knotts returned to his chair and sat down. He laid his cane across the table in front of him. "No, we're picking up something in Jamaica from the *Andrews* for that. You get the nukes."

Devers, the more serious of the two submersible operators, leaned across the table and peered at Knotts. "Are these nukes hot? They've been down there a long time."

"Maybe these nukes are what caused this monster to grow so big," Matthews suggested. "I remember the *Godzilla* movies. Fuck that."

A private report for Knotts' eyes only had suggested the same thing, the reason the timetable for the mission had been advanced by two weeks. "Don't worry about it. You've got a Geiger counter aboard the Nemo. Use it."

Matthews raised his hand in the air as if he were a student in a class, and then brushed it across his sandy blond hair. Knotts nodded at him. "What is it, Matthews?"

"I just don't want to come back glowing in the dark. My girlfriend can't sleep with a night light on."

Bates was more serious with his question. "What if we can't capture this creature alive?"

"My orders say alive if possible. If it becomes a threat to this ship, then we blow it the fuck away."

Bates smiled and tapped the tabletop with his trigger finger. "Yeah, I like that."

Knotts turned to Starnes, the chief engineer. Starnes was older than Knotts, pushing sixty, but he knew more about ships' engines and loading freight than any man alive did. "Once we sedate this bastard, you will deploy the lift bags, and the *Nemo* will secure them around the creature. Once on the surface, we call in the *Andrews'* Chinook, lift it onto the deck, and strap it down. Reports say it can breathe air, but we'll keep it wetted down as a precaution."

Starnes scowled. "If it's really two hundred feet long, that's a lot of weight to distribute evenly."

"You'll manage," Knotts assured him.

"Mighty considerate of the Navy to lend us a helicopter," Matthews piped up. "I didn't think they liked us much. Aren't they supposed to be helping this professor fellow?"

Matthews had a point. Normally, inter-departmental rivalries prevented cooperation between civilian intelligence agencies and the military, but someone at the top considered this operation significant enough to set aside those differences and conflicts and had applied sufficient pressure to assure cooperation.

"Professor Hicks and his party are expendable. The Navy is using their expertise to locate the creature. If they make the capture first, so much the better. The *Andrews* will still deliver it to us."

"What are we going do with it," Devers asked, "send it to Sea World and teach it tricks."

"I have no idea, Devers, and I don't particularly care. We deliver it where we're told and go on to our next mission. Clear?"

"Clear."

Knotts could tell no one was happy with the parameters of the mission. Too much was left to chance or under the control of others. That increased the chance of a mistake, something that could cost lives. He knew that they were also expendable. He thought some incentive might improve morale.

"Do this right and we stand down for thirty days."

Bates rubbed his hands together. "A month in paradise."

"Screw up, and I'll shove my cane up your ass."

"Is that it, Colonel?" Devers asked.

He was the only one that used Knotts old military title and even he avoided using it in public. To anyone they encountered, Knotts was just Captain Knotts, or whatever name he was using at the time.

"I'll brief everyone once we're on station. Until then, make your preparations."

"And make your wills," Matthews added.

Knotts frowned, hoping no one died this trip.

12

Oct. 29, Kingston, Jamaica –

To Josh, the past two days had become a cycle of hectic preparation and bouts of deep soul searching. His mentor, Professor Hicks, was joyous at the prospect of discovering and studying a new species, devoting his hours at the Caribbean Maritime Institute between coaxing the Navy into supporting his plan to capture the creature, and convincing the administration of the Institute to loan him their inland marina as a holding pool for the creature. Though as a marine biologist, Josh's curiosity was aroused by the prospect, he couldn't help but dwell on the carnage he had witnessed. Part of him simply wanted the creature destroyed.

The television stations carried news of the deaths in the Caymans and of the *Neptune* disaster, as well as his photos, but so far, he had avoided the fates of Doctor Chase and his three fellow survivors, who were being held in protective custody, or so the Jamaican authorities claimed. Josh was quite sure the Navy had something to do with it, a ruse to keep them from the swarm of reporters that had descended upon Jamaica. Germaine and Bodden had escaped incarceration only through the intervention of Professor Hicks. Germaine was frequenting the local bars in an attempt to recruit two new deckhands for his crew.

A large supply of the animal sedative MS-222 had arrived, as well as a hypodermic rifle the size of a bazooka. If they were successful in stunning the creature, a CH-47 Chinook helicopter would transport the creature to the bay. A Marine marksman proficient with the hypodermic rifle would accompany them on the

Miss Lucy. For their protection, a Navy frigate, the USS *Andrews*, would provide escort. Professor Hicks had been against the idea, but Josh agreed with the Navy this time. A ship the size of the *Miss Lucy* would provide a quick snack for the creature if they failed in capturing it.

The photos of the giant fish, isopods, and Bristle worms had stood the marine biology field on its head. Discovery of a live specimen of the extinct *ceresiosaurus* had upended archeology as well. Slight variations in the fossil records of *c. calcagni* indicated a robust, evolving creature. Small slits on the neck proved to be gills, and closer examination of the teeth signified a wide spectrum of food prey. The large eyes proved *C. calcagni* was well evolved for life in the dark stygian depths.

The tabloids had begun calling the creature Cere in an attempt to humanize the beast, like Nessie of Loch Ness monster fame. Josh saw no humanity in it, only a perfectly adapted survivor of an earlier age when monsters prowled the land and swam the oceans. A creature ideally designed to capture and devour large prey. He had witnessed too many humans going down that massive gullet to humanize it.

Professor Hicks was not a large man, but he commanded attention with his energized five-feet-six-inch frame. His gray eyes darted in all directions, missing nothing, as preparations for the creature's capture proceeded. He brushed back his silver hair from his wire-frame glasses and pointed at a crewman moving one of the thick neoprene bands that the helicopter would use to transport the creature.

"You there! Handle that carefully. It's not a bed sheet."

Josh suppressed a smile. The irascible professor brooked no lackluster attention to detail from his students and expected none from the Navy. Josh had overheard a few of the crewmen calling him 'the Commander'.

"They'll get the job done, Professor," Josh said.

"Perhaps, but they're taking their damn sweet time about it."

"This is just a job for them, not an expedition to capture a piece of history."

The professor clasped his hands behind his back. "Yes, I suppose so. How about you, Josh? What are your feelings?"

Josh hesitated before answering. How did he feel about their endeavor? Excited? Frightened? Perhaps a little of both. "The creature is worth studying, of course, but I can't help feeling the risk might be too great. I've seen what it's capable of." He added, "There are other things out there beside the *ceresiosaurus*. Something has upset the balance of nature. It doesn't bode well for mankind if this repeats itself throughout the world's oceans. If we lose the oceans, we will cease to thrive." He turned to the professor. "Have you heard of any similar occurrences?"

"No, but every catastrophe begins with a single event."

"What event began this horror?"

Professor Hicks shook his head. "I fear we did?"

Josh was startled. "Us? You mean mankind?"

"The Navy has sent me samples of the sea lice that invaded Grand Cayman. They are highly radioactive."

Josh digested this bit of information while his mind conjured vivid images of Godzilla rampaging through Tokyo. "From the Cayman Trench? Do you believe it's a natural source?"

Hicks sighed. "I fear not. Doctor Yellin from the Institute confided that a Russian freighter believed to be carrying nuclear warheads was sunk in the Trench during the Cuban Missile Crisis in 1962. I believe that to be the source of the radiation."

Josh was incredulous. "I've never heard this before."

Hicks frowned as the seaman tossed the straps into the helicopter in an untidy heap. "You wouldn't. We barely averted a war that sad October. It was a time of great secrets, before the internet made such things virtually impossible to conceal."

The professor continued, "Small sea creatures with rapid reproductive cycles, such as chemosynthetic bacteria and other single-cell organisms would mutate first. With sulfides of copper and iron flowing from hydrothermal vents, they would have an ample food source to grow larger. Tubeworms, clams, and shrimp would feed on them, and so on up the food chain."

"That doesn't explain the ceresiosaurus."

Hicks smiled. "We may never explain that." He shrugged his shoulders. "Perhaps we don't know as much as about the sea or about evolution as we imagined."

Josh was relieved that the phenomenon was a result of mankind's folly rather than an act of nature and confined to the Cayman Trench, but couldn't help wondering about all the nuclear testing carried out in the Bikini Atoll and other islands after WWII. Would they produce monsters as well?

Josh faced the lagoon, now cleared of boats. A heavy, steel mesh fence had been placed across the entrance to contain the creature. "Will the mesh hold? It sank the *Neptune*." He remembered the grooves slashed in the hull caused by the creature.

"A ship is easy to sink. It takes but a single fractured seam. Water will do the rest. The mesh will hold. Once the creature is inside the lagoon, we may observe him at our leisure. My worries are confined to the capture."

A two-hundred-foot creature and a fifty-foot boat – Josh had given those statistics considerable thought as well. "Yeah, mine, too," Josh confided.

"From your observations of your previous encounter, I agree with the premise that the creature hunts by sound. Even its enormous eyes would be useless at five miles deep. Using the sailboat will reduce the chances of it attacking. Besides, we will have the Navy with us for any emergency."

While the frigate was well armed with a Phalanx close-in-weapons system, six MK-46 torpedoes, and a 76 mm MK-75, rapid-fire cannon, the idea was to capture the creature alive, if it cooperated. None of that heavy firepower would be of any use in an emergency if the *Miss Lucy* strayed between the creature and the frigate.

"Well, I must see to the transfer of the MS-222. I'll see you at dinner."

Josh watched the professor stride across the parking lot, his steps quick and energetic. He was in his element, a new discovery to examine, the danger the creature posed dismissed as irrelevant. Josh harbored no such quixotic fantasies. He was out of his depths and sinking fast. He wanted nothing more than to go home to Texas, but he knew he could never walk away from such an opportunity without regrets. It was the opportunity of a lifetime. His name would go down in history with such notables as Jacques

Cousteau, William Beebe, Rachel Carson, and Robert Ballard – if he survived.

He spotted Germaine strolling up the road with two men carrying duffle bags over their shoulders, his new crew. One of the men was dark, tall and lanky with Rastafarian dreadlocks. The other was slightly shorter with a scar on his right cheek. Germaine directed them to the *Miss Lucy* and came over to Josh.

"I see you found a crew," Josh said.

"Two of Jamaica's finest," he chuckled. "They're okay when they're sober."

"Did you tell them we're after a monster?"

Germaine winced. "They saw what happened to George Town. They feel safer at sea."

"Are we ready?"

"Whenever the professor gives the word. The sails are repaired and the hull is tight. Plenty of grub and beer aboard. Have you met our Marine marksman?"

Josh shook his head. He had met Corporal Elansky briefly, but wanted to hear Germaine's opinion of her. "Not yet."

Germaine rolled his eyes. "She's got a rod up her ass, a real stickler. She should be a joy to have aboard."

"As long as she's a good shot."

"The way she cleans that cannon she brought aboard, she should be." Germaine smiled. "Makes me jealous."

Josh smiled. The captain of the *Andrews* had informed Professor Hicks that Elansky had held the record for the highest scores in marksmanship for the last two years. As a female Marine, Corporal Nina Elansky had worked twice as hard as her male classmates in weapons school to earn their respect. Her good looks had been more hindrance than help. He hoped Germaine or one of the crew didn't try to put the moves on her. He had learned that she also held high marks in self-defense.

"The professor wants to leave just after dark. We don't want any of the news people to try to follow us. Can we?"

"Any time. Where are we headed?"

"We'll sail a direct course to the *Neptune*'s last location, and then in a spiral pattern until we make contact. The *Andrews* will remain a few miles off our course."

"With that creature out there, it can ride up my ass. I'll feel safer."

Josh smiled. "With the new underwater detection gear the Navy loaned us, we'll be able to spot the creature a mile away. If we get a good shot, the MS-222 should knock it out within minutes. Then the Chinook moves in to pick it up, and you come back here a hero."

"A rich hero," Germaine added, referring to the bonus the professor had promised him if the capture was successful. "Tide goes out at eight. I guess I had better go make sure my new crew knows port from starboard."

Josh had developed a fondness for the gruff captain of the *Miss Lucy*. For all his hardness, Germaine was a deeply caring man, overcome with grief by events, but too stubborn to give in to his anguish. By plowing ahead, he sought to mitigate his pain. Josh suspected that Germaine would have accompanied them in search of the ceresiosaurus even without the chance for a bonus. He wanted to see the creature killed. Its death would assuage his guilt at surviving.

Josh understood because he was trying to not succumb to survivor's guilt as well. He was the lone survivor of Little Cayman. If he had died that night, the world would not have learned of the danger it faced. That made his choice a straightforward one. He owed it to his mentor, Professor Hicks, and those in danger to do what he could to stop the creatures up from the depths. It seemed as if Fate had taken control of his life and was directing his steps. He only hoped he didn't falter.

By six o'clock, preparations were complete. The steel mesh barrier across the lagoon was in place, secured at each end by massive concrete pylons buried ten feet in the earth. The *Miss Lucy* was ready to sail, and the Chinook helicopter was loaded onto the *Andrews* and her crew aboard. Josh would have enjoyed a night on the town, but knew he couldn't avoid the reporters lurking outside the Institute's gates. It wasn't from any reticence from publicity on his part, but rather that they might note the fear in his eyes.

The Institute provided a farewell dinner for the expedition participants, complete with an open bar, of which Germaine and his crew made good use. Josh nursed a Red Stripe beer with his meal, which began with Janga soup, a freshwater crayfish dish energized by the heat of scotch bonnet peppers. Callaloo and saltfish, a Jamaican favorite, spicy conch fritters, and curried lentils followed. His eyes were watering uncontrollably by the end of the meal, and his tongue was roasted, but Germaine and the others, even Professor Hicks, who was used to spicy Tex-Mex dishes, showed no signs of discomfort. A dessert of raisin bread pudding with candied sweet potatoes and a Jamaican rum sauce cooled things down sufficiently for conversation. Josh enjoyed a second beer and listened to Professor Hicks expound upon the significance of recent events.

"If, as we suspect, high levels of radiation are the root cause of the extraordinary growth of these creatures, then it follows that we could encounter the same problem in the future at other locations where nuclear weapons were tested. Perhaps we are lucky that the Russian freighter sank to the depths of the Cayman Trench instead of a shallower location. Imagine the catastrophe of high radiation levels in coral reefs or in local fishing waters. Here, we have only to deal with the results of high radiation levels and not the radiation itself.

"Oh, I see by some of your faces that you think I trivialize the problem. I assure you that I don't. We face not only a gigantic monster capable of sinking ships, but a host of other creatures just as deadly."

"Why the effort to study this bastard?" Germaine asked as he slammed his drink on the table top. "Why not just kill it?"

Several heads nodded approval at his suggestion. Not everyone agreed with Professor Hicks or approved of his commandeering the Institute for his expedition.

"It may come to that, but consider this. We do not yet know the extent of the danger we face. Suppose this ceresiosaurus is not the only one in existence. Indeed, it is highly likely that it is not. They are reptiles and require both sexes to reproduce. What if it isn't at the top of the food chain? These are questions to which we must learn the answers. We can't afford to kill a single creature and consider the danger over."

"What about the sunken Russian freighter?" Doctor Samuel Estes asked. Estes was the Director of Public Relations for the

Institute. Unlike his colleagues, he was ecstatic over the notoriety the Institute was receiving in the press. "Are we going to attempt to recover it?"

Hicks shrugged. "That is up to the Navy. They have the equipment and the knowledge to descend to those depths and survey the situation. I hope the warheads can be safely retrieved and disposed of. Our task is to capture the creature for study."

Germaine finished his drink, but it was clear to Josh that he wasn't satisfied with the professor's answer. He whispered something to Bodden that brought a smile to the mate's face, and then stood. "Me and my crew are heading back to the *Miss Lucy*," he announced. "We sail in two hours. Don't be late."

Germaine caught Josh's eye and nodded toward the door. Josh rose and followed him outside. He appeared less intoxicated than he had inside. Josh suspected his behavior had been a façade, the tough sea captain act. A light drizzle was falling and wisps of clouds cloaked the moon like a tattered veil. *Or a shroud*, Josh thought; then shivered at his morbidity

"Your Navy friends aren't being exactly truthful to you," Germaine said. The rain didn't seem to bother him.

Josh was taken aback by the captain's claim. As far as he knew, the Navy had been very cooperative. "What do you mean?"

"Bodden's been asking a few questions around the docks. There's another ship a few miles off the coast."

Josh hadn't heard of a second Navy ship, but it didn't surprise him. "What kind of ship?"

"The kind painted all black and gray with no name or registry showing. No flag." Germaine's scowl revealed what he thought of the idea of a ship with no name.

"Bodden must be mistaken."

Germaine cocked his head to one side. "How much of that MS-222 was delivered?"

"A couple of gallons. More than enough. Why?"

"Bodden saw a skiff from the other ship load up drums of that stuff. They also loaded some pretty sophisticated sonar gear."

Josh shook his head in disbelief. "No, Bodden's wrong. He must be."

"The men on the boat didn't look like any normal crew. They were all young, clean-cut, and built like American football linebackers."

"Coincidence," Josh replied. "Maybe *their* captain runs a tight ship."

Germaine ignored Josh's barb. "What do you know about *Nemo*? Bodden overheard two of the men talking about *Nemo*."

Josh swallowed hard. The name struck a chord. He had heard rumors about the *DSV-5*, a deep-sea submersible vehicle sold to an unknown group a few years ago. They had reportedly named it the *Nemo*, Latin for no name, after the fabled captain of the *Nautilus*. He had dismissed the tale as preposterous at the time. Now, he wasn't so certain. A nameless ship, gallons of sedative, sophisticated sonar gear, and a missing deep-sea submersible all pointed to one thing – a second clandestine operation.

"CIA black ops?" he suggested.

Germaine nodded. "Something ain't right about this whole deal. While we're playing tag with Cere, it looks like the CIA is going down in the Trench."

Josh glanced back toward the door. He could hear the group laughing politely at one of the professor's notoriously bad jokes. "I should inform Professor Hicks."

Germaine grabbed Josh's arm. "Don't say nothing. Don't forget about our Navy lady friend with the rifle."

"You don't think ..."

"I don't think nothing, and I don't trust nobody."

"Why are you telling me this?" He shook free of Germaine's grip. "Do you trust me?"

"Look, lad, I like you, but you're a college boy tied to the professor's coattails. You've got higher ideals than I do. You travel in different circles. I'm here for the money, but if I think you're a danger to me or my boat, I'll drop you, the old man, and the lady sniper over the side in a heartbeat."

Josh stared at Germaine trying to judge the truth in his words, but he couldn't read the captain. Was he capable of tossing them over the side? Had he abandoned the three divers he claimed were eaten by Viperfish? "I'll keep quiet for now, but if you try to harm the professor..."

Germaine smiled. "I don't want to harm anyone. I'm no pirate, though there's some in these waters that don't fly the skull and crossbones," he said, a clear reference to the black ship. "If you do right by me, I'll stick with you, but I don't trust the Navy, and believe you me, they know all about the black ship. You shouldn't trust them either."

Josh didn't like keeping secrets, but if Germaine was right, he and the professor were caught in the middle of chicanery of the biggest order. If the black ship had a submersible aboard, its occupants had two goals – capturing one of the ceresiosauri and recovering the Russian nukes for purposes of their own. Their reasons for capturing a second specimen eluded him for a few seconds before it dawned on him that a creature like the ceresiosaurus or the other mutated specimens would make good weapons if unleashed upon an unsuspecting enemy. Unregistered nuclear warheads of Russian origin would fetch a large price on the black market.

Perhaps he was being too skeptical of the black ship's motives, allowing captain Germaine's paranoia to influence him. The submersible could be another part of the same operation, a back-up plan, and recovering the warheads, the source of the radiation, simply part of the overall operation. The Navy could have its reasons for the secrecy. After all, knowledge of the warheads had been buried for over forty years. Relations with Russia were at an all-time low. Public knowledge could cause considerable diplomatic problems.

Still, he would keep a close eye on Corporal Elansky.

13

Oct. 29, freighter *Pandora*, Cayman Trench, Caribbean –

Captain Simon Knotts stood on the bridge of the *Pandora* and watched the crew ready the Deep Submersible Vehicle *Nemo* for its dive. A crane in the massive sub bay suspended the submersible by the diesel-filled buoyancy tank that rode above the spherical cabin like a dirigible. In a way, that's what it was. The diesel tank was lighter than water, supporting the sub. Without it, the sphere would drop like a stone to the bottom where the tremendous pressure would crush it like a soda can.

A hatch in the bottom of the freighter was open, revealing a pool of seawater designed to allow the DSV *Nemo* to be deployed unobserved. Technicians bustled about on raised walkways around the pool checking each connection and fitting. The ten-foot-diameter sphere held two men in cramped quarters. He could see Devers through the Plexiglas porthole waving at him. He lifted his hand and returned the wave. A second, smaller, robotic operated vehicle lay nestled in a niche beneath it. They would use this ROVER to locate the warheads. Then the *Nemo's* twin manipulator arms would snag the nukes and place them in its belly basket. If they were lucky and all went well, the *Nemo* would be down less than twelve hours. Knotts never expected things to go well. If they did, they wouldn't need his expertise.

He glanced down with contempt at the walking cane he needed to negotiate the steps. His bad leg prevented him from making the dive himself. He had tried it once. The hours of confinement were a torture for his knee. Devers and Matthews would make the dive.

Matthews was an experienced ex-Navy submariner from the dry state of Arizona, while Devers had worked at Woods Hole before the Company had lured him away with more money. Knotts had faith in Devers' ability and in the equipment, but he had no faith in luck. As he watched the winch lower the DSV-5 into the water, he lit a cigarette and hoped.

* * * *

As the *Nemo* reached a depth of three hundred feet, the titanium alloy hull groaned as gaskets sealed under the pressure. From his position in the small sphere in the sub's nose, the clear Plexiglas gave Devers a 240-degree view around him. They were leaving the Epipelagic Zone where sunlight penetrated the depths and most of the ocean's plants and animals thrived. Below them, lay darkness and unimaginable pressure.

Beside him, lying on his belly, co-pilot and remote arm technician Matthews, stared at the gauges as the craft sank. Matthews, a tall, lanky man, appeared uncomfortable in the sphere's confining space, but he never complained. Like Devers, he loved diving. Devers, barely reaching five-six, sat comfortably in the cushioned pilot's seat manning the single joystick controlling the sub's descent.

Four independent electric motors operated four four-bladed propellers, two fore and two aft, each capable of moving forty degrees for delicate maneuvering. The batteries supplying power, lights and, more importantly at deep depths, heat, would last eighteen hours. Neutral buoyancy was maintained by the bag of diesel fuel inflated like a metal balloon above them. The sub pumped water into holding tanks to descend and expelled it to ascend. Additional lead ballast could be dropped to aid the descent.

In theory.

Devers had been diving enough to know that a thousand things could go wrong. At eighteen thousand feet, water pressure was eight thousand pounds per square inch, enough to crush the metal hull like crumpled aluminum foil. One tiny hole in the foot-thick hull or a crack in the Plexiglas port, and water would burst in like a sieve. Underwater rivers could twist the sub like wringing a cloth rag, and thermals could slam it against the bottom. If the reports he had read were true, they had one more problem they might encounter – sea monsters.

"Coming up at fifteen hundred feet," Matthews announced.

They were entering the Mesopelagic Zone, the aptly named Twilight Zone. As pilot, Devers had very little to do during the descent. This gave him time to worry. He tried to force images of crushed soda cans from his mind. And remember his last leave in Savannah. That cute redheaded Southern belle he had met at Paula Deen's *The Lady and Sons* restaurant had managed to keep him occupied for three long days and nights. Her slow drawl hadn't affected her nimble tongue, and her Southern Baptist upbringing hadn't curbed her sexual appetite. In fact, he had been hard pressed to meet her needs, a challenge he relished. He couldn't remember if her name was Lila or Lilly, but he remembered her number.

A shudder ran through the sub. Matthews cast him a quick panicked look.

"Just a small current," he assured his companion.

At eight thousand feet, the middle of the Bathypelagic Zone, midnight reigned. They encountered a flurry of small shrimp and feeding squid. The shrimp glittered briefly in the sub's searchlights, and then vanished into the inky blackness, pursuit by the squid in a silent ballet. The freighter lay another six thousand feet below them at the edge of the Abyssopelagic Zone, the Abyss, resting on a ledge that sloped downward for a thousand feet before dropping off into the depths of Cayman Trench. They would have to move carefully to avoid dislodging the precarious freighter and being carried to the bottom with it. Fourteen thousand feet was pushing the sub's operational limits. It couldn't withstand the crushing ten-thousand psi pressure of the Trench.

"Sonar picking up something," Matthews announced at thirteen-thousand-five-hundred feet.

"Headed in that direction," Devers said, adjusting the controls.

His breath became a mist in the air as he spoke. Even with the electric heaters at maximum, the temperature was only forty-five degrees. In spite of the chill, beads of cold sweat dotted Devers' forehead. His hand gripping the joystick was cold and clammy. The sub vibrated as he increased the rpms of the propellers.

The lights illuminated a tiny slice of the blackness around them, reaching outwards a distance of only seventy feet. Without the sonar, the sub would be flying blind. Even so, the bottom appeared abruptly at the edge of the lights. Devers hit the reverse thrusters. The propellers kicked up a cloud of sediment that obscured their surroundings.

"It's above and to the right," Matthews said, as he scanned the sonar, guiding Devers.

Devers crept along the steeply sloping bottom in the direction Matthews indicated. The rear half of the freighter, as pristine as the day it sank, loomed ahead. Currents had kept it free of sediment and growth. Two eel-shaped hagfish tussled over a bit of food. The name, *A.K. Pokhomov*, stood out clearly on its hull.

He called the ship above to inform them of their discovery. "*Nemo* to *Pandora*. We've located the stern. Starting a search pattern for the rest of the ship."

"Watch your time," Knotts replied.

They had been down six hours. That left twelve to reach the surface with their find, but they need to ascend long before then or risk running out of power. They had, at most, four hours to locate and collect the nukes.

The nukes would have been stored in the ship's forward hold. If that section had slipped down the slope, it was gone forever. The Pandora's sonar indicated a single metallic mass. It couldn't resolve the sonar reflection any further. As he moved up and across the slope, he noticed the large gash in the hull where the torpedo had struck.

"Didn't the action report of the destroyer that sank the Russian say they fired from off the port beam?"

Matthews pulled out his I-pad and pulled up the copy of the report. "Yes. Two torpedoes from port side."

"This hole is on her starboard side."

Matthews shrugged. "Maybe the captain was wrong."

Devers doubted a captain could get that confused even in the heat of battle, but replied, "Maybe."

"Getting another signal," Matthews called out a few minutes later. "Ten degrees starboard. Radiation level is rising."

Devers adjusted the controls and slowed to a crawl. He had been assured that the steel hull of the *Nemo* was sufficient to negate background radiation, but only if the nukes were still intact. Knotts believed that at least one casing had been compromised, and Devers trusted Knotts more than he trusted the Company.

"How bad?" he asked.

"One hundred millisieverts, more than we would get in a year topside. Short-term exposure won't be bad, but I wouldn't want to live here."

A dark shape appeared ahead. "There she is," he said.

The aft section of the Russian freighter had landed bow first amid a jungle of large boulders and skidded to a stop. A three-hundred-feet-long gouge in the sea bottom indicated its path down the slope. Sections of hull plating lay scattered along the trail. A crane, bent double, protruded from the dirt like a thumbtack. Winches, steel cable, a funnel, and other debris littered the area. The ship had cracked in two just aft of the cabin. The cavernous area of the forward cargo hold yawned like an open mouth. Devers settled the *Nemo* on the bottom twenty yards from the wreckage.

"I'll send in *Spot*."

Spot, the five-foot-long remote rover, was equipped with three cameras, a bank of sensors, and an oxy-acetylene cutting torch capable of burning through most debris. Handling the controls as if playing a video game, Matthews' nimble fingers guided the rover to the opening and inside. Its powerful spotlight revealed wooden crates and steel barrels jumbled into an untidy heap, woven tightly together with a mesh of steel cables like a giant spider's web.

"We're going to have a difficult time cutting through that mess," Matthews said.

"See if you can maneuver around it. We don't have time."

The view screen revealed a small gap to the right side of the tangled jumble. "It looks just big enough to squeeze through." Matthews smiled at Devers. "It'll be like deflowering a virgin."

"Like you've ever met a virgin," Devers needled.

The focus of the rover's camera narrowed as the small robot wormed down the tight opening. Devers jumped when a grinning skull leaped into view. He suppressed a shudder as Matthews panned the camera to reveal a complete skeleton wearing tatters of a Russian seaman's uniform. The cause of his death was still apparent after forty-two years. A piece of steel protruded through his ribcage, splintering two ribs.

"At least he died quickly," Matthews commented.

A few yards further, the tunnel split, one continuing straight, the other going off at an angle.

"Which way?"

"Take the straight one."

The passage ended at a dead end within ten yards. A farm tractor and assorted plows and tillers blocked the tunnel. The rover couldn't cut through so much debris.

"So much for that," Matthews sighed.

"We'll have to try the second one."

Spot couldn't turn around in such a tight space. Matthews maneuvered the rover backwards until it reached the second tunnel. The tunnel widened and seemed promising, but it too ended, this time in a disorderly pile of wooden crates, some of which were crushed and splintered. Matthews whistled softly as the rover's lights illuminated the objects scattered around the crates.

"Munitions," he whispered, as if his voice could set the explosives off.

Large caliber artillery shells, belts of machine gun ammunition, boxes of hand grenades, bazooka shells, and boxes of rifle ammunition lay sprinkled around the area like confetti after a parade.

"They must have been expecting another invasion," Devers said. "We can't do any cutting here. Back it out, and for God's sake, be gentle. We'll have to cut in from the outside hull." Cutting through the hull would take hours, time they didn't have, but he could see no other way to locate the warheads.

It took Matthews twenty minutes to reverse the rover through the narrow, twisting corridor, cursing at every tight turn. He was perspiring profusely by the time the rover was free of the tangle. Devers decided to move the *Nemo* to the starboard side of the ship opposite the cargo hold. He had seen blueprints of the *Pokhomov's* layout and suspected the nukes would have been stored in a small compartment with its own steel door separating it from the rest of the cargo. If he were right, cutting through the hull would save time. If he was wrong, they would have to abandon their search.

He was surprised to find a rent in the ship's hull adjacent to the compartment. A second explosion had pierced the cargo hold, ripping a large hole in the side. Two steel hull plates had been forced together by the pressure of the explosion, causing them to buckle outward, leaving a two-foot-wide gap.

Devers smiled. "That makes things easier."

After the sediment caused by their approach had settled, Matthews used the rover's camera lights to illuminate the interior of the compartment. As the camera panned across the room, Devers spotted three conical objects strapped to metal cradles. The Soviet hammer and cycle was painted a bright red on their sides – the nuclear warheads. To his dismay, the fourth cradle was empty. It had been ripped from its moorings and was tossed around the room during the sinking.

"Three out of four's not bad," Matthews commented. He checked the Geiger counter. "High but not deadly. They're intact. The fourth one must have been damaged and thrown clear of the wreckage. That's where the stray background radiation is coming from."

"We need to find it." Devers was no scientist, but he understood that rumors of giant sea monsters and leaking radiation were not two separate issues.

A look of concern crossed Matthews' face. "Why? We have three of them. The other one might be too hot for us to handle."

Devers ignored him as he started the engines to move the *Nemo*. "Use the Geiger counter to pinpoint the location."

Turning the sub in a slow circle, the Geiger counter picked up a higher radiation count downslope of the wreck. He moved down the steep slope slowly to limit the dirt the sub raised and improve visibility. He crawled back and forth across the slope, avoiding large boulders. The numerous boulders and debris from the wreck made the search difficult. Each pile of debris had to be investigated. After an hour and a half, Devers had begun to give up hope.

"It's getting hotter," Matthews called out.

They were at the edge of a precipice. The slope dropped off sharply for three hundred feet, ending on a flat plain that continued for several hundred feet before continuing its descent to the Trench. Devers carefully piloted the sub down the side of the wall until he reached the plain. Pieces of smaller wreckage had ended up there. He swept the searchlights across the plain until they picked out the fourth warhead, sitting upright near the edge of the wall.

"The meter's going crazy," Matthews warned. "It's hotter than hell. We're too close already."

Devers could see that the warhead had been severely damaged in its descent. The cone was truncated and an access plate had been ripped away, exposing the delicate wiring. Retrieving it would mean certain death from radiation poisoning. They would have to settle for the three intact nukes.

"It's a job for someone else," he said to Matthews, to his immense relief.

"Good. I may want to make babies someday."

A shadow passed beneath the sub just at the edge of the lights. Devers was tossed from his seat on top of Matthews as the sub rolled abruptly to one side.

"What the hell was that?" he asked as he crawled off Matthews and back into his seat.

"Maybe a rock fell on us," Matthews replied, but sounded as if he didn't really believe it.

Whatever had hit them had come from the bottom. No rock could jump up and hit them. "Whatever it was, I'm taking us back up."

The sheer sides of the cliff loomed dangerously near the sub as it rose, but Devers suspected he knew what had hit the sub and wanted to use the wall as protection. He considered abandoning the salvage altogether, but knew that he or someone else would have to do the job eventually. He guided the sub back to the forward cargo hold. They were unmolested during the two hours it took to cut away a section of hull and retrieve the remaining warheads. Once the three nukes were safely ensconced and sealed in the basket beneath the sub, Devers began to relax. However, his relief was short lived.

"I'm picking up something on sonar," Matthews said. "It's down slope and moving toward us.

Devers swung the spotlight toward the direction Matthews indicated. At the edge of the beam, dark shapes began to appear. The sediment raised by their movement obscured them from view.

"Let's get out of here," Matthews urged.

Devers ignored Matthews' plea. He was curious. He kept one hand on the throttle, but didn't move. When the shapes became visible, he wished he had. A dozen creatures resembling pill bugs like he had played with as a child scurried toward the sub. Each was larger than the Plexiglas bubble he and Matthews were inside. Curiosity gave way to self-preservation. He powered up the engines to lift the *Nemo* from the bottom. The propellers revved but the submersible didn't move.

"They're on the skids," Matthews cried. He turned to Devers. "What the hell are those things?"

Devers knew. He had seen the photos. "They're what attacked Little Cayman."

Matthews' face paled. "Get us out of here," he screamed.

"Use the arms."

Matthews stared at Devers uncomprehending for a moment, and then his face relaxed into a wry smile.

"Yeah," he said.

He used the sub's manipulator arms to swat at the creatures as if they were gnats buzzing his head. The creatures were large and nimble, but the steel arms crushed them as if they were cardboard boxes. Devers rocked the sub to help dislodge the creatures from the skids. They might not be able to damage the Plexiglas bubble, but he suspected they could rip the thinner material of the buoyancy bag. He dropped the lead weights and the sub surged upward. They were free.

"Can we leave now?" Matthews asked.

"One more thing to do."

"What?"

He stared at Matthews. "Use *Spot's* torch to ignite the ammunition in the cargo hold. The explosion should bring half the mountain down on top of the fourth nuke, and seal it up for good."

Matthews shook his head. "Negative, man, *Spot* cost a small fortune. They'll take it out of our pay. Besides, it might not work."

"It'll work," Devers assured him. "We already sold our souls to the Company. So they'll own our asses for a few more years."

The radio range for the remote rover was less than five hundred feet. He hovered the sub above and to one side of the *Pokhomov,* as Matthews threaded the tight tunnel with nimble *Spot* until it reached the ammunition. Choosing a 76 mm artillery shell from a pile of shells, Matthews used the smaller manipulator arms of the rover to place it beside a large crate of munitions. The shell was not fused, but the cutting torch could easily ignite the powder charge inside. The blast would set off the entire store of munitions. Devers hoped the resulting explosion would be large enough to bring the entire slope down on the ledge and bury the fourth warhead.

Matthews wiped his perspiring forehead on his sleeve and licked his dry lips. "It won't take long for *Spot* to burn though a brass shell casing, so once I ignite the torch, you put the pedal to the metal and get us the hell out of here."

The camera flared as the torch ignited. The flame was directed at the shell casing, but the bubbles from the torch blurred the image. Devers dropped all the remaining ballast and the sub began to rise. Below them, the area around the ship was alive with more of the black bugs. He hoped they enjoyed the ride back to the depths that spawned them.

The explosion came a minute later. Light flared from every rip and opening in the ship. Then it swelled like a balloon as the ammunition ignited. Finally, it burst open along the seams, spewing shrapnel across the slope. Because of the intense water pressure, the gas-filled bubbles created by the explosion looked small, but they grew rapidly as they rose toward the surface. The shock wave hit the sub twenty seconds after the explosion, sending it into a wild spiral, nose down, that tossed its occupants around the cabin like dice in a cup. Devers cracked his elbow on the hull, numbing his right arm controlling the sub. He quickly grabbed the joystick with his left hand, fighting to level out. Matthews slammed headfirst into the control panel, knocking him out. Biting back the pain, Devers stared out the porthole. The forward section of the

Pokhomov was gone, disintegrated. The slope around it heaved and buckled like a shaken blanket before sliding downward, and raising a cloud of sediment that quickly engulfed the *Nemo*.

Devers was pleased with himself. The nuke was buried beneath thousands of tons of debris where it could cause no further harm. They had the remaining three nukes in the basket. In his mind, the mission was a success. He just hoped his superiors saw it that way. Matthews groaned as he came to, rubbing a bump on his forehead. The radio came alive.

"We picked up an explosion on sonar. What the hell happened down there?"

Devers ignored Knotts' frantic call. He reached over and switched off the radio. He had six hours of peace and tranquility to enjoy on the ride to the surface before all hell broke loose. He lay back and closed his eyes, thinking about Lila, *or was it Lily*, in Savannah.

14

Oct. 30, *Miss Lucy*, Cayman Trench, Caribbean Sea –

As luck would have it, less than four hours after leaving Kingston, the weather worsened. A twenty-knot westerly wind raised ten-foot waves with frothy whitecaps that slammed into the sailboat's hull like sledgehammers. The tiny boat heaved and pitched as if each roll would be its last, but Germaine kept the ship afloat by years of seamanship and by his refusal to give in to the whims of the sea. He rode the waves like a consummate surfer, using its power to shove the boat back up the next wave's back.

The crew clung to the masts and booms, gathering the sails before the wind shredded them. The professor had locked himself in the head, where the sounds of retching rose and quieted in rhythm with the boat's frantic motions. Corporal Elansky sat by herself as if unconcerned by the weather, as she dismantled and cleaned her rifle. Josh had thought himself immune to seasickness, but his stomach was rebelling at the constant swaying of the overhead light.

"You're doing better than the old man."

Josh looked up to see Elansky grinning at him. "I've sailed in rough weather before, but this is pushing it, even for me." He nodded toward the head. "The professor hasn't had much experience at sea."

"Strange for a marine biologist, isn't it? His books are very educational."

"You've read his stuff?" He was surprised that a sniper read books about marine biology.

"I thought his book on star fish declination of the Pacific coast was very compelling."

"Do all Marines follow marine biology professors?"

She rubbed a part of the rifle with a soft cloth, examined it, and then laid it with the other parts spread out around her. "I like to know whom I'm working for."

"What about me?"

"Joshua William Peterson, born 3rd December, 1991 in Waco, Texas. GPA of 3.8. You swim, dive, surf, like to play paintball with your friends, and prefer Chinese food to Tex-Mex."

"How did you ... Do you have a dossier or whatever on me?"

Her laugh was soft, not condescending. "No, I pulled your college file. The professor told me the rest."

Josh relaxed. "I see. I know nothing about you."

"Nina Haley Elansky, corporal. Born March 22, 1990 in Schuylkill, Pennsylvania. No siblings. Parents dead. I don't get seasick, I hit what I aim at, and I prefer scotch when I drink, which isn't often."

"Why are you here?"

"I'm a Marine. I go where they send me."

"You didn't volunteer for this mission?"

She replaced the last part in the rifle and laid it on the seat beside her, patting it gently as if it were her pet. "They said they needed someone with my special skills for a mission. I volunteered. When they briefed me, I thought, this is a shot no one else will ever have the opportunity to make, so I accepted."

"You're not curious?"

She leveled her eyes at him and replied, "No."

"Are you stationed on the *Andrews*?"

"No."

"The other ship?"

Her reaction was slight, but her eyes betrayed her. "What other ship?" she asked. She knew about the black ship, or at least suspected that something strange was going on. He wondered how much she knew. He decided to heed Germaine's advice about secrets. "Nothing, I thought someone said another ship would join us."

"Not to my knowledge."

Josh nodded. "My mistake."

The boat rolled violently, throwing Josh across the couch into her shoulder. When he tried to right himself, his hand brushed her breast. She leaned away but smiled. "I don't get frisky with anyone until after the job's done."

Embarrassed, Josh moved back to his side of the couch. "Sorry."

"Don't be. I enjoy a good roll in the sack as well as anyone, but business comes first."

Josh wasn't sure how to respond to her, but Professor Hicks broke the moment as he staggered out of the head, pale and slightly woozy. He braced himself against the wall as he moved to a chair across from Josh and Elansky and collapsed, groaning, "I didn't think it would be this bad."

Taking pity on him, Elansky replied, "It'll just last a few more hours. By morning, the sea will be calm."

"I hope so," Hicks replied, but his expression betrayed his doubts.

Elansky sat ramrod straight with her hands on her knees. She was unperturbed by the rough voyage or by the loud rumblings of the professor's stomach, audible even over the creaking of the boat. Josh tried hard not to stare at her, but couldn't help stealing discreet glances. She intrigued him, beautiful but deadly. He wondered why such a lovely woman would choose to go into the sniper trade. There were many women Marines, but killing someone at a thousand yards was different from normal combat. It took a special kind of person; one with powerful concentration and extreme calmness in the face of danger. It also took someone cold and calculating, he reminded himself. He wondered if she would look so calm when she saw the ceresiosaurus.

Twice more during the early morning hours, the professor visited the head. After his last visit, he lay down on one of the bunks and managed to fall asleep. Elansky remained seated in her chosen position with her eyes closed as if meditating. Josh thumbed through an old Playboy magazine, admiring Miss April of 2011.

"Do you prefer brunettes?"

Startled, Josh almost dropped the magazine. He hastily closed it and laid it on the table. Elansky stared at him with a grin on her lips.

"My girlfriend was a brunette."

"Was?"

"She died in an auto accident. I…uh…haven't dated much since."

"Sorry. I didn't mean to hit a sore nerve."

"It's all right. I'm learning to cope."

She frowned. "Clearly you're not. I can see the pain in your eyes. That's all right. It shows you care."

Josh nodded, surprised by her depth of understanding. "Thanks."

"The wind's dying down."

Josh looked up at the overhead light. It was barely swaying. "You were right."

"Snipers study the wind and weather. We're like sailors in that respect."

Was she subtly reminding him that she was a killer? "Have you ever hunted big game?"

"You mean shoot something other than people? No, I don't hunt for sport. I kill as a soldier kills. I just do it solo."

"Don't you usually have a spotter or something?" He didn't know much about Marine protocol, but he had watched a few movies about snipers. They usually had a companion.

This time, the pained expression was on her face. It disappeared quickly. "I had a spotter. He died on our last mission. I haven't chosen another one yet."

So she's suffered a loss too. Welcome to the club. "Sorry."

"It happens." She glanced out the porthole. "It's getting light outside. Why don't you get some shut eye?"

"I'm too nervous to sleep. What about you?"

"I don't sleep before a mission."

"This one is a little different, isn't it?"

"You mean tranquilizing an extinct sea monster? It's one for the books."

"Are you afraid? I mean …"

"You mean I'll be up close and personal. I'm excited. I get to shoot but not kill."

Something in her voice betrayed her feelings. "Does killing bother you?"

"Only a fool likes to kill. It's my job. I do it because most can't. I have a special skill set. I can save lives." She paused. "When you stare at a face through a telescopic sight, you see the lines on their face. You see their eyes. I remember the face of every person I've killed. They don't go away. It's like a gallery of the dead in my head."

"It must be rough. I'm sorry."

She shook her head. "Don't be. I live with it. It's what I chose." She stood and crossed the room to stare out the porthole. "It's going to be a clear day. Good." She looked at Josh and smiled. "If you don't mind, I need to be alone to prepare myself. It's a ritual I do."

Josh stood. "Uh, yeah, sure. I'll check on Germaine."

She resumed her position on the couch, laid the rifle across her lap, and closed her eyes. Josh noticed tightness in her jaw now, and one hand was clenched in a fist. He watched her large, firm breasts rise and fall with her breathing for a moment, and then left.

Bodden was at the wheel. Germaine sipped coffee while propping one foot on the aft starboard rail. He held a cigarette in his other hand. The other two crewmembers were rigging the gaff foresail on the aft mast for added speed. Germaine shouted occasional insults at their ineptness, but to Josh who had helped raise the sails once before, they seemed to move adroitly and speedily. Finally up, the sail caught the wind, and the boat surged forward.

The sea was much calmer, but wind-driven spray from the bow splattered Josh as he walked out the door onto the deck. Germaine saw him and called, "Beautiful day."

"Are we making good time?"

Germaine inhaled, exhaled a cloud of smoke swiftly ripped away by the wind, and shrugged. "About sixteen knots. We're tacking against the wind right now. We'll pick up a few knots when we change direction."

"Change directions?"

"We headed a bit east last night to avoid the worst of the storm," Germaine explained. "The wind's from the southeast this morning." He used the coffee cup as a compass to indicate the directions. "We'll head due west shortly to reach the area Professor Hicks expects to find the beast."

"Is the sonar operating?" The Navy had augmented the *Miss Lucy's* sonar gear with modern, government-issued equipment.

"I decided to keep it off until we get where we're going. If you're right about the creature detecting sound … well, we might want to sneak up on it."

"Any word from the *Andrews*?"

"No messages, but I caught a glimpse of her before dawn. She's following about eight miles to our east. I just bet her captain's bitching about having to crawl along behind a sailboat."

Germaine didn't look too perturbed by the idea.

"How's the professor?"

"Still sleeping. He had a rough night."

"And our lady friend?" Germaine grinned and winked.

Josh shrugged. "She's getting ready for her shot."

"She's a cold one. Beautiful but deadly." He closed his eyes and shook his head one time. "I like that in a woman."

"What about our other friend?" Josh asked, meaning the black ship.

"A quick blip on the radar a few hours earlier, but then nothing else. She's out there all right, but she's keeping well clear of us."

"She's headed for the Russian freighter for a bit of salvage work. I don't think she'll bother with us."

Germaine raised an eyebrow. He flicked his cigarette over the side and watched it drift away. "Then why are they traveling with a Navy frigate?"

"You think they're after the creature? Then why is the Navy helping us?"

"Doubling their chances. If we capture it first, all they have to do is move in and take it from us."

"You're paranoid. The professor would go straight to the press as soon as we returned to port. They'd never get away with it."

Germaine nodded. "If we returned to port."

Josh stared at Germaine. Was he suggesting …? "You're crazy. They would never do something that stupid. Even if they sank us, someone might survive."

"Not if we were dead before we sank." He turned toward the cabin. "The corporal is a killer. Why send a killer to capture a sea monster?"

"Because she's good at her job." As his words sank in, he realized the captain was getting to him. "She wouldn't." He wasn't sure why he was defending her. He didn't know her or what she was capable of doing. Was he letting her good looks color his opinion of her? "She wouldn't," he repeated.

"Maybe, but I'm keeping that shotgun you brought aboard handy. I picked up some shells in Kingston. If you're right, no harm done. If you're not … I won't give in so easily."

"You're wrong about her."

"We'll see."

The two new crewmen stood staring at them. "Get below and eat breakfast," Germaine bellowed at them. He pulled another cigarette from the pack in his pocket and lit it, and then turned to Josh. "There's a Webley revolver behind a loose board in the bulkhead of my cabin above the door if you need it. It fires a .455 caliber slug that can knock a man backwards at twenty paces. Remember, there's more out here to worry about than our feisty little sniper."

He walked back to the cabin and took over the wheel from Bodden. Josh remained on deck considering what Germaine had said. He might be paranoid about Elansky and the black ship, but he made sense about other things to worry about. The closer they got to the Trench, the likelier they were to encounter more creatures from the depths. Looking at the surface of the sea, it appeared tranquil and safe, beautiful even, but the sea was a shadow hiding monsters in its dark folds, nightmarish creatures that haunted the wildest dreams of the insane. They were real and they were deadly. He couldn't let his professional curiosity overwhelm his common sense.

It was odd that water could be so dangerous. The human body was composed of up to seventy percent water, but water wasn't man's element. Adapted for dry land, humans had barely explored the depths of the seas. To remain beneath the water for more than a few minutes, he must carry his own air supply. To explore the depths, he must surround himself with a pressure-proof shell of steel and Plexiglas. The depths were as foreign to man as the dark side of the moon. Only a tiny fraction of the ocean's bottoms had been observed, and what has been seen was strange and mysterious.

Whether created by nature, or as they now suspected, by man's folly, the creatures of the Cayman Trench were dangerous and deadly. Killing them would be difficult, capturing one even more so. Common sense dictated a safe retreat to land, but men such as Professor Hicks, and admittedly, himself, were driven to understand what brought these creatures into being. Sometimes curiosity was a dangerous compulsion.

As he moved forward, the sharp odor of Germaine's cigarette smoke mingled with that of frying bacon. Germaine was humming softly to himself as he leaned against the ship's wheel. Two sandwiches lay in a plate on the chart table, as well as a thermos and a cup. Germaine glanced over his shoulder as Josh entered the cabin.

"Bodden brought up some bacon and egg sandwiches, and coffee. Have some breakfast."

Josh wondered how the aroma of food cooking was affecting the professor's touchy stomach. To Josh, the smell was enticing. He poured a cup of coffee, picked up a sandwich, and took a bite.

"Tell Bodden thanks," he said around a mouthful of crunchy bacon and soft scrambled eggs with cheese.

"We received a radio message from the *Andrews*. One of her choppers spotted something in the water about fifteen miles from here, a lifeboat. There are three people in it, but they didn't see any movement."

"Survivors from the *Neptune*?" He was thrilled that more people might have escaped the sinking ship, but had they survived the long exposure?

"Possibly. They're sending out a boat to pick it up. The chopper is remaining in the area."

"We should go."

Germaine cocked an eyebrow at Josh's suggestion. "Why? We're still a long way from our destination. Let the Navy handle it."

"They might have seen something."

"If they're still alive," Germaine reminded him.

"We should go." Was concern or curiosity what drove him to insist? He couldn't drive the old man who had spotted him, Crabtree, from his mind. He had wanted to commit suicide. Had the creatures done the job for him, or was he on the lifeboat?

Germaine shrugged and turned the wheel a few degrees to starboard. "Makes no difference to me." He leaned over the steps leading below and yelled down, "Bodden, Odette, Miguel! Get aloft and adjust the sails."

The three men raced onto the deck and began moving the sails to catch the best breeze. Elansky followed a few moments later. She held the tranquilizing rifle in her arms and a .45 rested in its holster on her hip.

"Anything?" she asked Josh.

"Just changing course. One of the *Andrews'* helicopters spotted a lifeboat."

She nodded and relaxed her stance. "Any survivors?"

"They don't know yet."

She moved to the door and glanced out. "The weather cleared. Good. It'll make the shot easier."

"If we find the creature."

Her face hardened, and she narrowed her eyes as she spoke. "It'll find us. It's a hunter."

"We're running silent."

"It's out there. I can feel it."

Her tone made him jumpy. "It's a big ocean."

"It's territorial. It knows its boundaries, and it'll know when someone enters it."

Josh followed her gaze to the water, but he could see nothing. What did she see? "If it's attracted to sound, it should follow the *Andrews*, not us."

She faced Josh. "Are they sending a launch to investigate the lifeboat?"

"Yes, why?"

"The creature might not attack something as large as the *Andrews*, but a motor launch might be worth the risk."

"It sank the *Neptune*," he reminded her.

"It was following the Bristle worms. The *Neptune* rammed it."

"How did you ..." He started to ask her how she knew about the *Neptune*, but realized that her superiors had probably briefed her. She undoubtedly knew more about the incident than he did. The captain would have sent out a distress signal of some kind. It would be unlikely he would not mention the cause of the distress.

"How's the professor?" he asked.

She smiled. "Poor man. He's awake, but he's not eating. He took some Dramamine with a cup of coffee. He'll be up on deck soon."

"He doesn't travel well, but it's difficult to keep him down for long."

"Do I detect admiration in those deep blue eyes?"

Josh blushed and averted his gaze, unsure if she was complimenting him or making fun of him.

"Did I embarrass you?" she asked.

"Not at all. You just caught me off guard."

"I do that with people. They can't figure me out and that frightens them. Are you afraid of me?"

"I've never met a woman who could kill at a thousand yards."

"Twenty-five hundred yards," she corrected, "but I'm more dangerous close up." She took a step nearer. Josh resisted the impulse to back up. She wore a light floral fragrance that tickled his nostrils. He found the scent arousing but slightly disconcerting emanating from a Marine. Germaine broke up anything that might have happened next.

"If you two are through playing house, the captain of the *Andrews* wants to speak with someone."

She smiled and walked to the rail. Josh swallowed hard and rushed to the cabin. He snatched the microphone from Germaine's hand.

"This is Peterson."

"Mister Peterson, this is Captain Tremaine. I've sent a launch to investigate the lifeboat. Our helo has confirmed three bodies aboard, but no movement so far. It's remaining on station to assist.

Sonar is tracking something large at a depth of three-hundred-fifty fathoms and rising fast about two clicks to our port. It might be your monster. I suggest you get here ASAP."

Germaine nodded and whispered, "Twenty minutes."

"We're on our way. We'll be there in twenty minutes."

"Don't be late. Out."

"Here we go," Germaine said. His hands gripped the wheel tightly. He kept his eyes focused on the horizon. If he harbored any trepidation about meeting the creature, he didn't reveal it in his stance. He appeared determined to get the job done.

Josh leaned over the stairwell and yelled down, "Professor. We're close."

A minute later, Hicks appeared, disheveled and pale. His glasses set crooked on his nose. He forced a smile to his lips. "Good morning, Josh."

"Are you feeling better?"

He nodded. "Yes, thank you. I should be fine." He adjusted his glasses. "Have they spotted the creature?"

"The *Andrews* has something large on sonar. They also found a lifeboat adrift. They've sent a launch to see if anyone is alive."

The professor grew concerned. "They shouldn't have. A small motor might entice the creature."

"It might be a lifeboat from the *Neptune*."

"Then let us pray there are survivors."

Josh glanced out onto the deck. Elansky was cradling the rifle in her arms as she sat on the hatch cover. She appeared calm but intent. A second shell containing MS-222 lay beside her just in case. They knew nothing of the creature's physiology, but based on its estimated weight, they had derived what they hoped was the proper dosage. Too little and it might attack. Too much and they might kill it, losing it forever.

The next few minutes were nerve racking. Germaine and Bodden were both as stoic as ever, but the two new crewmen stood together whispering with looks of fear on their faces. They had heard the rumors, but desperate for work, they had still come. What type of man would willingly face a monster? Josh wondered the same thing about himself.

The *Andrews* appeared over the horizon, smoke pouring from her stack. A second speck, the helicopter, was hovering so close to the water that it appeared to be floating on the surface.

"Should I switch on the sonar gear?" Germaine asked.

"No," Hicks answered. "The helicopter should have dropped a sonar buoy. Our receiver will pick it up. That way we won't be sending a signal."

Germaine switched on the sonar receiver. A steady beeping filled the cabin. "If I'm reading this correctly, our Cere is two hundred feet down and circling the lifeboat."

Now Josh could make out the lifeboat. It looked like the sister to the one he had escaped in, but he couldn't read the name. The *Andrews* launch was alongside. The helicopter, an S-70B Seahawk, was a large craft, a Navy variant of the UH-60 Blackhawk. Its powerful rotor blades raised small waves around the two boats. They rocked in its wake.

The radio startled Josh as Captain Tremaine announced, "One passenger is still alive, but two are dead. We're retrieving them now."

Professor Hicks took the microphone. "Captain, you should have the helicopter move away. The creature is near."

"We're following it on sonar. The helo is standing by for the rescue."

"I'm afraid I really must insist. The noise, the vibration is attracting the creature. They all could be in danger."

"Professor, a Seahawk carries two Mk-46 torpedoes and a GAU-17/A mini-gun. It's a lethal anti-submarine weapons platform. It's quite capable of …"

"We're here to capture it, not kill it."

After a moment of silence, the captain of the *Andrews* replied, "Affirmative, Professor. I'll advise them to move away."

Hicks sighed with relief when the helicopter rose and moved back toward the *Andrews*. However, his relief was short lived.

"It's surfacing!" Germaine yelled.

The *Andrews'* motor launch lifted into the air as the ceresiosaurus breached beneath it. The launch rolled off the creature's broad back, spilling the crew into the water. It crashed upside down onto the lifeboat, crushing it. Now, four men were floundering in the water, including the lone survivor from the lifeboat. Josh watched helplessly as the creature lifted one of the men from the water in its enormous jaws and bit into him. One severed leg fell into the water. The man's scream was faint, blown away by the wind, as the creature swallowed him and submerged.

Josh had glimpsed the ceresiosaurus for less than a minute on the *Neptune*, and it had been dark. In full daylight, it appeared much larger and more menacing, a mythological creature from a macabre fairy tale. This was no Nessie, no harmless myth for tourists to seek to photograph. This was a specimen from the Jurassic Age, evolved over millions of years to be a deep-sea predator. It might have been the basis of many of the ancient sailor tales of sea monsters, when maps had 'Here be dragons' emblazoned on their edges.

Germaine slammed his fist on the wheel and cursed, urging the *Miss Lucy* to go faster, but they were still several hundred yards away. They could do nothing to aid the men in the water.

The *Neptune's* lifeboat had cracked in two beneath the weight of the launch and was gone, sunk beneath the water, its cargo of dead with it. The survivors clung desperately to the wreckage of the upside down launch. The helicopter saw what was happening and reversed course. The Seahawk reached them quickly and hovered thirty feet above the men, as a slender cable with a rescue belt lowered to them. They could be brought up only one at a time. Josh feared for their lives.

As the *Miss Lucy* neared the wreckage, Elansky took her position beside the forward rail. Josh hoped she got her shot. Their carefully crafted plans to lure the creature into the area with the *Andrews* had fallen apart. It was as if the *Neptune* had reached up from its grave with its lifeboat to stir the waters.

One man slipped his shoulders through the belt. The Seahawk began lifting him from the water. One of the helicopter crew leaned out the door steadying the cable. Dangling like bait on a hook, he proved too difficult a lure for the creature to resist. The massive head, half as large as the helicopter, rose from the water until it was level with the screaming man. It turned its head one way, and then other, reptilian fashion, to observe its prey. The Seahawk couldn't fire on it without hitting the man suspended from the cable. It attempted to pull away. The creature closed its jaws over the man and submerged.

The weight of the creature on the cable dragged the six-and-half-ton helicopter down. Its twin GE T700 401-C turboshaft engines were capable of producing 3400 horsepower, but they were no match for the ceresiosaurus' strength. The fifty-four-feet diameter rotor blades churned the air valiantly, but to no avail. The weight of the creature was too much. The helicopter rolled until it lay at an impossible angle. The blades hit the water, sending a spray of water over the survivors. Then, the blades snapped off, beheading one of the men in the water. The man operating the winch hung suspended by his arms from the open doorway. He finally let go and spilled into the water. The chopper landed upside down on top of him and sank rapidly. An underwater explosion hurled a plume of water fifty feet into the air. A thin column of smoke rose from the helicopter's watery grave. Josh watched but didn't see any of the four-man crew surface. Now, two men remained in the water. The *Andrews* was approaching rapidly but was still half a mile away.

"We have to help," Josh said.

Germaine nodded. He yelled to the crew, "Man the hooks."

Josh stared at him. "Hooks?"

"We don't have time to drop sail. Besides, I don't want to become a sitting target. I'll steer as close as I can, and we'll use boat hooks to snag them."

"What if you miss?" the professor asked.

"If we have time, I'll make a turn and try again."

"If we don't?" Hicks demanded.

Germaine didn't bother looking at Hicks. "Then maybe they die. Look, I've seen a lot of people die lately. I'm getting used to it. I came along to capture or to kill this monster to keep it from destroying more cities or sinking more ships. Two more lives more or less don't matter to me. I'm not stopping."

Josh recognized the anger in the professor's eyes and sympathized with his plight, but he also understood Germaine's reasoning. He was trying to protect his boat. He realized the danger they all faced even by making this attempt at rescue. The creature was feeding. Presenting him with more targets proved nothing.

Bodden manned one boat hook and the Rastafarian crewman the other. Both survivors were flailing in the water off the port side of the boat twenty feet apart. They had spotted the *Miss Lucy* and they were frantic. They didn't realize that their frenzied motions might attract the creature. Both men wore uniforms. The lone survivor from the lifeboat had met his fate miles away and days later than his fellow passengers, but the same creature had ended his life.

The gap between the *Miss Lucy* and the men in the water narrowed quickly. Germaine pushed the boat to almost 19 knots. At that speed, it would take precision piloting to pass close enough to reach them with the hooks without skewering them or running them down with the hull. Germaine kept his course true, missing the first person by less than three feet. Bodden's hook snaked out and latched onto the first man's uniform. The motion of the boat slammed him into the side with a dull thud, but Bodden reached down and grabbed the man's arm, pulling him aboard. The second hook ripped the lifejacket from the other person, who quickly grabbed it and hung on for dear life. After a handful of harrowing seconds, this one was also lying on the deck coughing up water from their lungs.

To Josh's astonishment, the second survivor was a woman, a coxswain. Her uniform shirt was torn open, revealing her breasts. She seemed unconcerned. She looked up at him, a smile on her oil-smudged face. "Thank you," she gasped.

"Thank these men. They saved you. Are you all right?"

"What about the others ... the chopper ...?"

Josh shook his head. "No one else made it."

She sat up, noticed her exposed breasts and crossed her arms. "What was that thing?"

The boat lurched to starboard as Germaine avoided a floating bit of debris. The coxswain grabbed Josh's leg to keep from falling. He helped her up. She was unsteady and coughing sporadically. She clung to his arm. The other sailor they had rescued was doing better, having swallowed less oil and water. He came over to the coxswain and took her arm. Germaine leaned out of the cabin door.

"Bodden, get them below."

Bodden and the other sailor escorted the coxswain into the cabin and below deck. Josh couldn't see Germaine stopping to deliver them back to the *Andrews*. They would remain passengers until the creature was captured or killed.

"The creature's making a run at the *Andrews*," Germaine yelled.

The frigate was four hundred yards off the *Miss Lucy's* starboard side. The creature's head broke the surface two hundred yards from the ship, streaking toward the ship like a torpedo. This time, the captain of the *Andrews* was taking no chances. All thoughts of a live capture had vanished with the loss of the Seahawk and the deaths of his men. The frigate's CIWS, Close-In-Weapons-System, opened up, stitching a line of splashes around the creature. The Phalanx consisted of a six-barrel rotary machine gun capable of firing seventy-five 20x102 mm armor-piercing tungsten rounds per second.

Unaware of what it was facing, but sensing danger, the creature submerged. It reappeared a few minutes later directly beside the frigate's hull, too close for the Phalanx or the 76mm MK75 rapid-fire cannon to fire at. The ceresiosaurus lifted its massive, claw-tipped fins and raked the frigate's side as it sped by, leaving three thirty-feet-long parallel gouges in the ship's four-hundred-forty-five-foot steel hull just above the water line. The sound of rending metal chilled Josh's blood. Almost immediately, the creature vanished in the frigate's wake. The monster was sending another ship to its doom.

15

Oct. 30, *Miss Lucy*, Cayman Trench, Caribbean –

To Professor Hick's dismay, the ceresiosaurus submerged after the attack on the frigate and did not reappear. Germaine didn't share the old man's disappointment. After witnessing the creature drag the helicopter into the water and almost sinking the *Andrews*, he was beginning to think he had made a big mistake. No amount of money was worth the risk. The creature was far more dangerous than they had anticipated.

For a while, it appeared that the frigate was in danger of sinking. With her two-hundred crewmembers in the water, the ceresiosaurus would have had a field day. The thirty-foot-long rip in the frigate's hull was just above the waterline, but underway, water was forced through the breach, flooding several compartments. This forced the ship to come to a full stop while quick repairs were undertaken to seal the breach and make the ship seaworthy. Men scurried about on the decks as pumps were positioned to drain the water from the flooded compartments.

He could do nothing to help them, so Germaine concentrated on keeping an alert eye for the creature. Neither the frigate's sonar nor the sonar buoy dropped by the Seahawk helicopter picked up anything. It seemed that Cere had left the area. In spite of this, the captain of the frigate kept the gun crews at their posts.

Germaine pulled alongside the frigate long enough to transfer the two surviving crewmembers, but Corporal Elansky chose to remain on board the boat, hoping for another opportunity at the creature. Germaine didn't intend to give her a chance. He was through. He had witnessed enough death in the last few days to last a lifetime. He called a meeting to explain his decision. He opened the discussion.

"That was a cluster fuck of the first order."

"Our initial premise is sound," Professor Hicks said.

Germaine rolled his eyes and scoffed, "Did you see the size of that thing and how easily it brought down that helicopter? Even if we manage to dart it," he glanced pointedly at Elansky, "it might roll over on us and crush us."

"The MS-222 should work very …"

Germaine waved his hand dismissively. "Quickly? How quickly? Seconds? Minutes? Ten minutes? It's too dangerous to capture. Let the Navy kill it."

"We might never have such an opportunity as this again," Hicks insisted.

Germaine slammed his open palm down on the table, startling everyone. "I won't risk my ship and crew."

Josh spoke up. Germaine detected a trace of bitterness in the young marine biologist's voice. "You allowed us to charter you under the premise of capturing the creature."

He jabbed a finger Josh. "I was a fool, and you encouraged me. I needed the money, but I don't wish to die in the manner we just witnessed. You can board the frigate and coax them into helping you capture the creature, but I'm of a mind that her captain won't listen. He almost lost his ship. Next time, he might not be as lucky. Next time, none of us might be."

Germaine glared at Hicks, but his eyes pleaded with Josh to understand. The boy had seen more death than most. Of them all, he best understood the power of the creature. Josh refused to meet his gaze and glanced away. Elansky stared at him with a slight smile creasing her lips, as if sensing his fear and deriving pleasure from it. At that moment, he hated her. She wasn't afraid, but he was, and his fear diminished him in her eyes. He didn't care. He owed her nothing. His eyes searched his crewmembers for their reaction. Bodden was unreadable as usual, but he would side with his captain no matter what. Clearly, the two new men were ready to leave. They were afraid and no amount of money would entice them to remain in the area with the creature. If he didn't return to port, he might face a mutiny.

"Drop us off on the frigate," Josh said. "We'll convince the captain that capturing the creature is better than killing it."

Germaine was disappointed in Josh's decision. He understood that he thought he owed allegiance to his mentor, but he had hoped for better from him. He nodded. "Good luck with that."

"What if I gave you a fifty-thousand dollar bonus?" Hicks blurted.

All eyes turned to him. Germaine swallowed hard and sank back in his seat. He cocked his head to one side and said, "Fifty thousand dollars? Are you insane?"

Hick's cleared his throat. "Perhaps, but I have the money in the bank. We can do a wire transfer over the internet if you wish. The money means nothing to me."

Germaine's pulse quickened. Fifty thousand dollars would allow him to pay off the bank loan and leave a few thousand to make overdue repairs. He glanced at Bodden, who, after a moment's hesitation, nodded his agreement. The other two crewmembers didn't look as happy with the offer. He would have to sweeten the pot or lose them. "Five thousand more for each of the crew, and you've got a deal."

Hicks smiled. "Done."

Germaine understood that Hicks was probably dipping into his life's savings. His reputation was at stake, and he was gambling his retirement on capturing the creature.

Josh didn't appear as happy with the professor's offer. "Don't do it, Professor," he advised. "It's too risky. You've seen what the creature is capable of."

"I must, my boy. Don't you see? This creature represents a lifetime achievement if I can study it and publish my findings. Any knowledge we glean from it might be invaluable against any future encounters with its kind."

Germaine knew Josh wouldn't win the argument. Hicks' mind was made up, and there was nothing more stubborn than an old man, especially one who believed himself right.

Josh must have realized it too. He hung his head and said, "Okay, I'll stay."

Hicks favored him with a smile. Elansky's expression was more difficult to interpret. She looked dumbfounded, but slightly pleased with Hick's decision. Germaine hoped he didn't come to regret it. He had an idea that might save their asses.

"The *Andrews* has to return to port for repairs. We'll be all alone out here. I suggest we rig a line to the sonar buoy the Seahawk dropped and tow it behind us at a safe distance, say fifty yards. The noise should attract the creature but keep him off our ass long enough for Dead-Eye here to make her shot."

Elansky favored him with a smile.

Hicks pondered his proposition for a moment, and then nodded. "That should work. If it follows us, it will present its chest and neck as a target, the most vulnerable spots."

As he listened to the conversation, Josh's attention ping-ponged between Hicks and Germaine. "The captain's right about one thing. If we miss or the tranquilizer doesn't work, we'll be sitting ducks. We can't outrun it." He turned to Germaine. "I don't think we can fool it like we did with the fire boat."

Elansky coughed softly to get their attention. She held a six-inch long shell in her hand. "Gentlemen, this is a .50 caliber explosive projectile. The tip contains enough high explosive to blow a hole the size of a dinner plate in that thing's neck. I don't care how big it is, everything dies."

Hicks stared at her in horror. "You intended to kill it?" he exploded.

Elansky remained unperturbed by his outburst. "It's my backup, Professor. I'll dart your creature, but I won't die for you."

She glanced at Germaine and smiled. His respect for her doubled. "I like your attitude." He turned to the professor. "I'll try to capture Cere for you, but if we fail, don't get in my way or I'll toss you over the side to slow the creature down."

He left the room, leaving Professor Hicks wondering if he was bluffing.

* * * *

Josh was of two minds about Professor Hick's overly generous offer to Germaine. He understood the professor's desire to continue the chase, but shared Germaine's fear of the ceresiosaurus. The sinking of the *Neptune* could have been an accident, but the attack

136

on the *Andrews* was not. A creature capable of inflicting such damage to a steel-hulled warship would have no problem turning the *Miss Lucy* into a stack of kindling.

Elansky producing an explosive-tipped bullet led him to wonder just where her loyalties lay. It didn't seem the kind of thing she would normally carry on a mission. Was her mission to assist them in the creature's capture or to destroy it? He wanted to trust her, but she was military and she would follow orders. Germaine, he understood. The *Miss Lucy's* captain was in desperate need of cash to pay off his boat and he would risk his life to obtain it. Without his boat, he would be nothing, just another landlubber. With it, he was a sea captain, lord of his domain. Between Professor Hick's desperate desire to capture Cere, and Germaine's reckless need to collect his bonus, it would be an interesting voyage.

The wounded frigate made temporary repairs and left, limping back to Kingston for more permanent repairs. As he watched the frigate disappear over the horizon, Josh began to feel dangerously exposed. In the event of an emergency, they could expect no help. Before departing, the captain of the frigate reported a large underwater disturbance on the bottom. The sonar signature was that of a massive landslide, but the initial report was closer to that of an explosion. Josh wasn't certain what to make of it, but suspected the black ship was somehow involved.

Germaine located the sonar buoy dropped by the Seahawk, secured it to the boat with fifty yards of nylon rope, and began sailing a zigzag pattern across the area, towing the buoy behind the schooner. The steady *ping-ping-ping* revealed nothing nearby except an empty ocean. Elansky took a seated lotus position atop the rear cargo hatch with her rifle across her lap and a pair of binoculars, intently watching the buoy as an eager fisherman watches his bobbing cork. Josh resisted the urge to start a conversation with her. Each time they spoke, he came away feeling as if he had been bested in a verbal jousting tournament. Instead, he chose Bodden.

The taciturn first mate was coiling a rope on the deck as Josh approached. He slid each section of nylon rope through his weathered hands as if familiarizing himself with its texture. In reality, he was looking for frayed rope.

"Do you agree with Germaine's decision?"

Bodden didn't look up from his task. "He's cap'n."

"But do you think it was a good idea?" Josh probed further. "Are you afraid?"

This time, Bodden stopped working and looked at Josh. His eyes were sad and weary. Crow's feet in the corners of his eyes and crevasses in his dark skin spoke of many years in the sun and weather, aging him beyond his years. "We've been together ten years. He takes care of me, and I take care of him." He pointed to the deck. "This is all he's got, all I've got. A man does what he's got to do to survive. Fear ain't got nothing to do with it."

He resumed coiling the rope, leaving Josh no clearer on Bodden's opinion about the wisdom of continuing the chase. He went where Germaine directed.

Professor Hicks was elated at Germaine's decision, practically dancing on the deck as he strolled from one side of the boat to the other searching the water, but Josh feared his intellectual curiosity overshadowed his common sense. Too often fame in academia didn't come with fortune. Even publishing wouldn't ensure a return of his squandered life savings. If capturing the creature failed, he would be looked upon as another Big Foot sighter, laughed at quietly behind his back by his peers. Josh would hate to see his friend and mentor reduced to the brunt of a joke.

His own feelings were a confused mixture of excitement, fear, and resignation. He couldn't disregard the ominous sense of dread that had descended on him since Germaine's decision. He had eluded death four times in the last week. Was he tempting fate, pushing his guardian angel's limits? At his age, death should be a distant thought, not a shadow lurking over him. He was young, not yet twenty-three. The professor was near the end of his life and wanted one last chance at fame. Germaine wanted to save his boat, and Elansky wanted her shot. What did he want?

For the rest of the day, they sailed back and forth in a lazy search pattern, each leg was ten miles in length, but the sonar picked up nothing. Their quarry had eluded them. He either had left the area or was too deep to detect. The professor's frustration grew more evident as the fruitless day wore on. He clasped his hands behind his back, pacing the deck with quick angry steps, talking to himself and shaking his head. He refused lunch or any attempts at conversation.

Around five o'clock, a speck appeared on the horizon. At first, Josh thought it was the *Andrews* returning, and his heart raced madly with hope. They would no longer be alone on the vast ocean. As he watched, he saw that it was indeed a ship, but not the *Andrews*. He was puzzled when Germaine turned the boat and headed toward it. As they approached, he realized it was the mysterious black ship they had heard about. It was motionless in the water, flying no flag and showing no name on its hull. By the plethora of antennae and communication dishes sprouting from the forward cabin, it was no mere freighter. He had expected a totally black ship, like a shadow, so he was surprised that the upper structure was gray rather than black.

The man Josh took to be the captain stood on the bridge watching them through binoculars. His bearing was decidedly military, though he wore gray slacks and a short-sleeved shirt instead of a uniform. The ship made no move to hale them or to contact them by radio. Germaine sailed the schooner in a tight circle around the freighter, and in Josh's opinion, coming dangerously close to the hull. Germaine's grim expression told Josh this was no mere sightseeing trip.

"Why are we circling this ship?" Josh asked, perturbed that Germaine would risk their lives in such a manner.

"I wanted to see the bastards close up."

Josh didn't understand Germaine's anger. "Why?"

Germaine wheeled on Josh so quickly that Josh jumped back. "It ain't right for a ship to not show her colors. She's up to no good."

Germaine's vehemence was new to Josh. He had never seen the captain so angry. "What can we do about it?"

Germaine cracked a grin. "Show them that *I* know what they're doing here."

"Now that you've made your point, can we continue our search? The professor is getting anxious."

"Aye. They know we're here, not that they give a furry rat's ass. They're after Cere same as us, and I aim to get it first."

Josh was worried about that. Without the *Andrews* supporting them, the Chinook helicopter would have to fly all the way back from Kingston. That meant that they had to keep the sedated ceresiosaurus afloat for at least an hour, maybe longer, before the helicopter could lift it. The *Miss Lucy* carried several floatation bags large enough for the purpose, but that meant that someone had to go in the water and feed cables beneath the sleeping creature. As the only certified diver, that task would fall to Josh, and he wasn't looking forward to being so near the sedated creature.

"You still think that they would kill us all to get it."

"If they're CIA, then they think there's a military use for the creature. Many a man's gone missing in the name of national security, and I'm not even a bloody American."

Josh wasn't sure he accepted Germaine's assumptions, but the captain's paranoia was contagious. He chanced a glance at Elansky, still sitting with her legs crossed on the aft cargo hatch. From the look of disdain in her eyes, she harbored the same feelings toward the black ship, as did Germaine. Before, she had been studying the sea for any sign of the creature, but now she stared at the black ship as if willing it to sink. He half expected her to load the explosive shell into the rifle and sink it herself at any moment. If she had reason to resent the ship's presence, then perhaps he should show more concern.

Professor Hicks also did not appreciate the ship intruding on their turf, though Germaine was the one who had encroached upon theirs. He stared at the hulk for a few minutes, and then rushed over to Josh, fuming.

"By what right do they remain here? No anonymous vessel can be benign."

"Germaine thinks it's the CIA or some other black ops group trying to get the ceresiosaurus."

Hicks puffed out his cheeks and expelled a deep breath. "They wouldn't dare. This creature is of vast scientific importance, not some government experiment." He paused a minute, and then said, "I'll bet they're here for the Russian nuclear warheads. The *Pokhomov* sank somewhere in this area." He relaxed and allowed a slight smile to dance on his lips. Josh didn't remind him that they could be there for both.

Germaine called out from the cabin, "I'm picking up something on sonar."

Both he and the professor hurried to the cabin. "Is it the creature?" Hicks asked.

Germaine shook his head. "No, it's smaller and metallic. It should surface over there." He pointed to a spot fifty yards from the black ship. A few minutes later, a pale yellow object appeared.

"It's a submersible," the professor shouted. "I suppose the rumors about the mysterious missing DSV-5 are true."

A loud groan in the water radiated from beneath the black ship, the sound of metal sliding against metal.

"It's submerging again," Germaine said of the submersible. "It's moving toward the ship."

"The ship has an underwater hatch for the submersible," the professor said. "That's what that sound was. This is an expensive operation."

"The CIA has deep pockets," Germaine announced, abruptly turning the wheel hard to port to steer them clear of the ship. "My curiosity's satisfied."

Hicks bounced against the bulkhead, but quickly regained his balance. He turned to Germaine. "I only half believed you about the black ship. I'm sorry I doubted you." He furrowed his brow. "If they indeed have drums of MS-222, they present a problem."

"Well, whatever they intend to do, we can't stop them."

Hicks nodded. "Yes, yes. We should continue our search."

"Why do you call it a black ship?" Josh asked. "It's black and gray."

Germaine stared at Josh for a moment. "It's a CIA mobile operations center, a black site. That's why it's called a black ship."

Josh felt like an idiot. His knowledge of the world was limited to textbooks. "Oh, I see." Properly chastised for his ignorance, he left Germaine at the wheel and went on deck. The professor was seated on the wooden bench just outside the cabin, facing aft, lost in thought. Josh didn't want to disturb him. He found a comfortable spot on a coiled rope, leaning against the forward mast. The vibrations of the mast as the sails popped in the breeze and the warm breeze on his face lulled him to sleep and to dream.

He was underwater, facing an amorphous dark shape, when suddenly a giant red eye opened and stared at him like an opening to the pits of hell. He opened his mouth to scream and water rushed into his lungs. Darkness overwhelmed him, smothering him. He awoke with the taste of salt water still in his mouth. His heart pounded as if starved for oxygen. He glanced around to see if anyone what witnessed his moment of fear, but no one had. His secret was safe.

They continued their search pattern until night fell. Then Germaine ordered most of the sails taken down to reduce speed. He or Bodden continued to monitor the sonar and the radar, but both were blank. They were alone on the sea. Their quarry had fled.

When the last glow of the setting sun faded, Elansky left her spot on the aft hatch cover. She stood, stretched her arms over her head, and, when she bent over to touch the ground, gave Josh an excellent view of her ass. Even the loose fitting fatigues she wore couldn't hide her obvious curves.

"Nice, eh?"

He turned sharply at Germaine's remark, feeling like a kid caught stealing candy.

"I, uh, wasn't looking," he muttered.

Germaine winked. "Sure, kid. Me neither." Germaine pulled out his cigarettes, briefly blinding Josh when he flicked his lighter into a flame and touched it to his cigarette. "Me, I've always appreciated the female form." He exhaled a cloud of smoke that settled around Josh's head. "Besides, it's kind of thrilling to think she could kill me with her bare hands."

Elansky crossed the deck to stand before the two men. She glanced first at Josh, and then at Germaine. "Gentlemen, are we calling it a night?"

Germaine smiled at her. "Our equipment is picking up nothing, not even a school of fish. We'll keep moving. I don't want to sit in one spot, but yeah, I think we're done for the night."

She nodded. "I could use a drink." She stared at Josh. "How about you?"

Any witty reply he might have attempted died in his throat. How could she disarm him with one glance? "Sure," he croaked, mentally kicking himself for acting like a teenager.

"Do we go below decks?" Germaine asked.

"No, I prefer staying up here," she replied.

"I'll have someone bring up some scotch. Dinner will be ready soon. I think we're having jerked pork."

Professor Hicks had gone below just before sunset and had not reappeared. He had been bitterly disappointed with the day's results, and his brusque manner conveyed that he wished to brood alone. He wouldn't be hungry. Josh gave him his space. From previous experience, he knew how moody his teacher could become and didn't want to spend the next few hours trying to salve his wounded ego. The professor was a good man but prone to bouts of melancholy that only solitude could cure.

Any guilt Josh might have felt over consoling his friend was assuaged by corporal Elansky's presence. She enamored him. He had never met anyone like her. The college girls he dated, even the ones not in college, all seemed to be cut from the same cloth – vacuous, petty, self centered, and temporary. Although nearly the same age, the gulf that separated Corporal Elansky and him was wider than the Gulf of Mexico. He had spent his entire adult life enmeshed in the world of academia. Elansky had fought in the deserts of Afghanistan, while he was busy bar hopping with friends, surfing, or diving. Her efforts made him look like a slacker.

Germaine brought out deck chairs and spread them behind the cabin out of the breeze. As the captain poured liberal amounts of scotch into their glasses, Josh was perplexed to see a Luna moth the size of his hand perched on the cabin's window. Amazingly, the moth had found the only source of light and spot to rest its weary wings for three hundred miles. It reminded him of how deep sea creatures sought out thermal vents, both as a source of nourishment and as a source of heat in the freezing depths. Nature, unlike Hoover, abhorred vacuums.

"To a successful hunt," Germaine toasted. Josh raised his glass.

Conversation died as the trio sipped scotch and watched the stars appear one by one in the night sky. They blazed brighter than stars over land or near a city, pinpoints of colored light on a black velvet background. Josh could make out the Big Dipper, Orion, and the Pleiades, but little else. He had spent most of his time staring down instead of up. He envied Germaine that much. He probably knew each star by name and could follow them across the globe. By the time dinner arrived, delivered by the grinning Rastafarian Odette, the liquor was working its way into Josh's system, relaxing him and kneading the tensions from his overwrought muscles. He glanced at Elansky, lying back in her chair, eyes closed, with her drink resting on her breasts. He wanted to talk to her, say something witty. Perhaps even teasing, but his tongue refused to cooperate. *Too bad the scotch won't loosen my tongue*, he thought.

Before they could take their first bite of their meal, Bodden sang out, "We've got company."

16

Oct. 30, *Pandora*, Cayman Trench, Caribbean –

"I ought to put you in the brig."

Knotts wasn't happy with the crew of the *Nemo*. Devers' initiative to blow up the sunken Russian freighter *A.K. Pokhomov* had cost him one of the four nuclear warheads. His superiors wouldn't be happy.

"You have three nukes," Devers replied. He closed his eyes and leaned back in his seat. "I don't see the problem."

Knotts, perturbed by Devers' nonchalance, slapped the desk with his palm, suppressing a smile when the submersible pilot jumped. "Your mission was to retrieve all four."

Devers leaned forward. "One was leaking radiation. Leave that 'do or die' shit to the Marines, Colonel. I'm a civilian."

"We're all civilians now, Devers, but we still have a job to do."

Devers erupted, waving his hands in the air. "You saw the video. Those giant pill bugs were isopods, normally six or seven inches long. Those things were six feet!" He stared at Knotts. "According to the reports, those creatures wiped out Little Cayman, so I played exterminator. Fuck 'em!"

Matthews, his co-pilot, had said nothing during the debate, but he nodded his head vigorously in agreement.

Knotts raked them both with his gaze, which he had been told, when focused, could make a man tremble. The video of the giant isopods had bolstered the Company's claim of a giant sea creature.

The attack on the *Andrews* cinched it. Until they captured the creature, the sea lanes wouldn't be safe to travel.

"We've still got a job to do," he said.

Devers rolled his eyes. "It's what I get paid for."

"Where else are you going to make 120K a year?" Knotts pointed out. "The *Andrews* is returning to port, but the schooner with Professor Hicks and his protégé is still out here. They've got a Marine sniper aboard who is quite capable of making her shot. We have to locate and capture the creature first."

"They've got a tranquilizer dart and a sailboat. We've got two hundred gallons of MS-222 and a fucking freighter. My bet's on us."

Devers' lack of concern bothered Knotts. He considered the professor a serious threat. The sailboat could travel silently, while the *Pandora* filled the sea with her sonar pings, propellers, and every reverberated creak and groan of its metal hull. It was like painting a bulls-eye on her hull. The *Andrews* was a well-armed missile frigate with a trained crew, and yet the creature almost sank it. His crew was a mixed collection of mercenaries, CIA technicians, and well-paid merchant marines. The special ops teams had experience, but the remainder took care of the ship and the submersible. They would be no good in a fight.

"I think you don't give the professor enough credit," he said. "He understands the habits of this creature better than we do. I wouldn't count him out."

Devers shrugged. "So, let him capture it, and then we take it from him. Wasn't that the idea?"

Devers was right about that. Knotts orders had included just such a provision, but unnecessary killing made him uneasy. Some of his ethically challenged colleagues considered anyone not one of them as the enemy. Knotts' years in the military had imbued him with a sense of honor that often clashed with his orders. To him, killing fellow Americans was a last resort.

"If it comes to that," he agreed.

Devers noticed the hesitation in Knotts' voice. He stared at Knotts. "Don't tell me you've got a conscience, not after ten years with the Company. Hell, I've just been with them three years, and I don't give a fuck about anything."

Matthews laughed. "You didn't give a fuck when you were working for Woods Hole."

"True, true, but I'm even more fuckless now."

Knotts slammed his cane down on his desk. "Enough!" he shouted. "I decide when and if we take such a course of action. Until then, I want you two back in the water. You'll carry four canisters of MS-222 with you. That should be enough to knock out anything you encounter. If you stun the creature, you'll deploy the lift bags and send him to the surface where we'll tag and bag him."

"Aw, Colonel, have a heart. I'm still stiff from the last dive," Matthews protested, stretching his arms for emphasis.

"I don't care if they have to pack you in oil like sardines. Get going." He stared at Devers, who remained sitting. "You're dismissed. You can leave my office now. We're headed to the Andrews' position when she was attacked. We'll be there in an hour and a half. Have dinner, take a piss, and get that DSV back in the water and find my ceresiosaurus."

He smiled as Devers and Matthews left his office. He enjoyed putting slackers in their place. Devers was good at his job, but he had no military training. He didn't appreciate the chain of command. He risked nothing but his job by being obstinate. Sometimes you had to make people like him understand who the big fish in the pond was. He knew Devers would do his job.

* * * *

By 1800 hours, the *Pandora* had reached proper coordinates and the *Nemo* was back in the water. By the expression on Devers' face as seen in the cabin monitor, he wasn't happy about it, but the two men soon fell into the routine of the dive.

"Four thousand feet," he reported. "Nothing on sonar."

He repeated his message every two thousand feet until the DSV reached the twelve thousand feet mark. "We're going to make a wide sweep of the area. Sonar at full. The bottom is another ten thousand feet below us. If we don't find anything, I'll take us to eighteen thousand, but that's it."

Devers was pushing it. Eighteen thousand was above the *Nemo's* rated depth, but Knotts had wounded his pride. Knotts decided to ease up a bit on him.

"Don't go below sixteen thousand. Don't take any chances."

"Copy that," Devers replied.

For two hours, the submersible prowled the black depths, finding nothing. Knotts' patience was wearing thin. It was like looking for a virgin in a Thai brothel. He was on the verge of cancelling the dive when,

"We're picking up something. Two thousand yards and closing."

Knotts pulse quickened. "How big is it?"

"Strange reading. It's more like a school of sharks, big but scattered."

"Be ready. Don't take any chances," Knotts warned.

The lights picked up a nightmarish creature, then several more. They were twelve to fifteen feet long and resembled harmless caterpillars, but all similarity ended there. Bristle worms. They were the creatures that had reportedly attacked the *Neptune*.

"Release one of the canisters and leave the area. Kill the bastards."

"Whatever you say, Colonel," Devers replied.

Matthews broke into the conversation. "I'm picking up something else."

"What is it?"

"I'm not sure, but it's damned big. It's as big as a sub. Doing close to twenty-five knots." Matthews' voice remained steady, but he spoke more rapidly. "It's almost here. The lights aren't picking up anything." A minute later, the camera jumped as the sub bounced wildly. "Wow! Something just passed beneath us. It felt like the wake of an aircraft carrier."

"Deploy the MS-222," Knotts ordered. "All of it."

"Negative. Not yet. I'm waiting until I'm sure it's the creature we're after."

A shadow appeared at the edge of the lights and hovered among the Bristle worms. With a quick snap of its jaws, it swallowed two of the creatures whole. Then it raced toward the sub. It was Knotts' first good view of the creature. The head was larger than the buoyancy bag of the submersible. It sat on a neck twenty feet long. The body was the size of two blue whales, over two hundred feet long, with claw-tipped flippers the size of orcas. It turned at the last moment and glided over the sub. The thirty-foot tail whipped by the sub just feet away from the Plexiglas porthole. Again, the sub rolled violently.

He heard Devers curse over the open mic. "Damn! That was close. Deploying the canisters now." He hit the switch on the console. The MS-222 was sealed in pressurized tanks, able to quickly pump the sedative into the water in spite of the great pressure. The canisters released. Devers dropped ballast to lift the sub away from the pressurized containers for safety. A cloud of chemical drifted around the sub, obscuring the outside cameras. The Bristle worms began to stop moving as the sedative took effect. They floated in the water, easy prey for the ceresiosaurus. It swam past with its mouth yawning wide, funneling the worms into its gullet.

"Pull out of the area and track the creature on your sonar until the sedative takes effect."

This time, Devers didn't argue. Having seen the creature's size, he was eager to leave. "Pulling back five hundred yards. I don't want to risk losing the creature. My God, did you see the size of that thing?"

"Something ain't right, Devers," Matthews called out.

"What?"

"The MS-222 isn't doing anything to it. In fact, I think it just made it mad. Uh, oh. It's coming back."

"Get out of there!" Knotts yelled, knowing his command was useless. The *Nemo* could never outrun the creature.

"Dropping all ballast," Devers said. Even over the speaker, his voice barely concealed his panic.

Suddenly, the outboard camera bounced violently and went dark.

"We lost our outboard camera and lights. Damn! One of the props is out too."

Knotts sat back in his seat. There was nothing he could do. Devers was fighting a losing battle to control the submersible. A loud screeching sound, like fingernails raking a blackboard erupted from the speakers.

"We're losing buoyancy," Devers cried out. His face was pale with fear. "It ripped the bag."

"Drop everything," Knotts yelled, "cameras, lights, Spot, everything." He doubted that the extra weight would make that much difference. Without the diesel in the buoyancy tank suspended above the pressure cabin, they would drop like a stone. He waited in silence for Devers to reply.

Devers looked up from the gauges. He now appeared calmer, resigned to his fate. "It's useless, Colonel. We're not going to make it back up. In fact, we're taking a nose dive to the bottom."

Knotts' voice broke as he said, "I'm sorry, Devers."

"Don't worry about us, Colonel. Our worries will be over in a few minutes. That monster is headed to the surface fast. You had better brace yourselves."

Knotts reached out and pressed the general alarm to alert the crew. The klaxon sounded throughout the ship. "Thanks, Devers."

"Passing seventeen thousand. The metal's groaning. It won't be long now." The cabin lights went dark. "Damn! I wish the lights were working. It's a whole new world down here. I'd like to …."

The radio squealed once, then became nothing but static. Knotts replaced the microphone. His hand trembled as he reached out to turn off the radio. He took a deep breath. He didn't have time for regrets. He had killed Devers and Matthews. Now, he had to try to save his crew.

* * * *

The *Pandora*, though a freighter, carried a wide array of defensive weaponry. Two .50 caliber deck guns and three GAU-type rapid-fire machine guns, carefully hidden from casual view, which gave the freighter as much punch as some Navy vessels. Knotts had hoped to capture the creature alive, but it had drawn first blood. His crew would never forgive him if he didn't allow them to draw second blood. On full alert now, the crew manned the heavy guns. Others stood on deck with machine guns supplied by five different countries, eager for their chance at revenge.

The sonar operator called out from the bridge, "Sonar is picking up a large object two clicks off the starboard beam, but it's deep. Another object is directly beneath us and rising."

Knotts stared at the water. A second monster? Could the *Pandora's* crew handle two of the creatures? As he stood there scanning the water with his binoculars, something Devers had said came to mind. He turned to the sonar operator.

"Are you certain that it's a second creature?"

The sonar operator hesitated. "Well, it gets fuzzy as it gets closer. It could be a large shoal of fish."

Their intruder wasn't the ceresiosaurus. It was the Bristle worms Devers had encountered. Either they had recovered from the MS-222 or there were more of them. "Damn! Tell the sub bay to make certain the pool doors are closed."

Even as he spoke, he heard the first gunfire from below. Almost simultaneously, dozens of Bristle worms emerged from the water around the ship. The big guns took out quite a few, but more took their place. Their claws clung to the metal hull like flies on glass, relentlessly creeping up the side of the ship. Men leaned over the rails to fire directly into them. Most of the creatures dropped back into the ocean, dead or injured, but enough managed to reach the deck to cause a panic. One crewman leaned too far over the rail and remained for too long. One of the worms grabbed him by the head and yanked him overboard. He surfaced briefly amidst several of the creatures before disappearing in a spreading pool of crimson.

The crew held the deck for as long as they could before retreating to the hatches of the cabin or ducking companionways below decks. Most, in their haste, failed to reseal the hatches behind them. The creatures followed like bloodhounds on the scent. Knotts knew the deck was lost. They would have to fight the creatures in the passageways. His main concern was the sub bay. He went to the intercom to call the chief engineer.

"Starnes, where are you? Answer me."

The intercom clicked. "This is Starnes. I'm a little busy now."

Knotts heard gunfire and screams in the background. "Are the bay doors closed?"

"Negative. They were on us before we knew what was happening. They're all over the bay now. We can't hold them off."

Damn! Knotts thought. They're all through the ship. "Get to the bridge if you can."

Starnes paused before answering. "Negative, Captain. These things have me cornered and all I've got is a .45. I'll try one more time to close the hatch doors. Sorry, Captain."

The intercom went dead. Knotts didn't try again. He knew he was soon going to lose another old friend. He had lost friends before, but that was long ago. Now, three deaths in one day were more than he could bear. A surge of anger built up in his chest, threatening to erupt through his pores like lava.

"I may be a crippled old man, but I'll show these things how a Marine fights."

He went to his cabin, pulled out the South Korean Daewoo K7 he kept under his bed, and grabbed two extra clips of 7.62 mm rounds. He descended the companionway to the next lower level. Men rushed by with weapons, but he paid them no heed. He was moving toward the sound of fighting, like a Marine. He rounded a corner and saw Bates and crewman named McCreedy kneeling on the deck firing at a worm clinging to the overhead pipes, which were bending under its enormous weight. Water cascaded onto the deck from a ruptured water pipe. He joined in firing at the creature. It finally dropped to the deck, but a second one appeared down the passageway.

Bates leaped up from the deck and ran to the metal shop two doors down. A six foot length of steel girder suspended on a winch from the conveyor track running the length of the passageway ceiling was in front of the door, left by a fleeing metal worker.

"Help me," he shouted to his companion.

The two men grabbed the rear end of the girder and pushed it toward the approaching worm. Knotts was frustrated that he could only stand and watch. As the pair gained speed, Knotts understood Bates' plan. The heavy girder struck the worm in the head. The momentum pushed it against the wall, momentarily pinning it. Before it could escape, Bates placed the barrel of his weapon against its head and fired. Blood and gore splattered the wall and Bates, but he ignored it. He looked back at Knotts and smiled.

"That's how you kill the bastards."

The three men continued down the passageway, sealing hatches as they went, but when they encountered a hatch folded in half and forced away from its hinges, Knotts fully understood the power of the creatures. As they went down one more level, one of the worms suddenly attacked McCreedy, as it grabbed his legs from beneath the steps. He fell forward onto the steps. Before Bates or Knotts could reach him, the creature closed its jaws tighter and severed both feet just above McCreedy's ankles. He screamed and rolled over, trying to fire his weapon at the creature, but his pain foiled his aim. Bates shoved the barrel of his M16 through the space between steps and emptied it, killing the creature. Knotts tried to staunch McCreedy's bleeding, but the wound was too severe and the flow of blood too great. McCreedy died quickly before Knotts could apply a makeshift tourniquet. They left him lying there.

Farther down the passageway, they spotted one Bristle worm devouring one of its injured brethren. Knotts considered letting it finish the job, but time was of the essence if he was to save his ship and crew. They poured almost a full clip each into the worms and left chunks of worm gore all over the deck. Worm gore was not the only thing staining the deck. Knotts winced when he saw trails of blood and parts of human bodies littering a junction of passageways where crewmen had been trapped and slaughtered. Firing had now become sporadic as crewmen died or ran out of ammunition. Three weapons lockers were located throughout the ship, but the attack had come so suddenly that only the men on deck had been properly armed. He came to a decision.

"I'm going to abandon ship. We can use the deck guns to clear the deck long enough to evacuate in the life boats."

Bates shook his head. He rubbed his arm where some of the worm slime had landed. "Those things won't stop coming at us long enough to load the boats. Men are trapped all over the ship."

"I know. I have to save as many as I can."

"We can't take the nukes, and we can't abandon ship and leave it floating."

Knotts nodded. "I know that too. I'll scuttle her after we leave."

Bates glanced down at Knotts bad leg. "You'll never make it out."

"Comes with the job."

"We'll have to clear a path first. Let's go."

The ship vibrated as the muffled sound of an explosion from below and toward the bow reverberated down the passageway. The lights flickered and went out. The emergency lights flashed on but quickly died. Knotts could sense rather than hear the absence of sound of the dead generator. The passageway was too dark to see his hand in front of him. He lit his cigarette lighter. In its soft glow, Bates was shaking his head.

"That was the generator room. It looks like someone is trying to beat you to the draw."

Knotts thought of his crew fighting the horde of Bristle worms in the darkness and shuddered. Facing the creatures in full daylight was bad enough. The intercom was dead. He couldn't even call to abandon ship.

"Come one," he told Bates, holding the lighter out in front of him to orient himself in the dark passageway. "We have to find some flashlights and get my crew off this ship."

"I'm not sure we can get ourselves off this ship alive," Bates replied.

"Crew first," Knotts said.

He pushed ahead of Bates and led the way down the passageway. He knew his chances of setting the scuttling charges and escaping were nil, but if he had to die, he wanted to take as many of the creatures as he could with him.

The captain always goes down with his ship.

17

Oct. 30, *Miss Lucy*, Cayman Trench, Caribbean –

Josh hoped Bodden's announcement had been the ceresiosaurus on the sonar. Instead, he pointed to a blip on the radar screen. "A ship," he said.

"The black ship," Germaine growled. His clenched jaw revealed his disgust. "Are they coming toward us?"

"No. They're dead in the water."

Germaine scratched his head. "What are they up to?"

"Perhaps they are deploying the submersible," Professor Hicks said from the steps. "If so, the ceresiosaurus may be in the vicinity."

"Let's take a look," Germaine suggested.

Josh noted that the professor had recovered from his earlier gloom. His eyes sparkled at the prospect of a second encounter with the creature. "It will be difficult to capture it in the dark," he said.

"We have a spotlight," Hicks insisted. "We can't squander this opportunity."

Josh thought the professor's zeal now bordered on recklessness. A spotlight and sonar were poor tools for pursuing a creature the size of four locomotives and an appetite for human flesh. That Germaine shared in the professor's fervor troubled him.

"I thought you were afraid of the black ship," he said.

Germaine shot him a fierce look. "I want to know what they're up to. If their submersible is on the bottom, they can't move. That's good for us."

He reluctantly agreed with Germaine's assessment. He nodded. "Okay. Let's go see."

Elansky entered the cabin, her glass of scotch still in one hand, her rifle in the other. Her eyes probed his. He refused to glance away, but he blinked first, ending their staring war. He felt as if he were being judged. He swallowed to hide his nervousness. "I'll man the spotlight."

He started out the door, but Elansky refused to budge. He brushed up against her as he pushed through the door. She leaned into him, her firm breasts rubbing against his chest. It reminded him of things he had too long neglected, like his sex life. She smiled up at him. "Don't worry. I hardly ever bite on the first date."

This time he found his tongue. "I've been bitten before. It doesn't hurt. Just don't break the skin."

"You're learning."

"We're coming up on the black ship," Germaine said, reminding them.

Josh reluctantly pulled away from Elansky. "I'll get that spotlight going."

As the schooner approached the looming hulk of the black ship, Josh noted that the entire ship was dark. No lights showed in portholes or from the cabin. No one was visible on the deck. He played the spotlight over the entire vessel, bow to stern. It was dead in the water, showing no lights, and making no sounds. It was a ghost ship.

"Have they abandoned ship?" Josh asked.

"No," Germaine said, "The lifeboats are still in the racks." He pointed to the four orange and white lifeboats near the stern. "But it's sinking. See, the bow is six feet deeper than the stern. It's got a hole in it somewhere."

Looking more closely, Josh noticed the slight slope to the deck. A rope hanging over the side near the bow swayed at an obvious angle. "Then where are they?"

The silence was ominous, playing on Josh's fears. Were they lying in wait for the schooner? Josh shook his head. No, they could easily run the schooner down or blow it out of the water with hidden weapons.

"Maybe we had better check it out," Germaine suggested.

Josh wasn't keen on the idea, but his curiosity was aroused. He eyed the twenty-foot-long rope hanging over the side. "Using that?"

"Unless you had rather swim under and come up through the sub hatch."

Josh sighed. "Climbing it is then." He looked toward Professor Hicks, who stood by the cabin door. "The professor can't make the climb."

"Then you, me, Odette, and Elansky go. I'll leave Bodden and Miguel here to watch the boat and the professor."

Josh turned toward the tall Rastafarian. Odette stood at the rail staring up at the ship. To Josh, he looked big enough to handle himself in an emergency. "Okay," he answered.

"I'll have Bodden pull up alongside the rope and tie off. I'm going to get your shotgun. I'll leave the Webley for Bodden. Elansky has her .45."

"There's another one in my bag," she said, rushing to her cabin.

Germaine nodded. "Good."

They made one more circuit of the ship but found no one. Bodden brought the schooner to a standstill just beneath the dangling rope and the two crewmen quickly lowered the sails. The only way to tie off was by throwing a rope over the bow anchor fluke protruding from the hawser pipe through which the anchor hawser traveled. Germaine proved his seamanship by lassoing the fluke with one toss. He secured the other end of the rope to a stanchion on the schooner. The waves pushed the schooner hard up against the hull, but tires hanging over the schooner's side prevented any damage as the boat rose and fell against the hull.

The dangling rope didn't reach the deck. It stopped just below the main mast. They would have to climb the mast and reach out for the rope. One slip, and a hard wooden deck would catch their fall, or they could fall into the narrow gap between the schooner and the black ship's hull and be crushed.

"I'll go first," Elansky said.

Germaine stepped back and smiled. "Be my guest."

She scrambled up the mast, timed her leap for the rope perfectly, and pulled herself up hand over hand to the deck above in less than a minute. Then she leaned over the rail with her pistol in her hand and signaled for them to follow her. Germaine went next. He slung the Remington over his shoulder and began climbing. He wasn't as nimble as Elansky or as quick, but he made it up the rope with minimal effort. Josh went next. From the mast, he eyed the yawning black chasm between the schooner and the ship. He took a deep breath and leaped. He grabbed the rope with both hands but swung like a clock pendulum until he could find a purchase with his feet. Steadying his swing, he began pulling himself up the rope slowly; breathing heavily by the time Elansky helped him over the rail. He was grateful for her outstretched hand. Odette reached the ship's deck with no problem, scurrying up the mast and rope like a cat. Once he had joined them, Josh glanced back over the railing and waved to Professor Hicks below on the schooner. The professor returned the wave and took his accustomed seat on the bench by the cabin to wait.

The spotlight from the schooner created more shadows than it exposed. Germaine signaled for Miguel to switch it off, leaving them only the wan light of the moon to guide them. Both Germaine and Elansky carried flashlights. Josh cursed his stupidity for not thinking to ask for one. The first thing the beams of the flashlights picked out was a pool of blood with a weapon lying on the deck beside it. Empty shell casings littered the deck.

Elansky picked up the weapon. "It looks like a Cugir 9 mm, made in Romania."

She handed it to Josh, who turned it over in his hands, examining it. His hands came away covered in sticky blood. Germaine snatched it from him, handing him the Remington shotgun instead. "Here, you take this."

Elansky rubbed the toe of her boot in the pool of blood, smearing it along the deck. "Whatever happened, it took place recently. This blood is still wet."

"Why are there no bodies?" Odette asked. His eyes darted around the deck, peering into the shadows.

Josh had wondered the same thing. The silence surrounding them was unnatural. They should be able to hear the throbbing of engines and generators running, conversation, the clanging of doors. The only sound was the waves lapping at the hull. He thought of the *Neptune's* demise and feared the same thing had happened to the black ship.

"Let's try the bridge," Germaine suggested.

As they ascended the stairs to the bridge, something large lunged from the shadows, slammed into Odette who was following last, and dragged him screaming to the deck. Both flashlights swung to pick out the features of a twelve-feet-long Bristle worm. Elansky fired four .45 rounds into the creature's head with little effect. Josh raised the shotgun, waited until the creature faced him, and fired at its eyes. It bellowed in pain as one of the eyes exploded, reared on its hind segment, and struck the stairs with a hard blow. Josh grabbed the railing to keep from tumbling over the side. He steadied himself and fired twice more, blowing a large hole in the Bristle worm's head. It fell across the bottom of the stairs.

Odette suffered a deep cut to his right leg where the fore claws of the Bristle worm had grabbed him. He ignored his pain and scrambled up the stairs and away from the creature on his hands and knees. He stared back at the creature's lifeless body, his eyes wide with fright.

"That be a devil," he moaned.

Germaine climbed the stairs to the bridge deck and yelled back down to Bodden.

"Start the engines and pull away. Circle the ship until we signal you."

"Shouldn't we go back?" Josh asked, alarmed that Germaine was sending the *Miss Lucy* away.

"I wouldn't," Elansky said. She pointed back the way they had come. Now, four of the creatures crawled across the deck toward them. She glanced at the .45 and shoved it back into its holster. "I need something bigger."

"Here," Germaine said, handing her the Cugir. "You're a better shot than I am."

Germaine led the way to the bridge. The wooden door had been smashed and shards of broken glass littered the deck. Like the rest of the ship, the bridge was deserted, but not all of the crew had escaped. A streak of blood ran halfway across the deck with bits of human bone discarded like so much garbage. Josh fought down a rush of nausea.

"This is some set up," Germaine commented, admiring the array of electronic apparatus not normally found on a tramp freighter. All of it was dark, powerless. Not even the emergency lights were on.

"Maybe they're all below decks," Elansky suggested.

"Only one way to find out," Germaine replied.

"Not me," Odette protested.

"Do you really want to stay here alone?" Germaine asked him.

He stared at Germaine, and then shook his head.

"Okay, then stay close." He looked at Odette's leg, still bleeding profusely. "Let's find a first-aid kit and attend to that wound. There should be one somewhere around here."

While Germaine attended to Odette's leg, Elansky kept watch, staring at the creatures below, busily cannibalizing their dead brethren. Each bite took a serving platter-sized chunk of meat from the creature. They appeared content enough devouring their own, so they ignored the humans. Josh came up beside her. "Do you think they're still alive?"

"No, but we still need bigger weapons to get off this ship. We'll find them below."

"How do you know?"

"The Cugir. If they have one, they probably have more."

Her reasoning made sense, but he wasn't eager to test her theory. "The ship's probably infested with Bristle worms."

She smiled. "You did a good job on the last one."

"I've had experience, but I'm not trying to become an expert."

After Germaine finished bandaging Odette's leg, he walked over to Josh and Elansky. His face was grim, made even harder by the harsh light of the flashlight. "The bite's not too deep, but his leg is already turning red and swelling. He's going to need more help than we can provide."

Remembering the passengers on the lifeboat, Josh said, "It's infected. Maybe there's more medicine in the infirmary," he suggested.

"Ammo first," Elansky replied, "then the infirmary."

They followed a passageway off the bridge until they reached a companionway leading down into the bowels of the ship. The rooms along the passageway, mostly filled with communications equipment and electronics gear, were empty. Standing at the top of the companionway, the beam from her flashlight was swallowed by the blackness below. Recalling his nightmare, Josh fought his imagination, which saw monsters in every shadow. Cautiously, Elansky led the way down the steps to the next level. More blood and bits of human flesh showed the creatures had indeed reached the interior of the ship. As they rounded a corner in the passageway, they came face to face with a dead Bristle worm blocking their path.

"Somebody got lucky and killed this one," Elansky said.

Josh was more worried that men armed with submachine guns had died. Faced with crawling over the dead creature or backtracking, they chose to search for another way down. They soon located a second companionway leading to a wider passageway. The overhead was a maze of pipes and electrical conduit. A steel rail used as a hoist track to transport heavy material ran down the center of the passageway. They passed several machine shops and a carpentry shop, not bothering to check them. Germaine closed and dogged each door they passed. Someone had pinned one creature against the wall with a steel girder using the overhead rail system and killed it. Josh applauded their resourcefulness.

They paused at the entrance to a small galley. A single long table ran down the center of the room. A grill, a microwave oven, cooler and a cupboard covered one wall. Untouched food remained on plates on the table. Glasses and cups filled with water and coffee sat beside the plates. There were no bodies or signs of struggle. It looked as if the diners had simply gotten up to fetch silverware and vanished. Josh felt the coffeepot sitting on an electric burner and found it was still warm. He picked up a slice of bread from a plate and nibbled it.

"Still fresh."

As they left, Germaine locked the galley door as well. The passageway ended at a set of double doors, both smashed and hanging askew from their hinges. Beyond the doors, they found signs of an epic battle – pools of blood on the deck and smears on the walls, a second dead worm, partially consumed, and hundreds of shell casings. Overhead pipes were bent and ruptured. A steady stream of water poured from a broken water pipe. Odette gasped and backpedaled when he discovered a severed human head lodged amid the tangle of pipes, as if one of the creatures had rammed the body into the ceiling and yanked it down, headless. The eyes were open and staring. The group quickly discovered more carnage. Several detached limbs lay scattered up and down the passageway, the remains of a grisly feast. Two weapons had been left behind as well. Elansky picked up a second Cugir and tossed it aside.

"Empty."

She found an odd-looking, short-barreled weapon, examined it, and smiled. "A Daewoo K7. It fires 1,100 9 mm rounds per minute." She checked the clip. "Full. A nice weapon made by the South Koreans." She seemed pleased by her find. She offered the Cugir to Odette, who was equally pleased to have a weapon in his hands.

Three quick shots echoed down the passageway ahead. Josh stiffened.

"Someone's still alive," Elansky said.

Without waiting for the others, she began running down the passageway toward the sound of the shots, her flashlight dancing on the bulkheads. The others raced to catch up. Josh caught a glimpse of her head as she disappeared down another companionway. As he caught up with her, he found her standing on the stairs above a Bristle worm facing away from her. She fired a short burst from the K7 into the back of the creature's head. Then she fired a second burst into the damage that the first burst had created. It was enough. The bullets dug into its tiny brain, and the Bristle worm collapsed at her feet, shuddering briefly before it died. Two men stood opposite the dead Bristle worm, their weapons pointed toward Elansky. The flashlights taped to the end of the barrels played over her. After a few tense seconds, they both lowered their weapons and flashlights.

"Glad to see you, corporal," the older of the two said. He wore slacks and shirt, both covered with splotches of blood and gore. He removed a black wooden cane tucked in his belt and leaned on it.

"Are there any more of you?" she asked.

The man with the cane shook his head. "I don't think so. They came up through the pool in the cargo bay and up the hull of the ship. They were on us before we knew what was happening."

"Who are you?" She spoke to the older man, clearly, the leader by the way the younger man deferred to him, but her eyes fixed on his companion.

"My name is Simon Knotts. I'm the captain of the *Pandora*.

18

Oct. 31, *Pandora*, Cayman Trench, Caribbean –

Josh was amazed that they had found someone alive on the death ship. He looked at the older man called Knotts, and saw a man who had resigned himself to death but fought to live, because that was how he had been trained, as a former military man. He had the bearing of a ship's captain, sharing some of Germaine's drive and determination, tempered by a hard edge, like forged steel.

"This is Bates, a specialist," Knotts said of his companion.

Elansky stared at Bates rather than the captain, and Josh had to admit that he cut quite a figure. Bates was slightly taller than Knotts, younger, leaner, and more muscular. He wore black slacks and a muscle-hugging black t-shirt. His sandy-colored hair and facial features reminded Josh of the old movie star, Tab Hunter, but with colder eyes, the eyes of a killer.

"What kind of specialist are you?" she asked.

Bates grinned. "Same kind you are, I think."

"*Pandora*?" Josh commented to stop the game of mutual admiration between Elansky and Bates. "An apt name for your ship."

"I'll wager this ship's had more than one name in her lifetime," Germaine said. He still kept a firm grip on his .45.

Knotts ignored him. "Are you from the schooner? Can we get to it? We need to get off this ship. It's sinking."

"Why is it sinking?" Germaine asked.

"Some fool decided to ignite a propane tank in a forward machine shop to kill the worms," Bates snapped. "He blew a four-foot wide hole below the waterline. He also blew the fuel feed to the generator. Now the bilge pumps are out."

"I sent my boat off after we boarded," Germaine replied. "I'll signal it when we reach the deck."

"Good, let's go," Knotts said.

"We're going to need more ammo," Elansky said.

Bates spoke up. "There's a weapons locker and extra ammo in the sub hold, but it's two decks below us and closer to the stern. We'll never make it."

"We'll never make it without ammo," Elansky insisted. "They're all over the deck."

Knotts glanced at the dead worm, and then back to Elansky. "Okay."

Bates turned and trotted back down the passageway. Elansky followed him. Josh was concerned by Elansky's quick trust of Bates and Knotts. He didn't trust either of them, but he trusted Elansky. Odette leaned on Germaine and limped along beside Knotts, who also struggled to maintain the fast pace set by Bates and Elansky.

"You said they came up through the sub hatch. Where is your sub?" Germaine asked.

Knotts' face clouded for a moment. "It's gone."

"When will it be back up?"

Knotts stopped and turned on Germaine. He stopped with his face only inches from Germaine. His jaw clenched and the grip on his cane tightened. "It won't. The monster you're after destroyed it. I sent them to their deaths."

Knotts failed to see Germaine's .45 pointed at his stomach. When Knotts didn't attack, he lowered it. "You mean the monster we're both after."

Knotts shook his head. "Not any more. I'll kill it if I can."

Germaine nodded, as if he understood the captain's plight.

"What were you diving for?" Josh asked. When Knotts didn't reply, he continued, "You were after the Russian warheads, weren't you?"

"That's classified."

"Not if they're on this ship," Josh insisted. "It's sinking."

"They're safely stowed away in a vault. We found them once. We'll find them again."

Josh shook his head in disgust. "You people make me sick. You weren't salvaging them. The Navy could have done that. You wanted them for your deadly toy chest."

"It's a dangerous world out there," Knotts replied.

"Yeah, thanks to the likes of you lot," Germaine said.

"Keep up," Bates called back to them.

With Bates leading the way, the group continued down the passageway and descended a longer companionway to a large open area serving as a garage. The room was too cavernous to distinguish all of its contents by flashlight, but several five-ton trucks, various automobiles, ranging from a brand new Mercedes SLS AMG GT roadster to a beat up, rusted out old Ford Bronco, and a dozen or so motorcycles almost filled the great space, leaving just enough room for a black 2006 Monaco RV. The crew of the *Pandora* was equipped for any vehicle necessity. Josh was willing to bet that most of the vehicles were bulletproof, prepared for any nefarious activity. A large door against the outside bulkhead allowed access for easy unloading.

"You don't happen to keep a helicopter handy?" Germaine asked Knotts, eying the garage's contents.

Knotts ignored him as they threaded their way through the neat rows of parked vehicles. Josh brushed against one car and his leg came away covered in the same slime that was on the Bristle worms. He instantly became more alert, but the only sounds he heard were their footsteps echoing in the cavernous compartment. He rubbed the slime off on a clean spot of another vehicle before the parasites could penetrate the material. They had almost reached the far end of the room, when Bates suddenly went into a crouch. He waved for the others to do the same. Josh lowered his head and cowered behind a green Toyota. A minute later, two large Bristle worms appeared from a side passageway, their multiple legs scratching at the metal deck. They paused, lifted their front sections into the air, and moved their heads back and forth, as if sensing the presence of food nearby.

Josh held his breath and tightened his grip on the shotgun, hoping they would go away. He had no desire to become a worm snack. The group was so intently focused on the two worms in front of them, they failed to see a third worm enter the garage from behind them until it banged into a car and set off the alarm. The high-pitched squeal and honking horn drew the first two creatures' attention. All three converged toward the six people crouched behind the vehicles.

Bates rose and fired at one of the two creatures. Elansky joined him. Bullets stitched a line of holes up and down its body but didn't stop it. Josh pumped a shell into the Remington and began firing at the second one. His shots, too, were having little effect. He was too far away. He rose and began walking toward the creature, pumping shell after shell into its head. Finally, one shot hit a vital organ. The creature thrashed wildly against the RV, smashing its window and caving in the side of the vehicle. It collapsed dead. Following Josh's example, Bates and Elansky concentrated their fire at the remaining creature's head and swiftly dispatched it as well. Elansky tossed him a questioning look at his foolhardiness. He didn't know what had come over him. He wasn't trying to be brave, He just wanted to retrieve the ammo and get off the ship.

Knotts and Germaine took the third creature, firing shot after shot into it, but Odette, pushed beyond his limits of his courage by fear, dropped his Cugir submachine gun and hobbled away between two trucks, quickly disappearing into the darkness. The worm, smelling the bloody bandage, ignored the ineffectual fire from the two men and followed Odette. Germaine's .45 clicked on empty. Knotts continued firing, but he had no clear shot at the creature's head as it weaved in and out of the row of trucks. Odette's wound was too great to allow a rapid retreat. As he crossed the open space between two rows of vehicles, he stumbled and fell. The worm was on him before anyone could get close enough for a clear shot. Josh broke out the driver's side window of the Toyota, reached inside, and switched on the headlights. Its alarm joined the others. The headlights silhouetted the creature rearing above Odette as he screamed in terror. Before Josh could fire, it sank its mouth into the hapless Rastafarian's chest. He gurgled out one last breath before dying.

Josh moved toward the creature, but Elansky grabbed his arm. "He's dead. The sound will draw others. We have to leave."

Josh stared at the Bristle worm as it slowly devoured Odette. His blood was racing. He wanted to kill it, but Elansky was right. They couldn't waste their ammunition. He had only three shells left. Bates picked up the Cugir that Odette had dropped, removed the clip, took out the remaining bullets, and handed them to Germaine.

"Reload your clip with these."

Germaine slipped the bullets into the clip of his .45 and shoved it back in. He nodded to Bates. "Thanks."

At the far end of the garage, Bates raised a round hatch in the floor. Josh peered into a sea of blackness. Bates' flashlight picked out a metal ladder, but it didn't penetrate the gloom to the floor. Josh had no idea how long the ladder was.

"This ladder bypasses an area infested with the creatures," Bates said, "but we have to pass through the sub pool."

"I thought you said it was full of worms," Josh said, disliking the idea.

Bates shook his head. "That's where they came in. They moved into the bowels of the ship." He hesitated before continuing, "It might be worm free."

"Might be?" Germaine asked, voicing Josh's thoughts.

"We need ammo and there's a weapon's locker right off the pool area."

Germaine glanced at Knotts. "What about him?"

Knotts overheard and said, "Don't worry about me. I've been making my way around this ship for ten years. I may be a cripple, but I'll manage." He grinned. "Besides, gravity does all the work."

Bates descended first, hands and feet on the ladder rails, sliding quickly out of sight. Knotts insisted on going next. "In case I fall on someone," he said. Elansky gave him time to descend and followed. Germaine went next, descending more slowly, clinging to the ladder with both hands. Josh cast one last glance at the Bristle worm outlined in the headlights that was still eating Odette, and then he followed Germaine.

Elansky's flashlight illuminated the end of the ladder for Josh. Bates played his flashlight around the hold. Much of the equipment, including the crane used to lift and lower the submersible was damaged. Smaller pieces of equipment were overturned and scattered around the deck. The sub pool was surrounded by a five-foot-tall rim with steel scaffolding containing equipment. Much of the scaffolding was ripped asunder. Here, the carnage was worse. As the worms had entered through the pool, defenders had concentrated around them, unaware of just how dangerous and difficult they were to kill. Pools of blood, chunks of human flesh, and shattered bones spoke of their fruitless efforts to stop the Bristle worms. They had managed to kill a few. The remains of their cannibalized bodies lay around the pool. The pool itself was a rectangle of darkness, a pitch-black mirror set in the bottom of the ship reflecting nothing, not even the lights of the flashlights. Water was beginning to push up over the side of the pool and spill onto the deck, streaming forward as the bow settled deeper in the water.

"Clear," Bates said. "The weapons locker is this way."

He pointed the flashlight beam to a narrow corridor leading off the sub bay. The first door they passed was a machine shop, the second a spare parts room, but the third door was marked Electrical Room. Bates unexpectedly stopped before it.

"Electrical room?" Josh asked.

"You don't expect us to label it 'Every kind of God-damned weapon you want' room."

Knotts removed a key ring containing dozens of keys from his pocket, selected a key, and opened a panel beside the door. Inside the panel was a palm print analyzer. He pressed a button, and the panel lit up.

"Battery backup," he said to Josh's questioning look.

He pressed his palm flat against the panel. A bar of light passed up the palm and back down as it scanned the wrinkles and ridges of his epidermis. Satisfied, with a loud click, the door opened. Inside was a wonderland of weapons. The ten-by-ten room held dozens of rifles, pistols, and heavier items, such as RPGs, LAWS rockets, and .50 caliber machine guns on racks lining two walls. Boxes of ammunition, grenades, and Claymore mines filled shelves on the third wall. Elansky's eyes settled on a SIG 556xi configured for 7.62 NATO rounds. She picked it up, tested the scope, and smiled. Josh discarded the Remington shotgun for an M16. Germaine took Elansky's discarded Daewoo K7. Knotts kept his weapon. Bates quickly handed out ammunition to them all. He also broke open a box of grenades and handed each of them one.

"Be careful with these," he warned. "They'll kill you as quickly as a worm."

Josh noticed that Bates hadn't chosen a weapon. "What about you."

Bates smiled. "I have something special in mind." He opened a Samsonite case, and pulled out a heavy, six-barreled Gatling gun. "This is a Hua Qing Mini-gun, a product of China. This ought to fuck with those bastards." He inserted a belt of 7.62 mm ammunition, slung it over his shoulder, and then glanced at Elansky. "Penis envy?"

"It ain't the size of the gun. It's the gunner."

Better armed, but not quite ready to tackle the Bristle worms again, Josh found himself wanting nothing more than to lock the door and hide. However, the ship was sinking. They had no time to waste.

"It's quicker to go back they way we came," Knotts said.

No one argued. He knew the ship better than anyone did. In the sub bay, the darkness was cloying. The flashlights poked a few tiny holes in the blackness, but revealed little. Josh spotted a portable battery-operated light stand against the wall. As Bates started up the ladder, he switched it on, savoring the relief as the light revealed a room clear of Bristle worms.

"That's better," he said, pleased with himself for his ingenuity.

Before Bates could climb another rung, the ship suddenly lurched as something stuck the bottom. Bates went flying from the ladder, landing on his shoulder, groaning as the impact dislocated it. Josh was knocked to the deck amid a tangle of steel cables. A geyser of water erupted from the pool, showering them all with cold seawater. As Josh climbed to his feet, the ceresiosaurus' head rose from the pool, slowly like a submarine surfacing. Its head swiveled until one of its large red eyes faced the lights. The creatures' roar was deafening, splitting the air of the cavernous room like angry thunder. Josh clamped his hands over his ears to shut it out.

Retreating up the ladder was out of the question. The creature could easily snatch them from the ladder before they reached the top, and shooting at it while climbing was impossible.

"Back into the passageway," Knotts yelled.

Josh struggled to untangle his feet from the cables, succeeding only in entangling himself further in his panicked haste. Elansky grabbed his arm and yanked, pulling him free of the worst of the snarl. He kicked off the last loop and scrambled away from the edge of the pool.

"Thanks," he said.

She ignored him, as she shoved him behind her. She raised the SIG and fired a burst at the creature. Her aim was true, hitting it in the head, but the powerful 7.62 mm rounds didn't penetrate deep into flesh that was dense enough to withstand the great pressures of the deep. Josh noticed Bates struggling to rise from the deck using only his good arm, holding his injured arm across his chest. He rushed over to help Bates to his feet and began pushing him toward the passageway.

"No, the gun," he yelled.

Josh eyed the creature, but it seemed fascinated by the lights. He recovered the Hua Qing mini-gun and joined the others in the retreat to the safety of the passageway. Just as he thought they had made it, the creature roared once more, slammed one of its fins into a pile of debris, and scattered it around the bay, showering the group with lengths of pipe, equipment, metal decking grates, oxygen bottles, and lead ballast for the submersible. A pulley from a winch struck Josh squarely in the back, knocking him flat. He heard a loud groan from Knotts and saw the captain of the *Pandora* pulling a sliver of steel from his leg just above the knee. Blood spurted from a nicked artery. He clamped his hands over the wound to staunch the blood.

Josh's back felt as if he had played tag with a freight train, but he managed to get to his feet, spitting out the water he had swallowed. He stood in knee-deep water. The creature had ripped a long gash in the raised structure around the sub pool, and water poured in at an alarming rate. The ship was sinking even faster than before. Germaine and Elansky had avoided the shower of debris and reached the passageway. Josh searched for Bates and found him lying in the water pinioned beneath a section of the crane used to lift the sub. He was still alive, but just barely.

He struggled to keep his head above water. When he saw Josh approaching, he yelled, "Leave me." Blood flecked his lips as he fought for breath.

"We'll get you out," Josh said, knowing the water would drown him long before they managed to lift the heavy piece of metal off him.

"No," he groaned as Josh tried to pull him free. "I'm pinned. Too late for me," he gasped. He smiled at Josh. Blood ran from his compressed lips. "Go."

The rising water quickly covered Bates' head. Josh tried to lift it above the water, but it was too late. A stream of bubbles broke the surface and then stopped. He felt the life leave Bates' body.

Elansky and Germaine had rescued Knotts. He stood between them with his belt around his leg as a tourniquet to stop the bleeding. Josh joined them in the passageway. The creature continued its rampage in the pool in its attempt to enter the ship. The bow was down another ten degrees, and the water was now waist deep in the passageway.

He handed the heavy mini-gun to Elansky. She gave her SIG to him to replace his lost M16. "Bates is dead," he said.

Knotts nodded. "So am I."

"What do you mean?"

"I mean I'll never make it back topside with this leg, and you can't carry me and fight worms." He turned to Germaine. "Help me to the weapons locker."

"Why?" Germaine asked.

"This ship is rigged with charges throughout her keel to scuttle her in minutes."

"I'm not going down with the ship," Germaine protested. "This is your command."

"My last command. I'll set the timer for ten minutes. That's as long as I can set it for. You should have enough time to make it. I'm sorry, but I can't wait any longer. I'm going to kill this creature. It's going down with my ship."

"What about the nukes?" Josh asked. All the talk of explosives and deliberately scuttling the ship concerned him. He wasn't ready to die. He certainly didn't want to go out in the heart of a nuclear explosion.

"They're sealed in a heavy vault. The explosion won't hurt them. All three are going back to the bottom where I found them. If I'm going out as a failure, I might as well fail at everything. Devers collapsed a mountain on top of the fourth one. It should be safe now."

Inside the weapons locker, Knotts sat on an ammo case as he unlocked a panel on the wall beside him. He entered a code on the keypad revealed and pressed ENTER. The clock began at ten minutes and started counting down. Josh set his watch's timer as well. The time was 12:20 a.m., October 31 – *Halloween, an appropriate day for the horrors around them*, he thought.

"Go," Knotts said.

The ceresiosaurus had forced its massive body inside the bay. Its claws raked at the bulkheads as it attempted to dig its way to its escaped prey. Given sufficient time, it would reach them, but not in the ten minutes, the *Pandora* had left to live.

"Let's go," Germaine said.

Josh took one last look at Captain Knotts, trying to fix the man's image in his mind. No one else would ever hear of his bravery, so the least he could do was remember him. Knotts pulled a cigarette from a pack in his pocket and tried to light it, but it was wet. He broke it in two and tossed it into the water rising around his waist.

The creature's pounding sent shudders through the ship, creating ripples in the water. Forcing a path through the rising water and floating debris was hard work and Josh was near exhaustion by the time they reached the engine room. The massive engines were silent. The Bristle worms had been there. Parts of bodies of both worm and human floated in the water. Blood smeared the otherwise pristine white bulkheads. One walkway had collapsed into the water, rupturing fuel lines. A strong odor of diesel fuel filled the room.

Following Germaine and Elansky, Josh forced himself up the stairs. Each step sent lances of pain racing through his back. As they crossed a walkway spanning the engines, a Bristle worm emerged from the shadows, blocking their path. Elansky didn't slow down. She pointed the Hua Qing mini-gun at it and pulled the trigger. The six barrels became a whirring blur as it poured hundreds of rounds into the creature. The 7.62 mm slugs ripped the creature to shreds, leaving only smoking chunks of flesh. The three of them plowed through the gory mess and continued to the hatch on the other side.

Josh checked his watch 12:23 – seven minutes to go.

Beyond the hatch lay a long passageway. Crew cabins lined the bulkhead. Thankfully, they encountered no worms, but their luck ended as they reached the last companionway leading to the top deck. More than a dozen worms milled about between them and the stairs. Germaine seemed ready to tackle them all to escape the ship, but Elansky stopped him.

"Give me your grenade," she said.

He handed her the M 67 fragmentation grenades they had taken from the weapons locker.

"Get into one of the cabins," she told them.

She edged closer to the worms. They still did not see her, but had become more agitated as they caught scent of the humans. Josh watched her pull the pins from two grenades, and then, using both hands, she flung them into the crowd of creatures. She threw herself flat on the deck and covered her head with her arms. Josh ducked his head back inside the cabin just as the grenades exploded. The 6.5 ounces of Composition B explosive in each grenade shattered it into hundreds of fragments of metal shrapnel that sprayed the companionway like shotgun pellets. The Bristle worms disintegrated into smoking piles of minced flesh and internal organs. The stench was overpowering.

Josh checked his watch – 12:26. Four minutes to get off the ship. Josh doubted they could make it.

They raced up the worm-slicked companionway and burst onto the deck. More Bristle worms patrolled the deck. Josh stopped counting at fifteen. The bow of the ship was now just above the water level. To his relief, Josh saw the schooner less than fifty yards off the port side of the bow, but to reach it, they had to pass through the army of Bristle worms, and they had no more grenades. The *Miss Lucy* was having problems of its own. Miguel stood on the deck shooting at Bristle worm heads as they surfaced, but the

Webley pistol was having little effect. The professor was standing on top of one of the hatches, holding an oar in his hands. It was a poor weapon against fifteen-foot long Bristle worms. The schooner was under siege.

Beside Josh, Elansky began firing the mini-gun, cutting a swath through the creatures. Josh joined in with the SIG. He had lost sight of Germaine, but he heard the schooner captain's Daewoo K7 still firing. They concentrated only on the nearest creatures, herding them away from the rail toward the center of the ship. Josh barely dodged one creature's mouth as it swung its head at him. He shoved the barrel of the SIG into its mouth and fired a long burst, blowing the creature's head off. Slime sprayed his shirt. He ripped it off and tossed it on the deck.

The *Miss Lucy's* spotlight swept over them. Bodden had spotted them. The schooner began moving in their direction, aiming for a point just aft of the sinking bow. Josh glanced over the side. It would be almost a ten foot drop to the deck of the moving schooner, but a broken leg was better than becoming a meal for the worms.

Germaine appeared from the throng of worms, ducking under one as it swung at him. He raised his K7 and fired into the creature's body at point blank range. He barely rolled away to avoid being pinned by the creature as it fell dead.

The schooner was almost at the ship. "Our ride's here," Josh called to Germaine and Elansky.

Elansky backed toward the rail, firing the Hua Qing until it was empty, the only sound coming from it was the whirring of the rotating barrels. She released the trigger and it stopped spinning.

"I'm out," she said, dropping the useless weapon to the deck.

Germaine threw his K7 at the nearest worm. "Me too."

Josh still had a full magazine in his pocket. He removed the almost empty clip from the Sig and popped in a full one. He handed it to Elansky. He was sure she could do more with it than he could. At the sound of the schooner slamming into the side of the freighter, Germaine leaped from the deck, neatly landing in the rigging of the forestaysail. He scrambled down to the deck. Josh waited for Elansky, but she shook her head at him, urging him to jump as she fired into the remaining Bristle worms. Josh checked his watch – 12:28. They weren't going to make it. He jumped, grabbing the mainsail boom with both hands to break his fall. A loud roar sounded from below decks of the freighter just as he jumped, the ceresiosaurus making its displeasure known. He swung to the deck and rolled until he banged his head into the hatch. He stood and looked for Elansky. She fired one last burst at the worms, and then, timing her leap perfectly, she landed on the main mast. She clung to it for a second before shimmying down.

Bodden had already begun moving the schooner away from the *Pandora*, but Josh knew they were out of time. He pushed Professor Hicks to the deck and yelled, "Everybody down!"

The first explosion went off exactly on time, but to Josh's surprise, it was soft thud deep in the bowels of the ship. Four more followed quickly, ripping out the freighter's guts. The bow disappeared beneath the waves.

That wasn't too bad, he said to himself.

Before the silent words could leave his mind, the deck of the *Pandora* heaved and buckled. Flames shot into the air from all hatches and portholes. Metal shrapnel rained down on the schooner. Everyone hugged the deck or sought cover in the cabin. Bristle worms along the rail of the freighter burst into flame or disintegrated from flying shrapnel. Now, the bow of the freighter was gone, and the rear deck was less than ten feet above the water line. The stern lifted a few feet, but settled. The freighter was going under fast.

The schooner was a hundred yards away from the blast, but the *Pandora* was not finished. The heat of the final explosion swept over them like a tsunami of flame, scorching wood, igniting sails, and singing flesh and hair. The ship shuddered as the shock wave traveled through the water. Any nearby worms would have been turned into jelly. The *Pandora's* captain had assured that no trace of the ship or the creatures remained.

Josh picked himself up from the deck, as Miguel and Bodden raced to extinguish the burning sails. He was stunned by the strength of the explosion. A few seconds late, and he and the others would have accompanied the *Pandora* to her watery grave. The nukes were gone, returning to the deep from which they had been salvaged. The ceresiosaurus was dead, the *Pandora* its new tomb. They had escaped with their lives but little else.

All things considered, Josh had had better vacations.

19

Nov. 1, *Miss Lucy*, Cayman Trench, Caribbean –

Halloween was over, and it would be one Josh would never forget. Instead of a glowing pumpkin, the orange flames of the *Pandora* disappeared behind them as the freighter vanished beneath the waves. Josh's back and arms stung from the blast of heat that had enveloped the schooner. His ran his fingers through his singed hair trying to undo tangled knots. Everyone on the *Miss Lucy* sported assorted cuts, bruises, and burns, but they had survived, all except for poor Odette and Miguel. Josh hoped Odette's Rastafarian god, *Jah*, accepted him. He hadn't known Miguel's religion, if he had one, but hoped that he found peace in death as well.

The sails were next to useless, peppered by shrapnel and holes burned by the fires. Germaine kept the engine running and took the wheel, eager to place distance between the schooner and the sunken freighter in case any Bristle worms survived the blast. With the ceresiosaurus dead, there was no longer a reason to linger in the area. He set the compass for Jamaica.

Josh tried to console Professor Hicks, who paced the deck with his arms folded behind his back. In the faint light falling across the deck from the cabin door, his small frame appeared even more shrunken. His dreams had died with the sinking of the *Pandora*.

"I'm sorry about the ceresiosaurus."

Hicks shrugged, but his dour face did a poor job of concealing his disappointment. "It happens. You were right. It was too dangerous to attempt to capture." He shook his head slowly side-to-side. "I don't know what I was thinking. The *Andrews* is damaged, the freighter and its crew are gone. We barely survived our encounter, though of course two of Germaine's crew did not. Perhaps it is for the best."

"A least you won't have to pay Germaine the bonus," Josh pointed out, hoping to lighten the professor's mood.

"True, but I shall still offer him ten thousand dollars, and the original five thousand to his crew and their families. It's the least I can do."

Josh thought it was a generous offer. "He'll appreciate that. What now?"

"I hope we can gain access to the carcasses of the creatures that attacked the Caymans. At least, we can study them and use our findings and your photos to prepare a report for our colleagues."

"Some good came of it all," Josh pointed out, trying to ease the professor's troubled mind. "The captain of the freighter had three of the Russian warheads sealed in a steel vault. They went down with the ship. The submersible crew created a landslide to cover the leaking fourth warhead. Once those mutated creatures die out, no more will be produced."

Hicks shook his head. "You don't understand, my son. These creatures were not created overnight. It might have taken decades and many generations of radiation exposure to produce them. Their gigantism will not disappear as long as they have a sustainable food source. They will continue to reproduce and to pass their mutated genes to their progeny. They will remain a problem to the area until they are sought out and destroyed. Many harmless species will pay the price for our stupidity in allowing a nuclear bomb to rest on the ocean floor."

The professor's words jolted him out of his self-imposed blindness. He should have known that it wasn't finished. He had avoided considering the long-term effects, concentrating instead on more immediate survival.

"That's someone else's problem," he said, trying to convince himself of his statement's validity more than to convince the professor.

Hicks sighed. "Yes, but we must study it."

"First, let's get back to Jamaica and then home. I'm ready for some dry land, preferably Texas."

"Yes, I suppose that is a good idea. I believe the Navy will be good enough to send us some samples."

Elansky sauntered onto deck wearing shorts and a long sleeve pullover against the chill of the night air. Her muscular legs were well tanned, and her pullover enhanced her large breasts, which Josh was surprised to see were unfettered by a bra. Out of uniform, she looked exquisite, a shapely example of womanhood rather than a cold-blooded killer behind a sniper scope. She carried three drinks in her hands. She handed one the professor.

"This scotch should relax us. I poured a rather liberal two fingers."

As she handed one to Josh, her hand remained on the glass for a moment after he grasped it, brushing her little finger over his hand. Josh took a sip and smiled. "Thanks."

Professor Hicks noticed the looks passing between the two of them and said, "If you don't mind, I will drink mine in the cabin."

As he strolled off, Elansky leaned against the rail and took a big swig of her drink. "I guess our expedition is over, huh?"

"I suppose so. The ceresiosaurus is dead. The only thing left is to study the dead creatures in a lab."

She sighed. "Too bad. I kind of liked this mission."

"Really?" Josh asked, intrigued by her comment.

"I got a tan, met interesting people, and shot monsters. What's not to like?"

"Interesting people?" he asked.

She moved closer, until the fragrance she wore drifted to his nose. He inhaled her heady aroma. She ran a finger across his bare chest, entangling it in a lock of blond chest hairs. "Well, you're a couple of years younger than me, but you're good looking. We click, but I don't think you will expect us to settle down and get married. That's not the way I operate."

Josh's heart beat a little faster. "If you're offering to sleep with me, I accept."

She leaned against him until her hips touched his. He felt a tingle that spread warmth throughout his body. He had tried to avoid intimate contact with her, settling for longing glimpses and daydreams, but she had made it difficult. Now, she was making it impossible.

"Who mentioned sleep?" she whispered.

Josh gulped down his drink, almost choking on the burn as it went down. "You took me by surprise," he wheezed.

"I'm a sniper, remember. We strike from hiding."

He took her hand and pulled her toward him, smashing his lips against hers to silence any more reminders of her profession. He wanted to see her as a beautiful woman, not a killer. She responded with more vigor than he expected, pressing him against the rail until the burnished teak buried into his spine. Pain erupted from his burns, but he didn't mind the minor pain. The pleasure radiating through his body more than made up for any discomfort.

She broke away. "I think you're as eager as I am."

"Damned right. Let's go."

"Before you do, maybe you'd better see this," Germaine called out. Cursing Germaine's timing, he cast a longing glance at Elansky and went to the cabin. Professor Hicks, Bodden and Germaine stood in a group staring at the sonar screen.

"What is it?" he asked, though the sinking feeling in his stomach presaged Germaine's reply.

"Another large blip on sonar, five clicks out and closing fast."

The ceresiosaurus. But how?

"How did it escape the freighter? I swore I heard it bellowing from below decks as we were leaving the ship."

"This blip is bigger."

"Could it be another school of Bristle worms or Viperfish?"

Germaine shook his head. "Not at this speed. Whatever it is," he added, "it's homing in on our engine."

"Do we dare shut it down?" Hicks asked.

"If we do, we're dead in the water. The sails are useless and it would take hours to re-rig new ones, if I had spares, which I don't."

Josh felt a hand on his shoulder. "Maybe it's Mama. I guess I get my shot after all."

Elansky had her rifle in her hand and the explosive tipped shell tucked inside the waistband of her shorts. Her expression was grim, but her voice couldn't hide her excitement. "How long do we have?" she asked.

Germaine glanced at the scope and made a rapid mental calculation. His face scrunched up as he arrived at an answer he didn't like. "If I push the engine, two and half hours, maybe less."

Elansky nodded. "That puts it here just after dawn. That helps. It makes it easier to take my shot."

Josh wasn't as confident of the outcome as she seemed to be. "Can't we radio the *Andrews* for a helicopter?"

"The *Chinook* isn't armed. Cere ate the other chopper, remember?"

"It could evacuate us." Josh knew he sounded desperate, but he didn't want to endure another encounter with giant sea creatures.

Germaine scowled. "I'm not leaving my ship."

"And I'm not missing my shot," Elansky added. "It's why I'm here."

Josh swallowed to hide his rising anxiety. Was he the only one on the boat that understood the danger? "You can take your shot from the helicopter."

"Too unstable. The sea is calm enough." She stared at him. "I won't miss."

"I don't doubt your skill. I doubt the efficacy of the MS-222. The dosage is just a guess. After seeing that thing close up, you might need more than one shot."

She reached down and caressed the explosive shell. "I've got back up."

"We still have a few hours," Germaine said. "I suggest you try to get some rest. Things might get a bit hectic at dawn."

Elansky slipped her hand into his. "I don't need rest."

Josh ignored Germaine's ear-to-ear grin, as she led him down the steps and through the narrow passageway to the first empty cabin they encountered. He knew he stank of sweat, singed hair, and Bristle worm blood and gore, but he didn't care, and she didn't seem to mind. She leaned her rifle against the wall and gently laid the explosive shell on a table. She ripped off his shirt while he dropped his pants. Her pullover came off next, revealing the most luscious breasts he had ever seen, melon-sized and firm, with large, dark nipples. As his lips found one, she pushed down her shorts. He wasn't surprised to see that she wore nothing beneath them.

He picked her up and laid her on the bunk, banging his head on the overhead bunk as he crawled in beside her. The bunk was narrow, forcing them together, but he didn't mind. There was no foreplay. That had been going on for days. Knowing that they would soon face death stoked their passion to a burning fire. She spread her legs and accepted him into her, groaning as he entered. Their movements quickly synchronized. They moved as one body, one being. Her vigor and strength forced him to summon reserves of strength he didn't know he had left after his recent trials. He forced the memory of his dead girlfriend from his mind. She had haunted his nights long enough. He would never forget her, but he knew he had to let her go.

He recognized that this was not love, just pure animal passion, as basic and as necessary as breathing. He gave in to the beast within him and let his mind empty of all thoughts except pleasing her. Her fingers raked the tender flesh of his back, but the agony only served to increase his ardor. She flipped him onto his back and rode him like a rodeo bull, lasting much longer than the required eight seconds. They climaxed together, his body going into uncontrollable spasms of pleasure. Her moans became louder until she stiffened and fell on top of him.

After a few moments of heavy breathing, she said, "That was good."

He nibbled her ear. "I'm glad. You almost killed me."

She giggled. "I'm not the only one who always makes their shot."

She snuggled up beside him and laid her arm across his chest, still breathing heavily from the exertion. He didn't know how far she wanted him to go in their post-coital relationship, so he settled for clasping her hand in his. It seemed the right response. She nibbled his neck and relaxed.

He knew the others had heard her moans of pleasure and probably his as well, but he didn't care. His desire had been a long time building. They lay entangled for ten pleasant minutes before she stirred. She crawled over him, lingering long enough for a final kiss, and dressed. Their lovemaking session was over. He lay there watching her until she picked up her rifle, tucked the shell back into her shorts, and opened the door. She looked back at him, smiled and said, "I'll see you on deck." Then she closed the door behind her.

He decided he needed a shower before dressing. The stream of water ignited his burns into patches of agony, but he used the pain to focus his thoughts. If a larger ceresiosaurus was headed their way, maybe Cere's mama as Elansky suggested, then the sedative dosage would have to be adjusted. If it were another monster entirely, then they would likely die at dawn like condemned criminals in old Westerns.

All of their plans had been designed for Cere. Now, they were gone out the window. They would have to wing it, and Josh hated uncertainty. Maybe it would be best to allow Elansky to kill the creature rather than attempt to capture it. She would be happy either way, but Professor Hicks would object strongly. His eyes when viewing the sonar scope had reacquired some of their earlier vigor. As much as Josh hated to disappoint his friend and mentor, maybe it was time to look to their survival.

He dressed in clean clothes and boots, forced a comb through his singed hair, and went out on deck. No one had followed Germaine's advice to rest. He was at the wheel. Hicks still stood by the sonar screen. Bodden leaned against the stern rail of the schooner watching the horizon behind them. Elansky had resumed her position on the forward hatch, her weapon across her lap. Josh wanted to go to her, offer some small talk or a thank you for the sex, but assumed she wanted to concentrate on her job. Since their lives depended on her aim, he wouldn't interrupt.

He did suggest a higher dosage of MS-222 for the dart projectile.

"It will still be guesswork," Hicks answered. "Without seeing the creature approaching, we don't know if it is a ceresiosaurus or some other gargantuan. However, I agree another dart should be readied with a higher dosage, but we might not get a second opportunity."

Josh thought it was time for his other suggestion. "Maybe it would be safer to simply kill the creature."

Hick's expression changed. He once again looked like an old man. "Believe me; I have considered just such an option. I have been so wrong in my assumptions and people have died. I am an old man and I am willing to risk my life. However, it is wrong of me to drag all of you with me. Perhaps, we should take a vote."

Germaine called everyone to the cabin. When they were gathered, the professor addressed them.

"We face a dangerous creature. Our lives are at risk. If you wish to kill the creature rather than attempt a capture, I will understand. Please offer your vote."

Germaine spoke first, "I still want that bonus." He turned to Bodden. "What about you?"

"I'll follow you," he answered.

All eyes turned to Elansky. "To me, a shot is a shot, dead or alive, I don't care, but it seems we can learn more from a live creature than from a dead one."

Josh knew where Hicks stood. He had been outvoted, so he saw no reason to voice his objections. They would only make him sound more frightened than he was. He nodded. "Very well, it's decided. We try to capture it." More softly, he said, "God help us."

20

Nov. 1, *Miss Lucy*, Caribbean Sea –

Sleep was out of the question. He was too restless to sit and wait, so Josh paced the deck. He ran several scenarios through his mind, but all of them ended with the *Miss Lucy* as a pile of debris and everyone on board dead. He had carefully refilled a dart with additional MS-222, and then added ten percent more for good measure. He still doubted the dosage was accurate enough or the sedative effective enough to sedate the creature before it could crush the schooner. Not quite resigned to death, but unable to foresee a long future, he decided to fight the dread threatening to overwhelm him and revert to a more clinical approach to their mission. He wrote down everything he could remember of his journey since arriving on Little Cayman Island, only leaving out his dalliance with Elansky. He took the journal and his cell phone and placed them in a waterproof bag. He attached one of the floats and laid it on the deck, where it could float free if the schooner sank. Someone, someday, might retrieve the journal and photographic evidence washed up on a beach and then use it to combat the creatures.

Knowing that the last few hours before dawn might be his last on Earth forced Josh to look back on his life, a kind of emotional retrospective. It was becoming apparent to him that he had been using the death of his fiancée to shield him from any future pain. He had withdrawn into the benign world of academia, venturing out of his comfortable shell only to spend a few hours with friends who he could not call close. He had no close friends, other than

Professor Hicks. He might add Germaine to that short list. The jury was still out on the captain.

Elansky was symptomatic of his life to date. He found her attractive and desirable, but understood that they had no future together. She wanted nothing more than sex from him, and he was more than willing to oblige. He thought he had feared her, but he had really just been afraid of her rejection. She had her chosen profession, and he had his. So many of his conquests – and he could add them up on one hand – had been short-lived dalliances, fitting into his schedule as he saw fit with no regards to anyone else's desires. He had been brutally selfish. He had thought he was simply being dedicated. Now, he could see the difference. He only hoped it was not too late to correct.

The steady ping of the sonar became a drone that dug into his subconscious like a steel spike, reminding him of what was to come. He should have known there was no way out for him. He had been drawn into the drama since he had first set foot on Little Cayman Island. His participation was as exorable as Odysseus on the island of Circe. He had no way out, nowhere to run. It was either face his demons or let them overpower him. His failure could mean the deaths of others, perhaps Elansky. She owed him nothing, but he owed her. He steeled himself for the inevitable.

The distance between the sonar blip and the schooner diminished rapidly. Josh peered at the eastern horizon, hoping for a glimpse of the sun rising, but saw only a faint lightening of the sky. Somehow, facing the creature in the dark was more frightening, more like struggling with a nightmare from which he couldn't awaken. He urged the *Miss Lucy* onward, to go faster, but the engine was pushing as hard as it could. Time was growing short.

Elansky finally moved from her spot. She stood, stretched, and walked to the stern to join Bodden. She cast one quick glance in Josh's direction, but her face revealed nothing. Josh longed for the Hua Qing mini-gun from the *Pandora*, but it was gone, sunk with the freighter. They had the SIG 556 with half a clip of 7.62 mm ammo, but it offered a poor defense against a two-hundred-plus-feet-long monster. If the sedative didn't work … he didn't want to think about it.

About two hundred yards behind them, barely visible in the darkness, a head slowly emerged from the water, creating a V-shaped wake behind it. The head continued to rise until it stood fifty feet above the water. It was a ceresiosaurus, but not Cere. Cere had perished in the Pandora. This was, as Elansky had guessed, Cere's mother, larger and therefore more dangerous. The creature reached the sonar buoy and plucked it from the water, ripping the nylon towrope from the schooner's stern. The trailing end of the rope snapped like a whip and rushed by Elansky's head, almost lashing her in the face. The pinging stopped abruptly. Now, the creature's attention focused on the boat.

Professor Hicks stood beside the cabin, watching the creature approach. He removed his glasses and wiped them on his shirt to clean them for a better view. He braced himself against the cabin with one hand as Germaine swung the boat to starboard in a hopeless move to outrun the creature.

"Keep it steady!" Elansky shouted. She raised the rifle to her shoulder and waited.

Bodden picked up a boat hook and stood beside her as if to protect her from the creature. Josh's heart threatened to climb up his gullet. It hammered in his chest like a racecar engine before the starter's flag dropped. His palms began to sweat. He wiped them on his pants. All he could do was to stand helplessly and watch.

When the creature was fifty yards away, she fired the dart. The report was louder than Josh expected as the projectile flew to the creature's chest and struck. It remained embedded in the creature's flesh. The pressurized container popped as it injected the MS-22 into its bloodstream. Elansky was taking no chances. She quickly fired a second dart, striking the creature in the shoulder. It, too, dug into the flesh and injected its load of sedative into the creature. Now, enough MS-222 was in the ceresiosaurus' bloodstream to knock out a small herd of elephants. To Josh's consternation, the creature continued forward without diminishing speed. It was almost on top of them.

Germaine spun the wheel to port, arcing away from the ceresiosaurus, but it craned its neck and snapped the top from the aft mast. Rigging and furled sails fell to the deck, almost knocking Elansky overboard. She leaped out of the way just in time. Bodden was not as lucky. The edge of the broken mast bounced off the boom as it fell and slapped him across the back, pinning him to the deck.

"Oh, my," Hicks groaned. He turned to stare at Josh. "I'm so sorry, my boy."

Josh rushed to the stern to help free Bodden. Elansky helped him lift the wooden mast from Bodden's body, but picked up her rifle as Josh dragged Bodden to the cabin. They had more darts and MS-222, but no time in which to charge them. He watched as she removed the explosive-tipped shell from her waistband and loaded it. It was time to try to save their lives.

The creature didn't give her the time. Germaine's maneuver had placed some distance between them, but not enough. It slammed its body into the side of the *Miss Lucy,* half lifting it from the water. The port rail splintered and Josh heard the sickening sound of the wooden hull cracking. The propeller buzzed as it spun uselessly in the air. Germaine cursed the creature as if it had injured him. The boat righted itself as it landed, and the creature slowed down.

"Check the hull!" Germaine screamed at Bodden, but the first mate was in no shape to comply. Instead, Josh raced down the stairs to see if they were sinking.

Water poured into the passageway from the engine room. He forced the door open and saw daylight through cracks in the hull. More ominously, water bubbled up from a larger crack below the waterline. He grabbed an armload of blankets from one of the cabins and tried to stuff them into the cracks. He managed to slow the small leaks, but the water pressure in the large hole simply pushed the blankets out each time he tried. Finally, he gave up.

"It's useless," he called out to Germaine, as he rushed up the steps. "The engine room is flooding."

Without power, they would be at the creature's mercy. Josh wondered why it hadn't finished them already. Back on deck, Bodden was coming to. Professor Hicks knelt beside him. He looked for Elansky and saw her standing amid the rubble of the mast, watching the creature. The ceresiosaurus remained behind them, trailing them from a hundred yards, as if it knew the schooner was sinking.

"I think it's slowing down," Hicks said.

"It should be down by now," Josh replied.

Hicks shook his head. "Its physiology is much different from other reptiles. I miscalculated the MS-222's effectiveness."

There was no time for recriminations. They had both made a mistake – the professor in seeking to capture the creature, and him for not insisting that they didn't. It would likely be their last mistake.

"It doesn't matter now. We have to try to save ourselves."

Hicks nodded. "Yes, tell her to use the explosive bullet."

The creature submerged, disappearing as abruptly as it had appeared. Was it leaving? Just as he was turning to Germaine, he got his answer. The schooner lifted into the air as the creature rose beneath it. Elansky fell, dropping her rifle. It slid across the deck to disappear beneath the rubble of the mast. Josh felt himself flying over the rail. He grasped uselessly at the air and landed in the water. The schooner slid from the creature's back, landing upright in the water, but the entire fore mast and bowsprit snapped like a felled tree and went over the side, trailing lines behind it. It acted as a sea anchor, slowing the schooner. The stern dipped lower in the water as the sea surged in. The engine flooded, leaving the damaged schooner dead in the water. For the *Miss Lucy*, only minutes of life remained.

Josh treaded water, waiting for the end. Germaine stepped from the wheelhouse and tossed something at the creature. Josh was surprised to see it explode. It was one of the grenades Knotts had given them on the *Pandora*. He didn't know Germaine had kept his. The explosion sent shrapnel flying into the creature's exposed back. It roared in pain and submerged, injured.

"Yeah!" he yelled in triumph. Germaine was not going down without a fight. His triumph vanished as the water swirled around him when the creature passed directly below him. He waited for the gigantic mouth to open beneath him and swallow him. The creature continued past him and surfaced ten yards away. He stared up at the enormous head and the reptilian eyes staring down at him and said a silent prayer for a quick ending, though he doubted it would be painless. Blood streamed from the wounds in the creature's back, but they wouldn't stop it from killing him.

"Josh!"

He turned to see Elansky standing on the sinking boat, pointing her rifle at the creature. Guessing her intent, he dove as deeply as he could. At the sound of an explosion, he surfaced. The ceresiosaurus was swinging its head wildly in agony, thrashing the water with its enormous fins. A fist-sized hole just below its head poured a steady stream of blood down its neck and into the water. True to her word, Elansky had hit an artery. The creature was dying. The question was would it die before it finished them all off, especially him? The creature's wild thrashing churned the water around him. He swam away and toward the schooner.

Germaine helped him aboard. Water was just inches below the deck. Bodden was removing the tarp from the *Miss Lucy's* lifeboat. Professor Hicks emerged soaking wet from the cabin with an armload of food and a small thermos of water. Somewhere along the way, he had lost his glasses.

"We did it," Germaine said, smiling. A piece of shrapnel had found his arm. It bled through his shirt.

"But your boat," Josh said.

"I've got insurance. I'll get another boat, this time with two engines."

"I think I got all I could salvage," the professor said as he dropped his supplies into the lifeboat. "I suggest we leave this place. Scavengers, you know."

Elansky dropped her rifle on the deck. It disappeared beneath the water.

"Thanks, Nina," Josh said. "You saved all our lives."

"You called me by my first name. Does that mean we're dating?"

"Until you become a Marine again."

"I've got a few days," she said, smiling.

The ceresiosaurus had stopped its mad thrashing. Now, its head slowly lowered to the water and it rolled over on its side, its fins sticking into the air like a final wave goodbye. The creature was dead. Soon, it would sink back to the depths that spawned it. They would have no specimen to study. *Just as well*, he thought. *Life needs a few mysteries.*

The schooner began groaning as air escaped its hatches. It, too, was dying. Josh helped Elansky into the lifeboat, and then the professor. He took a seat beside Elansky and let her settle into his arms. Germaine was the last one off his boat. He shoved the lifeboat off the deck as the schooner sank beneath it. They moved off a few yards, on the opposite side of the boat as the dead ceresiosaurus. Josh was adrift on the ocean for the fifth time in a week. He hoped it didn't become a habit.

21

Nov. 3, Kingston, Jamaica –

All his wounds were healing, but his dreams would be haunted by nightmares for some time to come. One did not face demons unscathed. Corporal Nina Elansky was gone, flying back to Guantanamo Bay for reassignment. Josh would miss her, but the day and night they had spent in bed together would last for a while. They would meet again, she promised, and Josh hoped so. She had dragged him from his self-imposed wall of indifference and planted him firmly back among the living.

The *Andrews,* apprised of the situation, had dispatched a helicopter to pick them up. Josh had reported the *Pandora's* sinking to Captain Tremaine and the loss of the Russian nukes. He disavowed any knowledge of the *Pandora,* as Josh assumed he would, and promised to convey Josh's report to the proper authorities. He was pleased that both ceresiosauri were dead, but refused to listen to Josh's warning that there might have been more than two.

Professor Hicks was eager to return to TCU and examine the specimens the Navy had provided. Josh thought that he, too, would be eager to resume his studies and put the incident behind him. To his surprise, he decided instead to go to Grand Cayman and help with the recovery efforts. Captain Germaine assured him that as soon as the insurance paid his claim, he would buy a new boat and take him there. He had already picked out a used twin-engine catamaran.

Mutated creatures still prowled the deep dark depths of the Cayman Trench. Undoubtedly, they would once again prove a nuisance for mankind, but for now, the world was breathing a sigh of relief. After helping in George Town, he would return to TCU and join the professor's research. However, for now, he had had enough of creatures up from the depths.